"Oh, I think we can give him something to broadcast," Dominic said, and before Polly realized what was happening, he'd pulled her into his arms. He pressed her close, his parted lips upon hers in a kiss that was really quite shocking. His fingers wound warmly into the hair at the nape of her neck, and his mouth teased hers in a way she'd never experienced before.

Polly's face was crimson with mortification and with aroused emotions she would have preferred had remained asleep. "How dare you!" she declared, then turned to hurry into the house.

Dominic gazed after her, his expression hard to decipher, then he walked quickly toward his own house.

Polly closed her eyes. Her lips still seemed to burn from his kiss, and she knew that in spite of the circumstances, she had found those few intimate seconds quite the most exciting imaginable. *Oh, Devil take him!* He was arrogant, presumptuous, selfish, and unkind, but oh, how easy it would be to love him!

The Magic
Jack-o'-Lantern

❧

Sandra Heath

A SIGNET BOOK

SIGNET
Published by New American Library, a division of
Penguin Putnam Inc., 375 Hudson Street,
New York, New York 10014, U.S.A.
Penguin Books Ltd, 27 Wrights Lane,
London W8 5TZ, England
Penguin Books Australia Ltd,
Ringwood, Victoria, Australia
Penguin Books Canada Ltd, 10 Alcorn Avenue,
Toronto, Ontario, Canada M4V 3B2
Penguin Books (N.Z.) Ltd, 182-190 Wairau Road,
Auckland 10, New Zealand

Penguin Books Ltd, Registered Offices:
Harmondsworth, Middlesex, England

First published by Signet, an imprint of New American Library,
a division of Penguin Putnam Inc.

First Printing, October 1999
10 9 8 7 6 5 4 3 2 1

REGISTERED TRADEMARK—MARCA REGISTRADA

Printed in the United States of America

Author's Note

Tradition has it that in nearly every home in England there is an invisible resident brownie to attend to all the small, overlooked tasks, and—in the country at least—to look after the bees. People are roughly divided into two categories: the minority who are very conscious of their supernatural fellow creatures, and the vast majority who remain in ignorance. Naturally, it is among the former that brownies find human friends to whom they are willing to appear; unfortunately, there are those who are sensitive to the supernatural but entirely bereft of scruple. Such persons are much feared by the brownie world.

Brownies do not resemble the elves and pixies of storybooks, but are covered with shaggy brown fur that is kept glossy by the regular application of a fine clove balm. They are about two feet tall, their faces wrinkled like old men or women, their arms and legs bare, and they have long tails that lash and twirl when they're angry. They have a great craving for all things sweet, and if unhappy or upset will go to considerable lengths to seek sugary comfort. An offended brownie will pack its bags and depart, leaving behind a house that feels empty, no matter how many souls reside within. But every brownie has an Achilles' heel: the invisible belt upon which he or she keeps the equally invisible keys of their house. Should this belt fall into the hands of one of the above-mentioned unscrupulous persons, its diminutive owner becomes a helpless slave. That aside, it has to be admitted that brownies are not always angelic; indeed, they can be very troublesome. When this happens, they become that most alarming creature, the boggart. Fortunately, this is a very rare occurrence, for most brownies never change at all.

This story concerns one brownie who *did* change. His name was

Bodkin, and he had looked after Horditall House, in the county of Somerset, since the fifteenth century. The hamlet of Horditall lay half a mile to the west of the main Bath highway, on the heights above the famous Cheddar Gorge, which cut from north to south through limestone hills. It was reached by an ancient Roman way, which after passing through Horditall deteriorated into a deeply rutted, high-hedged farm track that led only to the pig farm of a rascally fellow by the name of Johnson, whose pastimes included an inland variety of wrecking. This profitable hobby had earned him the nickname Wrecker Johnson. It was well deserved.

Bodkin had always been happy with his lot, but for the past three years the master of the house had been the rich but miserly Mr. Hordwell Horditall, whose already bulging coffers had swelled still more when he inherited the property from his late cousin. It was a fact that a man of Hordwell's wealth could and should have lived in luxury, but his only concession to the good things of life had been the retention of his deceased kinsman's servants and two carriages.

Hordwell was one of the psychic minority who were well aware of brownies, but although he was mean and grasping, Bodkin felt sure he wasn't of sufficiently wicked disposition to pose any threat. Nevertheless, having a miser for a master wasn't at all agreeable, and Bodkin would long since have marched out of the house were it not for Hordwell's pretty niece and ward, Polly Peach, who on the unfortunate demise of her parents in a carriage overturn on Westminster Bridge had come from London to reside with her uncle. Polly was very susceptible indeed to the supernatural, and detected Bodkin's presence from the moment she arrived. She and the brownie got on so famously that he not only stayed on at Horditall House, but was happy to make himself visible to her.

Polly was the twenty-year-old daughter of Hordwell's sister, Maria, whose exceedingly fortunate marriage to a rich London banker had bestowed a most agreeable inheritance upon her only child. The heiress to the Peach's Bank fortune was a very independent minded young woman who, in spite of her considerable expectations, had never been permitted to move in the very highest circles. This was due to her father's low opinion of aristocrats, so many of whom banked with him, and who continually ran deep into debt through gambling, womanizing, and the various other vices that seemed compulsory for the highborn. The banker was therefore not at all ambitious for his beloved daughter to marry into a title—unless it was for love, of course—and had she fallen for a lowly doctor or lawyer, he would have accepted it, because her happiness was what mattered. But Polly had yet to have her heart even mildly affected by a prospective suitor.

The late Mr. Peach's stingy brother-in-law held very different views regarding Polly's marriage. In his opinion it was his duty to acquire a suitable husband for an heiress who would come into the Peach's Bank wealth when she reached the age of twenty-three, and would one day be the recipient of the Horditall estate as well. Matters of the heart had no place in his calculations, but a title was *essential*. Polly—ever her father's daughter—was equally set upon love and romance, and so the battle lines were drawn, spirited niece standing up to determined uncle.

This is the story of what happened in the days leading up to Halloween in the year 1800. It started on October twenty-eighth, which happened to be Bodkin's birthday, although nobody knew how old he was, not even the brownie himself. Hordwell had been in Bath spa for several weeks, leaving Polly behind at the house. He'd gone allegedly on the sole account of his gout, but in reality also to connive at a particularly contentious aristocratic marriage contract behind the back of his obstinate niece. Thus Polly was to hand when Bodkin happened upon an act of her uncle's so heinous that the dismayed brownie realized the miser posed a threat to browniedom after all. It was such a shock that for the first time in his life Bodkin became a boggart.

Chapter 1

It was fall, the October sun was warm, and Polly was tending the garden. Trowel in hand, her basket on the grass beside her, she knelt in the morning sunshine, planting carnation and sweet william slips for next year. The garden was her pride and joy, because since her arrival she had single-handedly rescued it from a jungle of thorns and weeds. The reason for its sad state was Hordwell's summary dismissal of the two gardeners, whom he had then declined to replace. Now, thanks to her endeavors, everything was a carefully nurtured blaze of autumn flowers—Michaelmas daisies, asters, goldenrod, and nasturtiums, to say nothing of a commendable display of late roses that had escaped the summer rampage of the dreaded greenfly.

There was one unusual thing growing in the garden, an American pumpkin plant. Such things were very rare indeed in England, and Horditall House only possessed one because Bodkin knew a brownie, who knew another brownie, who looked after a very grand country house owned by a renowned horticulturalist lord. This lord had recently returned from the New World with all kinds of wonderful new plants and seeds, but somehow he had neglected to plant the pumpkins. His brownie, never one to tolerate waste, had prudently shared the seeds among his friends, and thus one had fallen into Bodkin's hands. Now the fruit of this protracted tale was flourishing close to the Horditall House beehives.

Polly knew that pumpkins were supposed to be eaten, but Bodkin informed her they weren't being grown for their culinary qualities. He declared, rather mysteriously, that his pumpkins were going to be renowned throughout the brownie world, but more than that he wouldn't say. Unknown to Polly, he had marvelous plans for Halloween, a very important festival for brownies, by whom it was also called Mischief Night. There would be all sorts of high jinks, and jack-o'-lanterns made from the traditional, rather puny turnips, but Bodkin perceived that the American pumpkin would make a much more impressive jack-o'-lantern, indeed it would make a jack-o'-lantern so wonderful it would be talked of ever after. So he tended his precious plant with infinite care, and the pumpkins had grown to a prodigious size.

Bodkin's bees droned contentedly in the hives, and doves cooed in the cote as Polly's trowel dug satisfyingly into soil that had benefited from all the recent rain, but then the peace was disturbed by the sound of an approaching carriage. She sat back on her heels in alarm, fearing her uncle had returned early from Bath. She felt disloyal for enjoying his absence, but he could be *so* disagreeable that his temporary absence had proved an immense relief. As for debt-ridden Lord Benjamin Beddem, the gentleman with whom he had been staying at Bath's renowned Royal Crescent, well, the least said the better.

Polly regarded the dissolute, overweight second son of the Duke of Lawless as one of the most odious persons in creation, and it was her misfortune that not only had he attached himself to her uncle, but also that he had asked for her hand in marriage. Lord Benjamin was a man in dire need of a fortune to save himself from the duns, and it was with money in mind that he bestowed such marked favor upon Hordwell, even to the extent of several times deigning to stay here in Horditall, which he clearly regarded as the back of beyond. Polly wasn't deceived by him at all, and rightly guessed that he had only leased the house in Royal Crescent, which it seemed impossible he could really afford, in order to impress her uncle, who was extraordinarily gullible when it came to the aristocracy. Hordwell so longed for a family alliance with the duke, who was one of the foremost magnates in the land, that he blithely overlooked the fact that every Beddem since the time of wicked King John had been a villain and philanderer. Sly Lord Benjamin had led Hordwell to believe that the irascible and difficult duke was about to disinherit his elder son, thus making Benjamin heir to the title. Hordwell was therefore convinced there could be no better match for his niece in the entire realm, unless, of course, there were to be a royal offer!

Needless to say, Polly wasn't taken in by either Lord Benjamin or his tales of disinheritance, and she said so in no uncertain manner whenever the opportunity arose, but Hordwell brushed her protests aside as he endeavored to secure the match of his dreams. She would as soon fling herself over Cheddar Gorge as become part of such a family of aristocratic scoundrels and seducers! All this ran through her mind as she gazed anxiously along the road. If it *was* her uncle's carriage returning, *please* let him be alone!

Adjusting the cream woolen shawl around her shoulders, she waited apprehensively for the vehicle to come into view beyond the stone wall and sentinel beeches. The sun dappled her face through the wide brim of her straw hat, and the gentle breeze lifted the wide white ribbons beneath her chin. She had lavender eyes and a heart-shaped face, and a thick ash blond ringlet fell over her left shoulder. Her slender figure was gently outlined by the soft folds of her blue muslin chemise gown, and she possessed the sort of pale, clear complexion that many a London belle would have died for. It might be thought she was little more than a defenseless porcelain doll, and indeed her uncle had made that very mistake, but such was not the case, for Polly Peach was not only spirited, but also accomplished, well read, intelligent, sympathetic, and thoughtful. She also had a deliciously impish sense of humor, which she often turned to great effect upon her uncle, although he rarely realized it.

At last the approaching vehicle drove into sight, and she was comforted to see it wasn't Hordwell's, but an expensive traveling carriage with a coat of arms on the door. Drawn by four excellent high-stepping grays, it was a gleaming equipage, green, with bright yellow wheels and polished brass, and for a split second Polly feared it might belong to Lord Benjamin, but then she remembered that her unloved suitor's colors were crimson and silver, whereas this liveried coachman wore green and gold. She breathed out with relief as the carriage drove past.

Because the window glass was lowered, she could see the solitary occupant, an exceedingly handsome gentleman with tousled dark hair and fine taste in clothes. A tall fawn beaver hat was tipped back on his head in a rather world-weary way, and a jeweled pin flashed on the creamy white neckcloth at his throat. There were discreet shirt frills peeping from the flared cuff of his tight-fitting sage green coat, and his gloved fingers tapped upon the window ledge as he glanced out. Polly's breath caught, for he was quite the most attractive man she had ever seen. Who was he? she wondered.

But then the effect was spoiled as she noticed the hauteur of his expression. For a long moment his eyes met hers, and as he looked coldly to the front again, her feelings were extinguished, as if doused with a bucket of cold water. She was piqued, and suddenly rather glad that the superior gentleman and his magnificently garbed coachman would very soon discover they'd been misled along this road, storm-driven ships lured by Wrecker Johnson. With a little clever manipulation of the signpost on the Bath highway, the pig farmer was wont to divert travelers through Horditall. Once these unfortunates had passed the hamlet, they suddenly found themselves in the narrow lane that led only to his property, where they were permitted to turn around only if they paid for the privilege.

Under any other circumstances she would have called out a timely warning to the coachman, for there was ample room to turn in the driveway to Horditall House, but since the gentleman clearly looked down upon her as a lesser mortal, he did not deserve to be rescued. In a short while now Mr. High-and-Mighty's elegant carriage would find itself in the farm lane, which was positively awash after the recent rain, and there would be no turning until reaching Wrecker Johnson's muddy, decidedly cramped yard. After the humiliating exercise of fending off some of the fattest pigs in Somerset, then paying the grasping farmer's fine, the prideful gentleman and his now filthy carriage would suffer the further indignity of having to drive past Horditall House again. If she caught his eye *then* she would treat him to a patronizing smile. And serve him right.

Chapter 2

Putting the carriage from her thoughts, Polly resumed her gardening, but then paused again as through an open upstairs window she heard Bodkin humming as he dusted and polished her uncle's bedroom. It was a sound that gladdened her heart. For exactly a year now Bodkin had been sunk desperately low because his former sweetheart, Nutmeg, had left him, but if he was humming again, maybe the whole sad episode was behind him at last. How appropriate that his recovery should happen on his birthday.

Nutmeg had come to look after a cottage owned by Hordwell just across the road from Horditall House, and she had seemed quite perfect for Bodkin. He doted on her, giving her presents of honey and honey wine from the Horditall bees, and it had come as a terrible shock to him when, on the eve of his birthday last year, his beloved suddenly left without a word. The evening before Nutmeg's disappearance, the brownie sweethearts had planned how they would celebrate his birthday—for which Nutmeg was going to make a special cake—then they said their usual fond goodnights at the stile at the bottom of her garden, and Bodkin watched as she hurried back to her house. That was the last he saw of her. Uncle Hordwell insisted that Nutmeg had simply decided to leave, and in the absence of any other evidence, that was what had to be believed.

The cheerful humming was so uplifting that Polly joined in as she returned yet again to her gardening. She and Bodkin had the house to themselves, and tonight they would have a special birthday dinner of all the brownies' favorite things, with the creamiest, sweetest dessert the cook could concoct. It wouldn't be as joyous an occasion as if Nutmeg were there to present him with the promised birthday cake, but she, Polly, would do all she could to make it his best birthday yet.

In the bedroom, Bodkin shuffled about his work, dusting here, polishing there. He'd always liked Horditall House, but now he only stayed because of Miss Polly. *She* was an angel, her uncle was a tight-fisted, devious, untrustworthy old curmudgeon. As he thought this, Bodkin glanced at the portrait of Hordwell on the wall above the fireplace, and blew a rather disgusting raspberry before going on with his cleaning.

His long tail swung contentedly to and fro behind him as he worked, and every now and then there was a tinkling sound from the keys on his belt. He had always been a little plump because of his weakness for sugar and honey, but he had become even more so since Nutmeg's departure because he comforted himself with sweet treats. He paused for a moment and sighed. How he'd loved her, and how foolish he'd been to think she loved him. She'd broken his poor heart, but today he'd awoken feeling better again.

He finished Hordwell's second-floor bedroom and began to busy himself along the lofty oak-paneled passage toward Polly's room, but then his humming broke off in surprise, for a door was open that was usually kept firmly padlocked. It was the one to Hordwell's study, a room the brownie had never even seen during the three years of the miser's ownership of the house. Hordwell kept it secure at all times with a patent padlock in order to prevent servants, brownies, and even Polly from prying into his private papers. In Bodkin's professional opinion the room was long overdue for cleaning, so he pushed the door open fully and went in with his duster at the ready.

The room was indeed in need of attention. Dust was thick on every surface, there was a musty smell in the air, the fireplace had not seen a fire in three winters, and the curtains looked as if they'd never been washed. The carpet was littered with untidy piles of documents and books, and there was such a clutter on the desk that Bodkin marveled the old miser could ever find anything! Hordwell did not deserve any consideration at all, but a brownie had his reputation to consider, and if the state of this room were to become common knowledge among the community, he—Bodkin—would be the target of much criticism.

Putting down his duster, he flung open the window, then began tidying the desk. Within moments an entry in an open ledger caught his eye. It referred to an agreement between Hordwell and Lord Benjamin Beddem, and the item agreed upon was—*Nutmeg*! She hadn't run away after all, but had been traded like a sack of flour to look after his lordship's elegant new rented residence in Royal Crescent!

For a moment Bodkin was so thunderstruck that he could not move, but then his mind began to race. His shaggy fur stood on end as pieces of a terrible puzzle suddenly fell into place. Why hadn't he realized before? It was so obvious. Oh, what a fool he'd been! He saw red, and the boggart hidden deep inside him came to sudden life. His tail started to lash, and he gave a howl of unutterable rage and dismay.

Polly heard from the garden and came running anxiously into the house. "Bodkin? Bodkin, what's wrong?" Another apoplectic howl issued from the next floor, so she gathered her blue muslin skirts to hurry up the dark oak staircase. "Bodkin?" she cried again, then her steps faltered uneasily as she realized the brownie was in her uncle's study, where not even she was allowed to go. Slowly she entered, and then halted in dismay as she saw the furious boggart-brownie, whose tail was now twirling so fast it was a blur.

Bodkin was too beside himself to speak, and jabbed a quivering finger on the open ledger. She went around the desk to read the damning entry, and her lips immediately parted on a horrified gasp. "Oh, Bodkin, I'm *so* sorry! Lord Benjamin is capable of anything, but I wouldn't have thought Uncle Hordwell would stoop so low."

"Well, he did, it's there in black and white!" cried Bodkin.

"I know." Then a thought struck Polly. "They must have stolen Nutmeg's belt, but how did they get it? She was invisible even to me, and she always kept well out of the way when anyone was around. I only knew about her because you told me, and my uncle only knew because I told him."

The brownie glowered at the ledger. "What does it matter *how* it was done!"

"All right, but *why* was it done? What possible reason could Lord Benjamin have for wanting to keep a brownie? They're hardly a fashion accessory."

Bodkin's face was ablaze with feeling, and his twirling tail threatened to lift his rear end from the floor. "He wants her because he will soon be able to make her visible to everyone, and make a great deal of money." Overcome once more, he picked up a sword-shaped letter opener, and hurled it at Hordwell's portrait. Brownies have amazingly accurate aim, some might even say magically accurate, and Polly's miserly uncle was stabbed right between the eyes.

She stared at the pierced canvas and then at the boggart-brownie. She had never seen Bodkin in such a state before. Indeed, he didn't seem like *her* Bodkin at all! "Money? What do you mean, Bodkin?" she asked, stepping aside because his tail was causing such a draft that several papers on the desk fluttered to the floor.

"People will pay a great deal to see a brownie." Bodkin grabbed his tail to stop its wild activity.

"Pay? Like a fairground attraction, you mean?" Polly was appalled.

"Yes. Just think how much was made from displaying that fake unicorn in London."

Polly nodded, for the unicorn had indeed minted a vast fortune for its owner before it was discovered to be merely a white horse

with a horn glued to its forehead. "Why do you think that is what
Lord Benjamin intends?" she asked.

"It *must* be what he intends. Just over a year ago, in spite of the
war, an Englishman who fits his description down to the last ounce
of blubber, slipped secretly into France to begin the purchase a
page from a book by Nostradamus. Last month a French brownie
risked coming to London to warn English brownies about it."

"Nostradamus? *The* Nostradamus? The sixteenth-century magi-
cian and prophet?"

"Is there more than one?" Bodkin replied archly. "Anyway, the
French brownie wanted us to be on guard because the page con-
tains a spell for making English brownies visible. It's apparently a
very expensive sheet of paper, and the purchaser has only been
able to pay in installments. When the French brownie left France,
he said there was only one more payment to make."

"And you think this mysterious Englishman is Lord Benjamin?"

"I know it," Bodkin replied. "Oh, why didn't I guess before? It
was staring me in the face, but I was too stupid to realize! Now
I've seen the ledger, it's so *obvious* that he is the purchaser."

"You still haven't told me why you think so."

"Because the French brownie described the scar the man had on
the little finger of his left hand," Bodkin explained, and Polly's lips
parted, for Lord Benjamin did indeed have such a scar. The
brownie went on. "As soon as he makes the last payment and re-
ceives the page, he'll make Nutmeg visible, then put her on show
somewhere. He'd have done it months ago if he hadn't been fighting off the duns. I think the cost of the page is one of the main reasons he's now so deep in debt!"

"Then surely the wisest thing he could have done was put his
purse away," Polly pointed out sagely.

"Maybe, but he has his eye on grander things, Miss Polly. If he
can stave off the duns, he'll make a huge fortune out of Nutmeg,
infinitely more than he outlaid in the first place, and much much
more than the unicorn, because she's real. It's too dreadful to even
think about." Tears welled from Bodkin's eyes, and he wiped his
nose with his arm.

"Oh, Bodkin, I don't know what to say." Polly was deeply saddened to think her uncle might be party to such a horrible design.
All she could hope was that he didn't actually know Lord Benjamin's reason, although it had to be admitted that if there was
money to be made, Hordwell Horditall was usually at the fore-

front. She tried to think of something comforting to say. "Take heart, Bodkin, for Lord Benjamin is now being hounded so much by his creditors, that I suspect he's no longer in a position to make the last payment."

"Unless Hordwell gives him the money," Bodkin replied, this new realization dawning with sickening clarity. "Hordwell Horditall would do *anything* to ingratiate himself with the aristocracy."

Polly lowered her eyes, for it was true. Her uncle wouldn't provide sufficient to settle all Lord Benjamin's debts, because such financial rescue was his lordship's sole reason for entering the proposed marriage. He would simply dangle the Peach's Bank carrot by agreeing to pay something. But did he know the full facts about Nutmeg? Oh, she hoped not, *prayed* not.

"Miss Polly, I cannot stay beneath this roof another minute! I have to go to Bath to rescue Nutmeg!"

"Please don't be hasty, Bodkin, especially when—forgive me—you don't seem quite yourself."

"Nutmeg is my sweetheart, and I'm going to get her back!" The brownie's moments of relative calm were over, and once again he was a boggart, incandescent with outrage. He grabbed a paperweight, and aimed it at Hordwell's portrait, this time at the chin in particular. The canvas ripped, and the paperweight buried a sharp corner into the wall paneling behind.

At this point, Polly realized the brownie was becoming a little hazy; indeed she could see through him. "Bodkin!" she cried. "Please don't become invisible to me, for I'm your friend!"

"I'm too angry with humans, even you!" he retorted ungraciously, then he unhooked the keys from his belt and tossed them onto the open ledger.

She heard rather than saw them land. "But I haven't done anything wrong!" she protested indignantly as he began to march toward the door. She barred his way, desperate to calm him down somehow. "At least discuss it all with me before you do anything rash!" she implored, watching in dismay as he grew even more indistinct.

"There's nothing to discuss," he retorted, scowling.

"You can't just leave. What about your bees? You are their guardian, and—"

"The bees will understand; indeed when I need them, they will come to me, no matter how far away I am! *Then* Hordwell and Beddem will regret what they've done!" he said, and pushed past her to stomp away along the passage, his tail no longer twirling, but lashing like a horsewhip.

Polly caught up her skirts and ran after him. "Bodkin, you cannot mean to set the bees on Uncle Hordwell! Or on Lord Benjamin! Oh, please promise you won't do such a thing!"

"From now on I'll do as I please," the boggart-brownie replied over his shoulder, becoming less visible by the second as he began to run up the back staircase to his little attic room. By the time he reached the top of the last flight of stairs, he had disappeared entirely.

Polly hurried up the stairs as well and stood in the doorway of the room, which had a sloping ceiling. She watched in dismay as a large square of red-and-white checkered cloth seemed to lay itself on the plain little bed that stood against one wall. Sunbeams danced through the open dormer window as the brownie's belongings, which were all quite visible because only his belt and keys could not be seen, were piled on top of the cloth. They included his fork and spoon, his brush and comb, an earthenware jar of the exceedingly potent mead he made from his honey, a large pot of the honey itself, and a small tin of clove balm. His knife he tucked into his belt. The cloth was tied into a bundle and fixed upon a brush handle that happened to be propped in a corner. Then the whole thing was jerked on his invisible shoulder. Next the top drawer of the chest beneath the window was opened, a ball of sturdy cord taken out, and the strange assortment bobbed past her toward the staircase.

Polly followed him downstairs and out into the garden, where he made for his pumpkin plant. Placing his things on the grass, he cleared the leaves around the largest pumpkin of all, then took his knife again and began to hack at the stalk. Polly was bewildered. "What are you doing? Why are you cutting a pumpkin?" she asked.

"I need it for Halloween," the boggart-brownie muttered darkly.

"Need it? Whatever for?"

"Never you mind."

Polly stared at the pumpkin. "But it's as wide as you're tall! How on earth will you carry it?"

"All brownies can carry three times their own weight without any trouble," he replied, getting up to haul the pumpkin from the bed onto the grass. Then he took some leaves to wipe it clean.

"You . . . you won't do anything really horrid with it, will you?"

she inquired uneasily, for now that he was a boggart, heaven alone knew what he had in mind.

"If I do, it will be no more than they deserve," he replied, then refused to speak again as he unraveled the ball of cord to wrap and knot it like a net so that the great orange-yellow orb was securely held. Then it, too, was fixed to the brush handle. Polly watched as the great load was heaved over his shoulder. For a moment she could tell that his little knees buckled, but then he gave a huge grunt, straightened, and set off down the garden path toward the gate just as the superior gentleman's carriage, now very dirty indeed, returned from the ravages of Wrecker Johnson's farmyard.

Chapter 3

After passing Horditall House the first time, the carriage containing the haughty young gentleman had driven blithely on, but on turning a sudden sharp corner, it found itself in Wrecker Johnson's waterlogged lane, where wild clematis tumbled over the high hedgerows and gossamer drifted clammily in the air. The vehicle's immaculate wheels were soon up to their axles in mud and deep puddles, the fine horses splashed with dirt and the dismayed coachman had no choice but to drive on. He was already in Sir Dominic Fortune's bad books for having drunk too much ale at the inn last night, and being the cause of a fracas, so he was certain that this disaster would signal the end of his employment.

As if on cue, Sir Dominic leaned irritably out of the window. "Where in God's name are we, Jeffries?"

"I . . . I fear I must have taken the wrong road back at the signpost, Sir Dominic. But I vow that this was definitely indicated as the way to Bath."

"If this is the road to Bath, I'm a Dutchman," Dominic replied cuttingly as he glanced down at the muddy water swirling in ruts so deep they resembled Cheddar Gorge itself.

Jeffries gazed desperately along the lane, and then his eyes brightened hopefully. "I see buildings ahead, sir. I believe it's a farm. We'll be able to turn around there."

Dominic sat back on the sumptuous brown leather upholstery. The last thing he wanted to do was go to Bath, but when inheritance of an uncle's considerable estate depended upon marriage, what choice did a sensible nephew have but to find a wife? Not that he really needed any more wealth, for he was already ridiculously well provided for, but another handsome helping did no harm. London was clearly the best place for choice, but right now the metropolis held too many painful memories.

He'd left the capital two weeks ago, but while his luggage and saddle horse were sent to Bath, he had traveled by way of friends in Winchester. The visit over, he'd made a detour of a few hours to see the wonders of Cheddar Gorge, and now he was finally en route for England's finest watering place. Pray God the spa was teeming with likely contenders for the title of Lady Fortune, for he wanted the matter over with as quickly as possible. It would be a loveless arrangement, because his heart was already given to a beautiful, but selfish and single-mindedly ambitious widow by the name of Lady Georgiana Mersenrie. Georgiana was the only daughter of the Duke of Lawless, and her late husband, an elderly Scottish lord of immense wealth, had left her with ample funds to make her Berkeley Square house one of *the* places for society to gather. She was one of London's foremost hostesses, a lady whose invitations were as sought after as vouchers to Almack's, but this wasn't enough. Her avowed intention was to be a duchess, and not just any duchess, for her designs centered upon Lord Algernon Lofty, the son and heir of the Duke of Grandcastle, England's richest and most influential nobleman.

Dominic sighed unhappily. So fixed was Georgiana upon her ambition, that she'd actually suggested he seek a wife elsewhere. This was hurtful enough, but how much worse it had been when she'd gone so far as to suggest it would be better if he removed to Bath to commence his search for a bride, leaving her to make certain of her duke-to-be. Without so much as a by-your-leave, she'd written to her second brother, Lord Benjamin Beddem, requesting him to accommodate her unwanted lover in his house in Royal Crescent! She could not have made her wishes more clear, and so Dominic had done as she wanted. What point would there have been in standing his ground? She'd made it abundantly clear that she would never marry him, so he had to get on with his life without her. Besides, he was thirty now, and it was probably time he took a wife. Any wife.

His thoughts were suddenly and very rudely interrupted by a cacophony of squawks, squeals, and grunts. What in God's own name—? The carriage jolted to a standstill, and he leaned out of the window again. To his horror he saw a walled farmyard that was even more muddy than the lane. At least, he hoped it was mud. A dozen or so enormous fat pigs milled around, and chickens flapped in all directions. The smell was atrocious, and he had to put a handkerchief to his nose.

Grinning broadly, Wrecker Johnson emerged from the farmhouse in his smock, breeches, and stout boots. He was a burly red-faced man, and was barely able to prevent himself from rubbing his hands together in glee as he surveyed Dominic's fine vehicle and elegant London clothes. "And 'oo might you be, zur?" he asked.

"Sir Dominic Fortune."

A title, eh? Oh, this got better by the second. Wrecker beamed at his victim. "You'll 'ave to 'elp me, zur, for 'twill take both of us to keep the pigs back while your dandy coachman turns your smart 'quipage."

Dominic shuddered. Help this yokel with his filthy fat pigs? Dear God above.

Wrecker strode through the quagmire and opened the carriage door. "Down you come, zur, for I can't do it on my own, not when they'm in such a panic."

Dominic knew the man was enjoying the situation, but could do little except bow to his wishes. With a resigned sigh, he alighted gingerly, closing his eyes for a moment as his gleaming top boots sank into the mud.

The farmer grinned. "That's right, zur. Don't worry now, your pretty footwear won't be sucked off when you walks. Leastways, I don't reckon so," he added doubtfully, as Dominic tried to take a step, then almost lost his balance because the mud gripped so well.

Jeffries did not dare to turn his head. His dismissal loomed ever larger, and he was pondering where he might find a new position as good as this one. Dominic glanced darkly up at him. "I'll make garters of your intestines for this, Jeffries."

"Yes, sir," the coachman replied resignedly.

Dominic returned the handkerchief to his nose as he addressed the farmer. "What do I have to do?" he asked, keeping an eye on the pigs, which seemed more like ferocious wild boars than domestic porkers.

"Most of 'em seem to have settled for this corner by me, so if you just round up old April and May over there, and bring 'em over, your flunky will be able to start turning your grand 'quipage."

"And what, pray, will *your* contribution be to the proceedings?" Dominic inquired. Playing the appreciative audience, no doubt, he thought.

"Me? Why, I'll be keeping the rest of my grand bacon calendar quiet," the farmer replied. "Or mayhap *you'd* like to take care of these ten, while I looks after April and May?" he offered then.

When it came to choice between ten or two pigs, the decision was easy. "You stay where you are."

Wrecker grinned. "A wise decision, zur."

With the handkerchief keeping only some of the stench at bay, Dominic squelched around the rear of the carriage toward April and May, who were two of the most monumental sows he had ever seen. If ever a man regretted giving in to the impulse to see Cheddar Gorge . . .

The following minutes were some of the most hilarious and entertaining of Wrecker's waylaying career. He roared with laughter at the sight of a London swell plowing through mud in pursuit of the two recalcitrant pigs. Even Jeffries was hard put not to grin, but Dominic didn't think it in the least funny. After falling twice and covering himself in mud—as well as ingredients less salubrious— he eventually managed to drive April and May to join their companions. Jeffries immediately began the laborious task of coaxing the nervous team into action again, and in five minutes had the carriage facing the way it had come.

Wrecker managed to control his laughter. "Don't worry now, zur, for when the mud and sh—" He cleared his throat. "Well, you know what I mean. When it dries, it'll come off easy enough. Leastways, it *should*." Dominic gave him a look that would have stopped lesser men in their tracks, but a thin skin wasn't one of Wrecker's qualities. "Right then, zur, that'll be sixpence," he declared brazenly.

"I *beg* your pardon?" Dominic replied, thinking he must have misheard.

"That'll be sixpence for the use of my yard and my services," the farmer repeated.

"If you think I'm going to—"

"Satan? Satan! Come out 'ere!" shouted Wrecker, and a very large, very black dog immediately emerged from the farmhouse.

As it bared its teeth and growled ominously, Dominic hastily took the necessary money from his pocket and thrust it into the man's hand. "With such a keen sense of business, you should go far, sir," he muttered, then clambered back into the carriage. Jeffries urged the horses forward, and the carriage jolted out of the yard back into the lane. Dominic sat on the spotless upholstery, smearing mud and mire everywhere. He stank like the proverbial dung heap, and he doubted if his own mother would recognize him. Damn all farmers, damn Somerset, damn everything!

It seemed an age before the carriage was on firm going again, allowing Jeffries to bring the bedraggled team up to a reasonable trot. As it drove through Horditall, Dominic's attention was drawn once more to the house where the young woman in blue had been tending the garden. To his relief she was no longer there, and so would not witness the ruination of his splendor. He leaned his head back, and closed his eyes. What an unutterably appalling day this had turned out to be.

If he had continued to look out at Horditall House, he would have seen a bundle of belongings and a large pumpkin on a pole bobbing at the double down the garden path, with Polly in anxious pursuit. On reaching the wall on the road, the bundle and pumpkin were flung amid the luggage at the rear of the carriage, and then there was a thud as something invisible jumped on as well. Dominic's eyes opened momentarily, as he heard the sound, and Jeffries turned his head, but there was so much luggage that he saw nothing.

The carriage bowled on, and Bodkin made himself as comfortable as he could. Clutching the pumpkin on his lap, for fear it would roll onto the road and be lost, he glowered back at the hamlet as it faded behind. He wrinkled his nose at the farmyard smell pervading the entire vehicle. But what did a foul smell matter? He was going to rescue Nutmeg, and in the process he intended to make the lives of Hordwell Horditall and Lord Benjamin Beddem a misery. He patted the pumpkin. "You're going to be the best jack-o'-lantern that ever was," he muttered, envisaging the diabolical face he would carve into it.

Polly gazed unhappily after the carriage, then turned to walk thoughtfully back to the house. Unless Bodkin could somehow be prevailed upon, in his present fury he was capable of causing a great deal of trouble, not only for her uncle and Lord Benjamin, but for anyone else who got in the way. Bath might never be the same again! This last prospect made her halt in horror. Now that she had seen a boggart for the first time, she knew how awful a creature it was. Bodkin had to be stopped. But how? It was clear she had to follow him in her uncle's second carriage, but she held out no hope of catching up with the arrogant gentleman's vehicle, which had been moving at a very smart pace when last seen. Uncle Hordwell was too mean to pay for blood horses, so his team would stand no chance of overhauling the four grays, even supposing she was ready to leave immediately. It would be Bath itself before she could prevail upon the boggart-brownie, or indeed upon Uncle Hordwell, who had to mend the situation regarding Nutmeg.

She didn't relish going to Lord Benjamin's residence in Royal Crescent, but since it was bound to be Bodkin's destination, she had no choice. It was out of the question that she should stay there, however, so no matter what her uncle might say, she would lodge at a suitable inn or hotel. She hoped the whole business would be resolved in a short time, and soon she would be back here again.

She hurried inside to issue instructions. It was twenty-five miles to Bath, but she reckoned to be there before nightfall.

Chapter 4

The Bath road descended very gradually from the heights of Horditall. It passed through rich farmland, where cattle and sheep grazed, the fields were plowed for winter, and the orchards were mellow with fruit. Smoke curled lazily from chimneys or hung above gardens where the autumn leaves were being burned. The swallows had gone now, and the hedgerows were heavy with rose hips and hawthorn berries, as well as sloes and the ubiquitous wild clematis—known as old man's beard—that rambled so thick and dusty white at this time of year. It was all very beautiful and tranquil, but Polly was too anxious to draw any enjoyment from the passing scene. There were still twelve miles to go, and the light was already copper and hazy as the sun began to sink.

Sitting impatiently in the slow-moving carriage, she willed the final miles away. She was dressed in an ivory woolen gown, with a three-quarter-length lilac velvet pelisse over it, and her hair was pinned up beneath a lilac velvet jockey bonnet. A long filmy white scarf fell from the back of the bonnet, and her hands were encased in gray kid gloves. Her reticule lay on the seat beside her, together with her volume of *The Castle of Otranto*, intended to make the time pass, but now discarded. She stared out of the window, wondering how far ahead the other carriage was. Almost in Bath, she judged, listening to the slow trot of her team as they negotiated a slight hill. *Oh, hurry, hurry, for I want this to be over with.*

Dominic's carriage was indeed coming toward journey's end. The sun was setting fast as his carriage bowled down into the Avon valley, then joined the Bristol turnpike on the outskirts of Bath. The resort tumbled down the valley sides to the river's edge, where the tower of the abbey rose in medieval splendor. Row upon row of handsome golden stone houses graced the steep slopes, and as the carriage rattled into the elegant cobbled streets, the oil lamps were already being lit.

Huddled amid the luggage, Bodkin was still in a boggart rage. He was wedged between a trunk and a portmanteau, and was very glad of his thick fur because the autumn evening had grown cold. All the way from Horditall, he had dwelt hard and long upon how to exact revenge upon Hordwell and Lord Benjamin; indeed those gentlemen's ears should have ignited as he imagined all kinds of dire punishment. Oh, they were going to rue the day they took his beloved Nutmeg away!

It should have been a simple matter to drive up to Royal Crescent from the edge of the town, past Marlborough Buildings, but that route was closed because of work on the road, so Jeffries had to continue into the center in order to approach the crescent from the other side. Dominic's hapless coachman was in better spirits now, for at the fateful signpost east of Horditall, he had been able to point out to Dominic that it had indeed been tampered with. There was no need to wonder who might do such a thing, for a certain farmer's eagerly outstretched palm was all the evidence required.

Dominic observed Bath's fine streets and squares, and noticed the preponderance of sedan chairs and bath chairs, as well as gathering groups of torch bearers—universally known as link boys—whose task it was to light the way through the darkness. Then he became aware of a great number of uniforms. Foremost among these he recognized those of his own former hussar regiment, the Duke of York's Own Light Dragoons, which he'd quit on his father's sudden death two years ago. What was afoot? he wondered. A review of some sort? A stir of interest crept over him as he hoped the entire regiment was in the vicinity, because if so, he'd be able to call on many of his old friends.

As the carriage progressed through Bath, he had to concede that in spite of his great reluctance to be here at all, the resort was very handsome indeed. But, oh, how much better he would feel if he were in London now, with Georgiana in his arms, his ring on her finger. No woman would ever compare with her. Still, when it came to his marriage bed, he could always *imagine* it was Georgiana he had between the sheets.

His fingers drummed on the window ledge as the carriage swung around Queen Square, where the railed central garden was graced by an obelisk. Please let his sojourn here be brief, he thought, his fingers pausing a moment as Jeffries maneuvered the team north out of the square toward the Circus. Passing the junction with George Street, he noticed the premises of the renowned pastry cook, Wilhelm Zuder. The illuminated windows displayed a magnificent selection of pastries, cakes, fudge, bonbons, jellies, preserves, honey, and all manner of other sweet delicacies. A queue of ladies, gentlemen, maids, and footmen was waiting at the oak counter, and the portion of the premises that had been turned into a tea shop was so crowded that not a single seat was to be had. Bodkin had also seen the pastry cook's. He feasted boggart eyes upon the treasure hoard of sweet temptation, and his conscience became nonexistent as he resolved to pay Zuder's a clandestine visit later on that night. It was his birthday, and he was going to sample everything on the premises without paying a penny!

The shop fell away behind as the carriage climbed up to the Circus, a fine ring of town houses intersected by three streets, one of which, Brock Street, led directly to the eastern end of Royal Crescent. At last the matchless sweep of Bath's most desirable address came into view. It was a truly superb sight in the final moments of daylight, a masterpiece of thirty town houses situated above sloping common land with an uninterrupted view across the Avon valley.

As Jeffries drew the carriage to a standstill outside of Lord Benjamin's residence, and Dominic prepared to alight, Bodkin peered over the side of the boot. He'd seen the name Royal Crescent written on the first house in the curve and could hardly believe his luck that his unknowing transport had brought him to the very street he sought! The brownie gazed along the pavement, belatedly wishing he'd thought of asking Polly the number of Beddem's residence. Nutmeg was in one of these houses, but which one?

Suddenly the front door of the house by which the carriage had halted opened, and several footmen emerged to attend to the unloading of the luggage. Bodkin jumped hastily down with his bundle and the pumpkin, and bent low as he hurried to the unlit entrance of the property next door, and from there he watched as Dominic entered his house. As the last item of luggage was carried inside, and Jeffries drove the carriage around to the nearby mews, the brownie emerged from his doorway to consider what to do next. How was he going to find out which house it was? Inspiration struck almost immediately. All he had to do was find the mews and ascertain which coach house contained Hordwell's carriage! The coach house would surely have the same number as the house to which it belonged! Yes, that was it. He swung his cumbersome things over his shoulder again and set off along the pavement. Soon he went around the large house at the beginning of the crescent, then disappeared from view.

It was very dark indeed when Polly's carriage reached Bath and was obliged to take the same circuitous route to the crescent. At Lord Benjamin's house, Polly paused apprehensively before alighting. Oh, how she was going to loathe the coming hours, for being anywhere near Lord Benjamin was always purgatory to her. He was a true scion of that long, long line of philanderers, clammy and lascivious, always eyeing her, murmuring supposed compliments, and trying to brush against her as if by accident. If ever there was a prime example of the house of Beddem, it was he! She climbed reluctantly down to the pavement and braced herself for the ordeal ahead. The air was cold, and her breath was visible as she went up to the door to rap the gleaming brass knocker. She felt a little embarrassed, realizing that unescorted ladies who called at doors after dark were frequently not ladies at all, but at least her name would soon dispel any such unwelcome conclusions.

After a moment a footman answered, but her name did not seem to convey anything at all. "Er, is Sir Dominic expecting you, madam?" he inquired.

"Sir *Who*?" Polly was startled, and further dismayed to see that the footman's livery was an unfamiliar green and gold.

"Sir Dominic Fortune, madam. This is his residence."

She glanced hastily at the number painted in black beside the door. Yes, she was at the right address. "There must be a mistake, I—" She broke off on a gasp as she saw Dominic descending the staircase at the end of the entrance hall. He had changed out of his dirty clothes, and after a good hot bath now wore a long gray paisley dressing gown.

He paused on realizing something was amiss at the door. "What is it?" he inquired.

"A Miss Peach has called, sir."

Dominic approached reluctantly. He inclined his head to Polly, not recognizing her at first. "Sir Dominic Fortune, your servant, madam. May I be of some assistance?" he murmured.

His eyes were a clear, steady gray; disconcertingly steady. She found herself blushing before their gaze, for she was again obliged to judge him the most handsome man ever. The intense feeling of attraction returned quite unnervingly, and she felt her pulse quicken with anticipation. Oh, this wouldn't do! She forced herself to recall his manner earlier in the day. He might be handsome beyond belief, but he was also unpleasant!

"Have we met?" he asked, beginning to realize he'd seen her somewhere before.

"Er, no, sir, we haven't. I . . . I was seeking the residence of Lord Benjamin Beddem, where my uncle is staying, but I've come to the wrong house. If you'll excuse me . . ." She turned to leave, but he spoke again.

"If we have not met, you seem strangely familiar, Miss Peach."

"Well, you may have noticed me earlier today," she confessed, facing him again.

"Indeed?"

"Yes, when you drove through Horditall."

His expression cooled. "Ah, yes, the gardening goddess who could so easily have spared me the ignominy of the pig farm."

Her eyes flashed at that. "And you, sir, could quite easily have omitted to be so disdainful when you passed."

"So I *deserved* to be covered in filth and rooked by that villain. Is that what you're saying?" he answered stiffly.

She didn't reply, but her expression spoke volumes.

He was stung into an accusation he knew had to be unjust. "I can only presume you are the ruffian's accomplice?"

She bridled indignantly. "I certainly am not, sir!"

His glance was filled with the disdain of which she'd accused him a moment before. "I'm relieved to hear it. Well, madam, unhelpful *you* may have been, but I will not stoop to that level. Since you reside in Horditall, I can only imagine your uncle to be Mr. Hordwell Horditall. Am I correct?"

"Yes, sir, you are."

"Then in a manner of speaking you have the correct address after all. Lord Benjamin is indeed the leaseholder here, but he has temporarily rented the property to me."

She was taken aback. "Then please, sir, can you inform me where I may find my uncle?"

"Lord Benjamin's father, the Duke of Lawless, has taken 1 Royal Crescent in readiness for the Christmas season, although he himself will not take up residence until nearer that time. Lord Benjamin decided he preferred the extra grandeur of that property to this, so he moved there a week ago, and naturally your uncle went with him."

Polly had noticed that the houses at either end of the crescent were very regal indeed. How sensible of Lord Benjamin to go there, and let someone else take up the lease here. Not only did he not have to pay a penny for the larger property, but he could impress Uncle Hordwell all the more. She wondered about Nutmeg. Was the brownie here, or had Lord Benjamin taken her to number one? Momentarily she pondered asking Dominic, but then discarded the notion, for not only did he seem the sort of man who would dismiss any notion of brownies even existing, but she could also see his luggage in the hallway, signifying he hadn't merely been in the Horditall area for a day's excursion out of Bath, but had come by that route on his way here. He was therefore unlikely to know about any of the staff, let alone an invisible brownie! She made herself look at him again. "Thank you for your assistance, sir." But as she turned away once more, he stepped quickly after her.

"Allow me to attend you to your carriage, Miss Peach."

"There is no need, Sir Dominic," she replied, not wishing to be in his debt for even so small a service.

"There is every need, Miss Peach, for in spite of your prejudgment, I am a gentleman."

"I did not question that, sir. I merely found fault with your conduct."

"As I in turn found fault with yours, so I believe we are even, Miss Peach," he said, taking her hand and drawing it firmly over his sleeve.

Polly said nothing as he escorted her across the pavement to the waiting carriage. He handed her inside, then bowed coolly before closing the door. He turned to instruct the coachman to turn around at the far end of the crescent in order to return to the first house on the corner of Brock Street. He remained on the pavement as the carriage drew away from the curb, but had gone inside by the time it drove past again. Polly was annoyed as she sat in the shadows, feeling not only that she had somehow been bested, but also that in spite of everything, she still found him diabolically attractive. Oh, how very vexing! She wanted to loathe every inch of him; instead she wondered what it would be like to be in his arms!

Chapter 5

The carriage halted once more, this time at the much grander entrance of the end house. Polly alighted again, forced thoughts of Sir Dominic Fortune aside, then went up the flight of stone steps that led to the pedimented front door. She employed the gleaming brass knocker, and the sound echoed through the house beyond. At last she heard footsteps approaching, and the door was opened by a footman in the crimson and silver colors of the Beddem family.

This time when she gave her name, it was recognized immediately; indeed the footman's reaction was such that she could not help but realize indignantly that Lord Benjamin's offer of marriage was common knowledge below stairs. And if the footman's deferential manner was anything by which to judge, her acceptance was regarded as a mere formality! She stepped a little crossly into the warmth of a stone-flagged entrance hall with walls that had been painted to resemble pale golden marble. Various doors led off on either side, and at the far end there was a curving stone staircase upon which had been laid green carpet. A glass-sided brass lamp was suspended from the ceiling, with four bright candles that cast a good light.

"Is my uncle at home?" she asked the footman.

"Indeed so, madam, but Lord Benjamin has been called away to London and will not be back until the morning of Halloween."

She could hardly believe her luck. "Oh, well, it cannot be helped," she murmured, for to give a whoop of delight would hardly be the thing.

"Mr. Horditall is in the library, so if you will please be seated, I will announce you." The footman indicated a dark mahogany chair.

"There is no need to announce me, er . . . ?"

"Giles, madam."

"I'll announce myself, Giles," she replied firmly. If the fellow thought she was to be Lady Beddem, she might as well use the authority bestowed by that mistaken belief. "Which door is it?"

He was a little uneasy as he indicated a door on the right, for there was a glint in her eye he knew did not bode well for her uncle. But what could a mere footman do when confronted by Lord Benjamin's bride?

As he turned to beckon another footman waiting by the door to the kitchens, Polly realized they were about to attend to her luggage. She spoke quickly. "Oh, no, please don't unload the carriage, for I intend to stay at a hotel or inn."

"I beg your pardon, madam?" Giles gaped at her.

"I believe I made myself quite clear," she replied, still making full use of her supposed future rank.

"Very well, Miss Peach." Bemused, he bowed, and then he and his companion withdrew below stairs.

Polly drew a deep breath, then opened the door. The library was warm and cozy, with dancing firelight moving over the fawn silk walls and biscuit-colored carpet. Two very fine mahogany secretaire bookcases stood on either side of the white marble fireplace, and there was a garniture of Bristol delftware on the mantleshelf. Above the fireplace was a portrait of one of the royal princes, she

wasn't quite sure which, and on other walls were various land-
scapes, some watercolor, some oils. The furniture was upholstered
in chestnut velvet, including the elegant sofa, and the Hepplewhite
fireside chair in which her uncle reposed asleep, his mouth open as
he snored.

In appearance, Hordwell Horditall wasn't at all what one would
have expected of so miserly a character, for he was plump and
rosy-cheeked, and outwardly seemed very amiable indeed. However, in his case appearances were definitely deceptive. He was
dressed in a beige velvet-collared coat and gray breeches, and his
marcella waistcoat buttons were strained across his ample middle.
His walking sticks rested against the chair, and his gouty foot was
cushioned on a stool before the fire. His small gray wig was askew
on his balding head, and his muslin neckcloth was undone, resting
crumpled against his stomach. On the table beside him were the re-
mains of a cold chicken supper and an empty decanter of port, neither of which could possibly be recommended for relief from gout,
and which would certainly not have graced his evenings at Horditall House because of their cost. His suppers there consisted of
bread, Cheddar cheese, and a tankard or three of ale. How very
agreeable for him to enjoy all this luxury at someone else's expense, she thought. Lord Benjamin's threadbare purse wouldn't
suffer either, for everything in this house was paid for by the Duke
of Lawless. She could just imagine the alacrity with which the
duke's reprobate second son had secured Sir Dominic to take over
his payments for the other house, and then moved in here.

She studied her sleeping uncle. Behold the unfortunate invalid,
she thought crossly, recalling how much fuss he'd made about his
painful foot prior to leaving Horditall. It was only too clear now
that his gout wasn't as bad as he'd pretended, and that he'd come
here with the ulterior motive of negotiating with Lord Benjamin
regarding her marriage! She bent to speak loudly in Hordwell's
ear. "Good evening, Uncle!"

He sat forward with a jolt. "Eh? What? Dear God above!" he
cried, and then his jaw dropped as he saw his niece. "Polly?"

"The same."

"Whatever brings you here?" he asked, snatching off his napkin,
and tossing it guiltily over the telltale supper.

"Don't attempt to gull me with napkins, Uncle, for I've already
observed your sins. You *know* you are forbidden port and chicken.

What is the point of coming here for the cure if you're going to disobey your doctor's instructions?"

"It is but a single fall from grace," he muttered, testing his gouty foot with great care on the floor. Then he seized his walking sticks and began to make much of hauling himself to his feet.

He expected her to rush to spare him such painful exertions, but she left him to it. If he was well enough to gobble chicken suppers and guzzle decanters of port, he was well enough to stand up to greet her! She eyed him heartlessly. "Be honest, Uncle, admit that you've really come here with marriage contracts in mind."

He ignored the remark as he hobbled over to peck her on the cheek. "Is all well at the house?" he asked.

"As well as might be expected under the circumstances."

"What circumstances?" he asked quickly, fearing an imminent assault on his purse.

"I wish to know about the agreement you have with Lord Benjamin concerning Nutmeg."

He was momentarily taken aback, but then recovered. "How do you know about that?"

Her heart sank that he did not deny it. "You forgot to padlock your study door. Bodkin found it open and went in to tidy up for you. The ledger was open on your desk."

"He had no right to go in there."

"I know, but he did, and so the truth is out. What have you to say?"

He rubbed his chin for a moment. "Well, it's all nonsense, of course," he said then.

"*Nonsense?* Oh, Uncle, how can you dismiss it like that? Nutmeg was Bodkin's sweetheart, and you allowed Lord Benjamin to take her like a piece of furniture!"

"It wasn't like that, my dear. Oh, please sit down, for my poor foot is very sore tonight."

"Good," she replied unsympathetically, but went to sit on the sofa.

"You're very cruel, Polly," he complained, easing himself carefully back into his chair.

"No, Uncle, you are the cruel one. How *could* you let Lord Benjamin take Nutmeg to put her on show at fairs and such things?"

"Eh?" He looked blankly at her. "What are you talking about? What fairs?"

She paused. "What do you know of the page of Nostradamus that Lord Benjamin is purchasing?" she asked then.

Hordwell's face was a puzzled blank. "Nostradamus? I don't know anything. Oh, for heaven's sake, Polly, stop talking in riddles."

He wasn't pretending to be ignorant on the matter. He clearly knew nothing, and for that at least she was relieved. But it didn't absolve him of the crime of handing poor Nutmeg over in the first place.

He eyed her across the firelight. "Well? What's all this about a page of Nostradamus?" he prompted. She told him what Bodkin had told her, and when she'd finished, he gave a disbelieving chuckle. "What superstitious rubbish. Spells, indeed. Polly, I did not give Nutmeg to Benjamin, nor did he take her, although he was certainly prepared to do so. Out of consideration for her well-being, I hasten to add, not any despicable motive. In fact, she left of her own accord, and I have no idea where she is. As to the entry in the ledger, well, that was made in anticipation of an actual transaction. You see, I intend to virtually rebuild the house she looked after, and it occurred to me that she might appreciate a temporary sojourn in the comfort of Bath. I was going to mention the subject to you, so that you could tell Bodkin, and he could explain to her. The intention all along was for her to return to her true home again as soon as the alterations were complete. But she disappeared before anything could even be put to her. Neither I nor Benjamin had anything to do with her departure, and she certainly isn't here in this house, or in the other one here in the crescent. Now, that is the truth, which you may take or leave, as the pleasure moves you."

Chapter 6

Polly hesitated, for there was an earnestness in her uncle's glance and voice that seemed to indicate he was telling the truth. "If that is so, Uncle Hordwell, perhaps you can tell me why she went without saying anything to Bodkin?"

"I have no idea. Maybe they had a quarrel, which he is omitting to mention," he replied, spreading his hands.

In spite of herself, she was convinced. "Very well, I believe you," she said.

He breathed out with relief. "Oh, my dear, I'm so glad."

"There's just one thing."

"Yes?"

"You must tell this to Bodkin as well. You see, as soon as he found that wretched entry in the ledger, he rushed here to Bath to find Nutmeg. He's in a terrible temper; indeed I would hardly know him. He's become a boggart, I fear."

Hordwell shifted uncomfortably. "Oh, dear . . ."

"I'm very worried about him, Uncle, for he was absolutely livid when I last saw him. In his present mood I fear he's capable of anything."

"That is the way with boggarts."

"You may count upon it—you and Lord Benjamin are to be targeted for some mischief, so the sooner we find him, the better."

"Find him? My dear, I can't even see him, let alone anything else. You may have seen him on countless occasions, but he's always remained invisible to me. No, I fear *you* will have to tell him."

"He's so disgruntled with the human race at the moment that he won't even let me see him. I only know he jumped onto Sir Dominic Fortune's carriage because he threw his things in first."

Startled, Hordwell sat forward. "*Fortune's* carriage?"

"Sir Dominic is the disagreeable person who has taken Lord Benjamin's other house here in the crescent," she explained.

"I know who he is."

"Yes, I suppose you do. Well, he was one of Wrecker Johnson's victims, and happened to be driving past just as Bodkin rushed from the house. I followed the carriage here to Bath, and went to the wrong house. It was Sir Dominic who directed me here."

"I see. Why do you find him disagreeable? I haven't met him, but have been led to believe he is a man of impeccable manners."

"He's too full of his own importance." Polly smiled then. "But I fancy Wrecker's pigs cut him down to size."

"Dear me. However, enough of him, and enough of this wretched Nutmeg business. Have you eaten? The cooking here is most excellent."

"I'm sure the Duke of Lawless would be flattered to know your opinion," she replied. "As it happens, I brought something to eat in the carriage."

"Nothing too lavish, I trust?" The miser in him was foremost.

"It was as nothing compared with succulent cold chicken suppers and the finest port," she replied pointedly.

He colored a little. "A guest must eat as his host provides," he said unctuously, then cleared his throat again. "Well, how very pleasant it is to have you here, my dear. It's unfortunate that Lord Benjamin has been called away to London, but he will return on Halloween. He has acquired tickets for the fancy dress celebrations at Sydney Gardens. The Duke and Duchess of York will be there as well. He's going as a devil, I believe, Lord Benjamin, that is, not the Duke of York."

A rather overweight devil, she thought ungenerously. "What are you going as, Uncle?" she inquired, thinking that he could just go as himself. Being a sly old skinflint seemed a perfectly acceptable guise for Halloween.

"Me? Oh, nothing. Fancy dress is optional."

"What a spoilsport, to be sure," she murmured, and then turned the conversation to the contentious but important subject of Lord Benjamin Beddem's marital intentions. "Uncle, I know full well that you aren't here just for your gout. You may as well accept that I will *never* marry Lord Benjamin, so please do me the kindness of recognizing the fact."

"We'll see, my dear, we'll see."

"No, Uncle, we won't."

"But one day you will be a duchess," he said, perplexed that any sensible young woman could turn down such a grand opportunity for advancement.

"A duchess? Well, that's always providing his lordship is telling the truth about his elder brother being disinherited, which I doubt very much." Lord Benjamin Beddem was so disreputable that she doubted if he even trusted himself! Her uncle was the only one to credit him with any semblance of honesty.

"He would hardly lie about such a thing."

"Why not? Uncle, he *knows* you won't question anything he says, so he feels at liberty to say anything he chooses!" A thought occurred to her. "Has he cozened you for money in recent weeks?" She was thinking about the costly page of Nostradamus.

"No," was the prompt reply. Hordwell shifted, then gave her a reproachful look. "Polly, enough of this. Are you intending to stay a while?"

"In Bath, yes, but not in this house."

"What nonsense. Of course you must stay here!"

"I hardly think it would be appropriate, Uncle."

"I insist that if you are in Bath, you lodge here," he said firmly.

"Uncle—"

"That is the end of it."

Polly felt a little like a worm on a hook. "Aren't you being a little free with the Duke of Lawless's hospitality, Uncle?"

"If Benjamin were here, he would insist as well."

"Oh, yes, I'm sure he would, but his motives would be questionable, would they not?"

"I do wish you wouldn't keep denigrating him, my dear, for he isn't the monster you seem to think."

"No, he's worse, and I refuse absolutely to stay beneath his roof."

"He isn't even here," Hordwell pointed out.

"I know, but—"

"Polly, it would distress me a great deal if you were to stay elsewhere. It would not be seemly, and it would reflect very poorly upon me. I am your guardian, or had you forgotten?"

"That's blackmail, Uncle."

"To be sure, and very necessary, too."

She considered a moment. If Lord Benjamin was absent, surely it would be all right for her to stay? She made a hasty decision. "If you insist, Uncle, but I only wish to remain in Bath until I've found Bodkin and convinced him that neither you nor Lord Benjamin have Nutmeg imprisoned somewhere. If I still haven't found him by Halloween, I will remove to an inn or hotel, and nothing you say or do will change my mind."

"We'll cross that bridge when we come to it," he warned, then gave a satisfied smile. "I'm glad you're here, my dear, for it means I have the use of a carriage again. Did I mention that the large carriage is being repaired?"

"No."

"It's most inconvenient, oh, not for the cure, to which I am conducted by means of a sedan chair, but certainly for everything else. For instance, apart from the Halloween junketing at Sydney Gardens, there is a ball at the Assembly Rooms the day after tomorrow, again attended by the Duke and Duchess of York. By the way,

Polly, did you know that four years ago the Duke of York took this very house?" He indicated the portrait above the mantelshelf. "Just imagine—we are guests beneath the very roof that once sheltered a prince of the blood."

"I am in awe," she murmured.

He frowned disapprovingly, for he found it astonishing that she was not as impressed as he by royal or noble blood. Putting her failings down to a lack of correct parental guidance on the part of his late sister and brother-in-law, he sniffed and continued, "As to the ball, everyone who is anyone will be there, but every hired carriage in Bath has been snapped up. The crush of traffic near the rooms promises to be unbelievable."

"Surely anyone with sense will walk," Polly ventured, thinking that walking seemed infinitely preferable to the madness of driving the short distance along Brock Street, around the Circus, then a few yards east to the Assembly Rooms, in the full knowledge that everything was bound to grind to a complete standstill anyway.

"Polly, you know it isn't done to *walk* to a ball!" he replied tartly, then went on. "On the day before the ball—that's tomorrow, of course—there is to be a fine army review on Claverton Down, at which the duke will take the salute of his own regiment of light dragoons. I confess that even though I have been invited to join Count and Countess Gotenuv's very select luncheon party in their tent at the review, and—"

"Count and Countess Who?" Polly interposed, never having heard of them before.

"Gotenuv." He chuckled. "Gotenuv by name, got enough by nature, for they are rumored to be fabulously wealthy. They're Russians, but the count is out of favor with the czar, so he and the countess were obliged to flee the country. Anyway, where was I?"

"Their select luncheon party at the review."

"Ah, yes. Well, their tent will be right next to the royal pavilion, and I had resigned myself to not attending due to lack of transport, but now we can go together, for I have no doubt the Gotenuvs will graciously include you among their guests."

"Uncle, you cannot keep imposing upon other people's hospitality like this. They don't know me, and I don't know them, so why on earth would they wish to include me in their exclusive party?"

"They are very well bred, my dear, and any such request from one of their guests would be agreed to without question."

"As you would agree if you were the host? I think not."

"Don't be ridiculous, Polly, for you know I would never have a tent at a royal occasion in the first place." Hordwell frowned at her, then went on. "Anyway, I was telling you about the Gotenuvs. They've taken the other end house here on the crescent, and are very well acquainted with Benjamin, upon whom they dote as if he were their son."

Which meant they were probably addled, Polly thought, further surmising that Lord Benjamin's interest in them would be purely mercenary. No doubt he intended to swindle them out of all he could. "Does the count play cards?" she asked shrewdly.

"Oh, yes. He and Benjamin spend many an evening at the green baize," her uncle duly confirmed.

Definitely addled, she decided, for who in their right mind would play cards with a debt-ridden sharp like Lord Benjamin Beddem?

"Well, Polly, no doubt you are tired after your unexpected journey. I will ring for a footman to take you up to whichever room is deemed best for you." He reached over to tug the bellpull.

After a moment Giles came. "You rang, sir?"

"I did indeed. My niece will be staying, so please conduct her to one of the guest rooms. Oh, and then refill this decanter."

Polly darted a cross look at him. "What of your gout, Uncle!"

"Show a little understanding, my dear. It helps with the pain, you know."

Especially when it's free, she thought as she followed the footman from the room.

Chapter 7

Earlier, on finding the mews belonging to Royal Crescent, Bodkin had immediately selected a comfortable hayloft in which eventually to spend the night. He'd tossed his bundle and the pumpkin up into the loft from the stable below, his aim so impeccable that both landed in the exact place he'd chosen. Then, after eating a little of his honey, he commenced his search for Hordwell's carriage.

He combed the length and breadth of the mews, but found no sign at all of either Hordwell's carriage or Lord Benjamin's. Having convinced himself he'd find Nutmeg straightaway, he soon wound himself up to a pitch, and it wasn't long before his frustration boiled over. Nothing would do but that he caused as much petty mischief as possible for the innocent grooms, coachmen, and other such staff whose domain the unhelpful mews were.

There was no one about as he muffled horses' hooves with rags, or when he moved the animals from stable to stable. Come the morning, Dominic's coachman, the hard-pressed Jeffries, would find four bay horses where there should be grays, and so on. Not satisfied with this, the boggart-brownie then tied numerous door handles together, tipped over some troughs, and hid some well-chosen items of harness beneath the hay in the largest loft. Chance decreed that because he was so busily engaged upon this nuisance making, he neither heard nor saw Polly's carriage being brought around to the stables appertaining to 1 Royal Crescent. When he deemed that sufficient temporary disruption would result from his mean-minded handiwork, he stomped off to Zuder's to console himself with as many free sweet things as possible.

While all this was going on, Dominic was taking a second bath, being quite convinced that the faint aroma of farmyard still clung to his person. The bath was in a small third-floor room set aside for that purpose. Blue and white tiles covered the walls, and there was a fine washstand and shaving mirror. A wall cupboard contained shelves of freshly laundered white towels, and the curtains were drawn at the window that looked out from the back of the house.

As he languished in the cologne-scented water, resting his head against the thick towel draped over the elegant copper bath, he felt that all trace of pig had at last been removed, but he remained considerably annoyed with Polly for permitting the farmyard incident to take place. Miss Peach might be pretty, but she was also prejudiced and totally without conscience. By what right did she judge him? If ever a young woman was in need of a sermon on the sins of presumptuousness, it was she!

He didn't open his eyes as someone came into the room to take towels from the cupboard and place them on the chair beside the bath. Nor did he glance around when the window curtains were

drawn more neatly, but he sat up sharply when he heard a long female sigh. A maid had come in while he was totally undressed? He
turned to remonstrate with the girl for breaching such an obvious
unwritten rule, but was in time to see the door closing. Had she
seen more of his anatomy than was seemly? At that he smiled
philosophically. If she had, it had hardly been his fault, and if she'd
sighed, maybe it was because she was so overwhelmed with admiration and desire! He laughed and lay back again.

A footman suddenly spoke from beyond the closed door. "Begging your pardon, sir, but a Major Dashington has called."

Harry, his closest friend in the regiment! Dominic reached de-
lightedly for a towel. "Show him up, show him up!"

"Very well, sir."

Dominic heaved himself from the bath and grabbed one of the
towels that had been placed nearby only a moment before. He
dried himself briskly and had just donned his dressing gown when
the major was shown in.

Major Henry Dashington—Harry to his friends—was a Scots-
man of medium height, with sandy hair, hazel eyes, a mustache,
and side-whiskers. He was in his hussar uniform of a gold-
braided blue dolman jacket, a wide red-and-gold sash, tight white
breeches, and spurred cavalry boots, with a fur-trimmed pelisse
fixed over his left shoulder. A saber and flat leather purse em-
bossed with his regimental badge was suspended from his waist,
and beneath his arm he carried a fine plumed bearskin. He
grinned at Dominic. "It's been a long time, you old rogue." His
Edinburgh accent was very pleasant, his smile and easy charm
even more so.

"A long time indeed! How are you, Harry?" Dominic replied
warmly, seizing his friend's hand and pumping it.

"Still in need of a good woman, but otherwise thriving," Harry
replied. Then he pretended to sniff the humid air in the room.
"Dear God above, Dominic, you smell like a whore!"

"I use the best cologne, I'll have you know."

"Purchased in a Covent Garden bordello?"

Dominic raised an eyebrow. "You know more than I about such
shocking low places."

"Is that a fact?"

"Yes. Besides, I can promise that you'd prefer to smell me now
than earlier today."

"What do you mean?"

"It concerns the filthiest farmyard in creation, and an impudent young woman who has managed to insert herself under my skin to a degree I can hardly believe."

"Do I detect a matter of the heart?"

"Certainly not!" Dominic glanced at the footman, who waited at a discreet distance in the passage. "We'll adjourn to the drawing room, and will require supper and a bottle of Medoc, or whatever good red is in the cellar."

"Sir." The footman bowed, then hastened away.

Dominic looked at Harry again. "How on earth did you know I was here?"

"I was in Zuder's, laying siege to a goddess with the reddest hair in England, when I saw you driving past. I sent a boy after the carriage, to see where you went."

"So you still have a penchant for redheads, eh?"

"And sloe-eyed brunettes, to say nothing of blue-eyed blonds. Ah, me. I fear the entire female sex is to my liking."

"Is your Bath redhead the lady of your heart?"

Harry leaned against the windowsill and folded his arms. "She's just the latest pretty face to catch my eye. There's no one in particular yet, whereas you . . ." He paused. "When last I heard, you were hopelessly in love with Lady Georgiana Mersenrie; in fact I was informed she was your mistress. Is that still so?" He watched as Dominic combed his damp hair in front of the shaving mirror on the washstand.

Dominic lowered his comb. "Georgiana is rather a sensitive topic. She was my mistress, it's true, and if she'd consented to be my wife, I'd have been the happiest man alive. But I fear I rank too lowly for her."

"Rank?"

"Dukes are all she will consider." Dominic reached for a cravat. Harry seemed relieved. "So it's over between you?"

"On her part, yes. Why?"

"Because she's here in Bath."

"Oh?" Dominic's fingers became still upon the half-tied cravat.

Harry nodded. "And she's not unaccompanied. The Marquess of Hightower is constantly at her side. He has recently been seconded to our regiment, and so has to be here. That's why I was a little uneasy to see you arriving. I thought maybe she was being unfaithful."

Dominic leaned his hands on the washstand and bowed his

head for a moment. So Lord Algernon Lofty, Marquess of High-tower, future Duke of Grandcastle, was still the target of Georgiana's ambition. He glanced up again. "I'll warrant she didn't want to leave London," he murmured, remembering how glad she'd been when he'd departed. She'd wanted him to be the other side of the country, far away from her, so he could well imagine her reaction on discovering that if she wished to keep her hold on Hightower, she'd have to come to Bath as well.

"You're right, for she complained loud and long about it last night at the White Hart Hotel, which has become our officers' mess for the duration."

"I'm suddenly filled with an inordinate desire to attend this review. Where is it to take place?"

"Claverton Down at noon, but listen to me, Dominic. She's making her interest in Hightower very plain indeed, so I suggest you avoid her at all costs."

"Wild horses couldn't keep me away."

Harry shrugged. "You never did heed my advice."

"Nor you mine," Dominic pointed out.

"True." Harry straightened from the windowsill. "What do you see in her, Dominic? She may be beautiful, but she's as hard as nails, and sincerity is a quality in which she is singularly lacking. The Beddems are without doubt one of the most disagreeable families in the land, and of them all, she and her younger brother, Lord Benjamin, are the worst. Even the Duke of Lawless himself stands in their shadow."

"Have a care, Harry, for although you may be an old and valued friend, you tread on thin ice when you speak ill of the woman I love. As for her brother, you happen to be beneath his roof right now, so it's equally inappropriate to denigrate him."

"Point taken." Harry was curious. "If you and Georgiana are no longer together, why has Beddem allowed you to have this house?"

"It was Georgiana's idea, a ruse to get me out of London. That's why I can be sure she didn't want to come here."

"Enough of her. What brings you to this neck of the woods? Bath doesn't exactly seem your cup of tea," Harry said then.

"I'm here to find a wife."

"Good God."

Dominic smiled wryly as he went to the door. "Come, I'll tell you all in the drawing room."

"I trust you mean to elaborate upon the intriguing subject of filthy farmyards and impudent young women?"

"Certainly, for now that I smell sweet again, I can be reasonably civil on the subject." Dominic ushered him from the room.

As the two gentlemen settled to enjoy their first glass of Medoc, Bodkin was having a wonderful time at Zuder's. He'd gained entry by shinning up a drainpipe from the narrow lane at the side of the building, and then climbing through a faulty skylight. The shop was now closed for the night, and its magnificent selection of sweet things was entirely at the disposal of a boggart-brownie who had no manners at all. A street lamp outside cast a poor light over everything as he set about ransacking the shelves and counter. Several carriages drove slowly around the corner, but no one observed the plate that mysteriously raised itself from the neat stack on the oak counter. Nor was there any witness as it piled itself with a mountain of pastries, cakes, meringues, fudge, and sugared almonds, before spiriting itself to one of the little round tables. A chair drew itself out, and then the goodies were set upon with such vigor that within minutes only a scattering of crumbs and a smear of cream were left.

Bodkin smacked his lips. "It's not what it would have been if Nutmeg had baked, but happy birthday to me anyway." Then he got up to replenish the plate. By the time a second mountain had been demolished, Bodkin's boggart self had gone into abeyance for a while, and was a little more placid. If he'd had any sense he would have left the shop at this point, but he was greedy, and filled the plate a third time. He wasn't hungry anymore, and had already had more than enough, but he crammed everything into his mouth, only stopping when he began to feel ill. He pushed the plate away and sat back with a groan, holding his bulging tummy. The smell of sugar seemed to press in on him from all sides, and suddenly he could bear it no more. Scrambling from the chair, he made his way quickly back up to the attic and out through the skylight into the blessedly cold night air. There he inhaled deeply, hoping the sick feeling would subside. He would never eat a sweetmeat again, never! Until the next time, of course . . .

He eased himself gingerly down the drainpipe up which he'd shinned so effortlessly a little earlier, then made his way back to Royal Crescent. Now, as well as feeling ill he also felt guilty. Instead of gorging on stolen sweet things, he should have been

scouring every house in the crescent for Nutmeg. It was too late
now, he felt too unwell to do anything except go to sleep. He'd let
his beloved down! A large tear rolled from his eye and disappeared
into his shaggy fur, and he quickened his pace, his feet pattering
along the quiet pavements. Once in the mews, he returned to the
hayloft he'd selected earlier and made himself as comfortable as
he could next to the pumpkin. He would sleep now, then resume
his search in the morning.

Chapter 8

The sun streamed into Polly's bedroom as she pinned her hair in
front of the dressing table mirror. Her room was on the third
floor, facing along Brock Street toward the Circus, and had gray-
and-white striped wallpaper. The rose silk four-poster bed stood in
a raised alcove, with a balustrade that separated it from the rest of
the room. Rose, gray, and white were also picked out on the ceiling plasterwork, and again in the specially woven Wilton carpet.
There was a carved black marble fireplace, a dressing table draped
with frilled white muslin, and a concealed door that gave into a
small anteroom that held the washstand and two tall wardrobes.

Polly grimaced as she tried to fix the knot in her hair, and then
tease ringlets over her left shoulder. She'd had to leave Horditall
without her maid, whose day off it had been yesterday, and who
had gone visiting no one knew where. Polly sighed, for this meant
doing it all herself, and today her hair seemed willfully determined
to be difficult. At last she put down her comb and stood up. Her appearance was not what she would have wished; indeed she felt
barely presentable enough for Horditall House on washday, let
alone breakfast at Royal Crescent! She smoothed her yellow-and-
white gingham morning gown, fluffed the lace at the neckline,
then draped her white shawl over her shoulders. "I'm afraid this is
the best you'll manage this morning, Polly Peach," she said resignedly, then left to go down to the dining room on the ground

floor, where her uncle had been waiting for some time for her to join him.

As she reached the ground floor, she heard concerned voices drifting up from the basement kitchens. By the tone, it was clear something untoward had happened, but she could only catch phrases here and there. Wrong horses? Grease on upholstery? Doors deliberately tied? Harness stolen? Halloween two days early? She was puzzled. What were they talking about?

The spacious dining room was directly beneath the second-floor drawing room, and also faced south down the sloping common to the Avon, as well as west along the magnificent sweep of the crescent toward the matching house at the opposite end, residence of the Gotenuvs. The walls were sand-colored, and there were ruched cream silk curtains at all the windows. Hordwell's regimen had commenced before dawn, when a sedan chair had conveyed him to the King's Bath to be immersed in the medicinal waters. On his return, well wrapped in warm blankets, he'd retired to his bed for an hour to cool down. Soon he would sally forth again, this time to the Pump Rooms to take the waters internally. He had commenced his breakfast when Polly entered, for the rigors of the baths had given him a very hearty appetite, and he'd tired of waiting for her.

He wore a mushroom-colored coat and mustard waistcoat, with cream breeches and top boots, and was reading the morning newspaper while applying himself to a plate of scrambled eggs, sausages, bacon, and deviled kidneys. The air was warm with the smells of food, coffee, and chrysanthemums from the bowl that stood in the center of the mahogany table.

Polly's little shoes tapped on the polished wooden floor as she approached the table. "Good morning, Uncle Hordwell."

"You're a little late, miss," he replied, spearing a sausage with his fork.

"Being without a maid is time consuming," she explained, as Giles hastened to draw out a chair for her.

Fearing an imminent request for a suitable maid to be hired, Hordwell gave her a beaming smile of approval. "You look excellent, my dear. The queen's own maid could not have done better."

"Rest easy, Uncle, for I intend to manage on my own," she replied, glancing surprise as Giles brought her a plate of breakfast that was scarcely smaller than her uncle's. Clearly the footman believed *everyone* from the country ate like hogs, she thought, as she

turned her attention to her uncle. "What has happened this morning? I overheard something about stolen harness."

Hordwell looked up hastily from his newspaper. "Stolen? Surely
not." He looked inquiringly at Giles. "Has something occurred?"

"Yes, sir." As the footman explained about the trouble discovered in the mews that morning, Polly knew instinctively that Bodkin's hand lay behind it. She also knew that the brownie wouldn't
have stolen any harness, just hidden it somewhere. Oh, Bodkin,
she thought with an inward sigh. She had been racking her brain as
to how to find the boggart-brownie. Now it seemed a visit to the
mews might prove productive. Failing that, she would visit every
pastry shop in Bath, for Bodkin was almost certain to take himself
along to one or another of them. Probably Zuder's, since that was
the one he would have passed at journey's end yesterday.

While Polly's thoughts rambled around Bodkin's activities,
Hordwell was concerned that his property might have received
some unwelcome attention. "What of my vehicle? Is all well with
it?"

"It escaped attention, sir."

"Excellent." The matter in the mews ceased to be of any consequence, and Hordwell resumed his breakfast.

The footman withdrew from the room, and as Polly poured herself some coffee, her glance was drawn out of a window that faced
along the crescent. Sir Dominic Fortune had just emerged from his
house to mount a fine bay thoroughbred brought around from the
mews by a groom. She paused with the silver coffee pot suspended
above her cup, unable to help surveying him appreciatively from
head to toe. He wore a pine green riding coat and white breeches,
with a green silk neckcloth, pale gray waistcoat, and top hat, and
he flexed his fingers in his tight gloves as he prepared to mount.

Polly felt her cheeks go warm and pink. She still thought he was
horrid, so *why* did she also find him so devastating? It was a paradox. She hadn't realized he could see into the room as easily as she
could see out, but to her huge dismay, he suddenly looked directly
at her, doffed his hat, and swept her a scornful bow. Embarrassment swept hotly over her, and she declined to acknowledge him
as with a shaking hand she continued to pour the coffee. A few moments later the clatter of hooves echoed as he rode past, and although she stole a surreptitious glance, he did not look again. The
omission annoyed her, which was another paradox.

Hordwell finished his gargantuan breakfast and folded his napkin. "Well, that will keep me going," he declared.

"It will keep your gout going, too," she replied.

"What an acid tongue you have, to be sure," he grumbled.

"It's no more than you deserve."

"I begin to pity poor Lord Benjamin!"

"Lord Benjamin? Why? What has he to do with this?"

"He'll be acquiring a veritable nag when he marries you."

She stiffened. "I keep telling you, I'm not going to be his wife," she replied.

"My dear, as your guardian, it is within my power to *arrange* your marriage."

She stared at him. "You wouldn't!" she breathed. There was no reply, so she spoke again. "Is that what you intend to do, Uncle? *Force* me into a marriage I abhor?"

He sighed. "Polly, can't you see that this a very advantageous match?"

"*Advantageous?* For whom? Lord Benjamin, I fancy, for his are the empty coffers!"

"You would have a title."

"Not much of one."

"His elder brother is to be set aside!" he snapped, then glanced around, forgetting Giles had gone. Seeing no one, he looked at her again. "At the very least, be civil about Lord Benjamin when you are enjoying his hospitality."

"I'm not *enjoying* anything, Uncle, indeed I'm only here because you insisted. I would much prefer to take a room at one of the hotels in town."

"That matter has already been discussed. I will not permit you to stay elsewhere."

No, in case you have to pay, she thought angrily, buttering a slice of toast. He wouldn't be obliged to meet her bill, for she had more than sufficient funds in her allowance, but the dread of having to dip into his purse was always uppermost in his mind.

Hordwell exhaled heavily. "You're a very trying creature, Polly. Most young women would leap at the chance of marrying into the nobility."

"I see nothing noble about Lord Benjamin Beddem," she retorted.

He felt it would be wise to change the subject. "I, er, presume you mean to accompany me to Claverton Down later?" he asked, deliberately changing the thorny subject.

"To the review? Yes, of course, if that is what you wish."

"Good, for I've taken the liberty of sending a note to the Gotenuvs, informing them that you will accompany me at their luncheon party."

"Informing them? Isn't that a little brazen? Surely you should have made a polite request?"

"Nonsense. The count is a very close acquaintance of Lord Benjamin's, and since you are a guest here as well as the future Lady—" He broke off hastily, not wishing to start another confrontation.

Polly gave him a look, then bit into her toast.

He cleared his throat. "I, er, trust you will drive to the Pump Room with me in the meantime?"

"Yes, that too, if you wish."

"I do, and have already canceled my sedan chair and ordered the carriage in readiness. Oh, by the way, I also wish you to accompany me to the ball at the Assembly Rooms tomorrow night."

She was dismayed. "But I haven't brought a ball gown with me!"

"That is easily remedied. A courier will await your instructions this afternoon. All you have to do is write a list of exactly what you want, send it with him to Horditall House, and the maids there will pack it all. The courier will then bring everything back here."

She relaxed a little, but only a little. "Didn't you say the Duke and Duchess of York will be present? Uncle, my gowns are hardly grand enough for royalty. I really should have a new—"

"Nonsense, you look exquisite in all your togs," he interrupted hastily, then glanced at the longcase clock at the far end of the room. His chair scraped as he grabbed his walking sticks and rose quickly to his feet. "Do be swift, my dear, for one is supposed to drink the water between eight and nine, and it's half past eight now. Ah, there's the carriage now."

She got up quickly. "I'll put on my spencer and bonnet," she said, and gathered her skirts to hurry from the room.

The carriage was not the only thing at the curb outside 1 Royal Crescent, for Bodkin was there too, albeit invisibly. The brownie had been up for some time, first observing with great pleasure the havoc he'd caused with his overnight mischief, and then taking a leisurely honey breakfast in his hayloft. After that he'd left the stable to start searching for Nutmeg, but just as he emerged into the sunlight, he recognized Hordwell's second carriage being driven out of the coach house pertaining to 1 Royal Crescent. Its presence could only mean that Polly had followed him to Bath, in the process leading him to the very house in which to find Nutmeg! Delighted, Bodkin ran after the carriage, jumped aboard, and held on tightly as it swung out of the mews on its way to the front of the crescent. As it swayed to a standstill, the brownie climbed down again and stood looking at the house. After a minute or so, the front door opened, and Polly emerged with Hordwell, who was hobbling on his walking sticks. Bodkin's eyes sharpened, for Polly was smiling and clearly not at odds with her uncle as she assisted him down the steps toward the waiting vehicle. The brownie stared at her in dismay. She'd taken Hordwell's side! She *approved* of what had been done to Nutmeg!

Feeling too betrayed to even howl with boggart fury, Bodkin edged past them and slipped into the house.

Chapter 9

Dominic had ridden to the Pump Room, in the certain hope that Georgiana and her duke-to-be would also go there, because it was *the* place to be seen in the mornings. Set right in the heart of Bath, alongside the abbey, the room was a splendidly elegant place, with harmonious and restful pale blue walls and exquisite cream-and-gold decorations. Great Ionic columns soared up to the high ceiling, and there were curved recesses at either end, in one of which stood a fine longcase Tompion clock that had been made especially for the premises. There was a clatter of crockery at the numerous little tables, and above the babble of polite conversations the small orchestra in the gallery could just be heard. A flower woman was selling the little herbal nosegays that were all the vogue this year, and which she had successfully pressed upon most of the gathering.

The famous water, which had an unpalatably rusty taste, was

served at a counter by a young woman in a crisply starched mob-cap and apron, who had pyramids of gleaming glasses arranged before her. It was expected of everyone that they should drink three glasses of the water, and then take tea while endeavoring to appreciate the daily concert on the gallery. It was a dreadful press of chattering groups, both large and small, a sizable number of unfortunates in wheelchairs, and numerous hobbling persons on walking sticks and crutches, all of which made Dominic's progress quite hazardous as he threaded his way around in search of Georgiana.

Suddenly he saw her. She and her uniformed dukeling were at the water counter, receiving their first glasses. Transfixed, Dominic gazed adoringly at the object of his affections. How breathtaking she was, with her raven hair, melting dark eyes, and matchless profile. As was the latest vogue, she had fixed the false white curls to her coiffure, and they looked perfect beneath the wide brim of her stylish orange silk hat. Her silk pelisse and gown were orange too, and there were pearls at her creamy throat. She was engaged upon the subtle art of flirtation, employing his nosegay to tickle the chin of Lord Algernon Lofty, the twenty-six-year-old Marquess of Hightower, which did very little for his allergy to flowers.

Dominic's expression soured as he looked at the future Duke of Grandcastle. Hightower was a tall, exceedingly thin young man, with straight mouse-colored hair, small brown eyes, and a receding chin. When not in uniform, he possessed a taste in fashion that verged on the theatrical on account of his delight in vivid colors. His partiality for a fearsome shade of mauve was often much discussed, but Bath was being spared today, for he was in uniform. However, the regimentals of the Duke of York's Own Light Dragoons, while splendid on the likes of Harry Dashington, somehow contrived to make Hightower seem more lanky and chinless than ever. The duke-to-be was not a pretty sight, and his claim to intelligence was questionable to say the least, but Georgiana was treating him as if he were the most handsome, romantic, and witty fellow in the world. *And* she was bestowing kittenish glances upon him, glances her discarded lover wished for himself!

Jealousy washed hotly through Dominic as his rival's sneezes rang out above the general racket of the room. Hightower was a fool, and grand title or not, surely Georgiana must realize by now how desperately unhappy she would be with such an article. Or was ambition truly her be-all and end-all? It was time to find out, and how better than by confronting her when she was with her dukeling? Let her see what she was throwing away in favor of his dukedom!

Taking a deep breath, Dominic pushed his way toward his goal, and Georgiana turned, almost as if she sensed his approach. Her dark eyes flickered, and her lips parted, then she seized Hightower's arm so violently that his glass of water splashed over his uniform. Her intention was to hurry him away in the opposite direction, but all she achieved was his yelp of horror as he hastily drew out a lace-edged handkerchief to mop his elaborately braided blue jacket.

In that second Dominic was upon them both, sweeping a gallant bow, then drawing her little brown-gloved hand to his lips. "Lady Georgiana, what an unexpected pleasure." He straightened and nodded coolly at her companion. "Hightower."

Lord Algernon's small brown eyes swung toward him. "Fortune," he muttered with equal brevity, then went on with his mopping up. He knew Dominic was Georgiana's previous lover, and disliked him accordingly.

Georgiana looked fit to have the vapors, for Dominic was the very last person she wished to encounter, but she managed a weak smile. "Why, Sir Dominic, I quite forgot you were here in Bath," she declared with monstrous untruthfulness.

Dominic didn't know what to say next, for her dismayed reaction wasn't at all what he'd hoped for. By presenting himself unexpectedly like this, he'd wanted to startle her into realizing he was the one for her after all. Clearly such a hope was in vain.

She recovered a little and took out her own scented handkerchief to dab at the marquess's soaked uniform. Dominic was subjected to a cross look. "That was ill done, sir," she declared accusingly.

Taken aback, Dominic stared at her. "Ill done? I . . . I don't understand . . ."

"Of course you do, sirrah. How *could* you startle me like that? There was no need, no need at all! Now look what you've done to poor Algie's regimentals."

Dominic's face was a study, but he allowed her to get away with it. "I apologize, Lady Georgiana, but in truth I did not mean to alarm you."

"Nevertheless, that is precisely what you did."

He didn't reply, for although he loved her to distraction, he wasn't going to apologize again!

She colored a little, and while the marquess's attention remained upon things sartorial, she decided to be a little cruel to Dominic, suddenly smiling at him in a most yearningly seductive way. Her lovely dark eyes promised every delight under the sun—and between the sheets—but her words were politely conversational for the marquess's benefit. "Have you been in Bath long, Sir Dominic?"

"I arrived yesterday, Lady Georgiana," he replied, plunging joyfully into her gaze. She *did* love him, she did!

"Are you going to Claverton Down to see the Duke and Duchess of York review Algie's regiment?" she asked then.

"Of a certainty I am, and the ball the day after. As to the regiment, it was mine, too, remember?" he added.

"Was it?" Her eyes were wide and innocent as she went on. "What of the Halloween festivities in Sydney Gardens?"

"Halloween festivities?"

"In the manner of all Vauxhalls, there is to be a bonfire, fireworks, and all manner of other entertainments. Fancy dress isn't mandatory, although it *is* rather expected, and dressing up is so much more fun than ordinary togs, don't you agree?"

"Er, yes, I suppose I do."

"The Duke and Duchess of York will be there, too, to light the bonfire, and tickets are naturally at a premium."

"Indeed? Well, I will endeavor to acquire one."

Having raised his hopes with such talk, she now chose to dash them again. "Well, to be sure I *may* acknowledge you, but after your clumsiness today, I may not," she declared witheringly, then turned to smile dazzlingly at the marquess. "Oh, Algie, I do admire men in uniform." She sighed.

Her contrariness made Dominic feel angry, as well as foolish, but nothing she said or did seemed to dent Hightower's doglike devotion, for that gentleman beamed adoringly at her. "Oh, my dearest Georgiana, how glad I am to hear you say that, for I vow I felt quite out of sorts at not being in my mauve."

Her smile became fixed. "Your mauve? Oh, I *much* prefer you in uniform," she said quickly.

Dominic's lips twitched. *She* did? *Everyone* preferred Hightower in uniform, for his beloved mauve was an assault upon the eyeballs!

Georgiana tossed another glance at Dominic. "I fear we must proceed with the regimen, Sir Dominic, so I trust you will excuse us . . . ?"

With a shock, Dominic realized she'd delivered his *congé*. It wasn't something to which he was accustomed; indeed he was usually the one to deal such things rather than receive them. Now it was his turn to color, and with an abrupt nod he turned to walk away. He was angry, and vowed never to approach her again, but he couldn't help glancing over his shoulder. Her lustrous gaze was upon him, and she gave him another of her yearning seductive smiles. Once again his emotions were in turmoil. He didn't know where he was with her! A prisoner of his worshipping heart, he found himself a table from where he could watch as she and the marquess sipped from each other's glasses, and gazed into each other's eyes. Dominic knew he was only torturing himself, but he simply couldn't help it. Where Lady Georgiana Mersenrie was concerned, he had no will of his own.

At that moment, Polly and her uncle were arriving at the colonnade that separated the abbey yard and Pump Room from the Bath street. Polly was deep in thought, for as the carriage had driven around the corner past Zuder's, she had observed a very strange scene inside. The assistants, and Herr Zuder himself, who was recognizable by his famous goatee beard and waxed mustache, had been gathered around a table close to the window. Scratching their heads and looking generally puzzled, they were clearly discussing something as mystifying to them as the overnight events in the Royal Crescent mews. Bells rang in Polly's head. Bodkin! Had the brownie recommenced his comfort gorging? She would have to make a point of calling at the shop on the return to the crescent.

She was aroused from her thoughts as the carriage halted, and with much groaning and complaining, Hordwell allowed himself to be helped down by two of the Pump Room's footmen. She climbed down as well, but her uncle hadn't shuffled more than a few yards on his walking sticks when he declared he must secure one of the wheelchairs that stood in line for hire. Polly was dismayed, for the chairs looked cumbersome to push, and she wasn't exactly muscular, but Hordwell didn't consider her at all as he plumped himself in the nearest one. He placed his walking sticks rather awkwardly across his lap, then gazed serenely ahead as the wheelchair man held out his hand for payment. With a sigh, Polly reached into her reticule, produced the necessary coins, then began to push the unwieldy chair toward the Pump Room door.

Her dismay increased tenfold when she saw the enormous crowd squeezed inside. She wanted to deposit Hordwell at a suitable table, then go up to the counter alone for his first glass of water, but he would not hear of it. Nothing would do but that she push him to the counter so that he could ask himself. Resignedly, she began to push him forward, apologizing to left and right as his walking sticks prodded various persons on the way. She passed Dominic without noticing him, nor did he notice her, for his eyes were fixed upon Georgiana. At the counter, Polly glanced momentarily at Georgiana, whose orange togs were perhaps the most modish in the room. She didn't know Georgiana was Lord Benjamin's sister, not that it would have made any difference to the ensuing fracas.

It started as Hordwell was handed his glass, and Polly turned the wheelchair toward a free table she'd noticed nearby. The dreaded walking sticks jabbed Georgiana's elegant posterior, and with a startled shriek, that lady whirled about, lost her balance, and fell against the marquess, who in turn fell against the counter. The pyramids of glasses went crashing, and in the ensuing shocked silence the only sound was Georgiana's hysterical shrieking. Every eye in the room was directed toward the scene, and Polly felt so dreadful that she could only stand there with her hands pressed to her crimson cheeks.

In a trice Dominic was on his feet to rush to Georgiana's rescue. He pushed past Polly, then stepped over the marquess, who had been dazed by one of the falling glasses, in order to stretch out a hand to his beloved. As Georgiana's trembling little fingers closed gratefully over his, and as he drew her to her feet, he flung a furious glance at Hordwell. "Have you no sense, sir? Walking sticks are not to be used as weapons!"

Hordwell gave him a cold look. "Walking sticks have more right in here than fripperies," he replied, then gazed ahead again, his expression one of stony indifference to the chaos he'd caused.

Dominic kissed Georgiana's fingers reassuringly. "There, there, all is well again," he murmured, before turning his outrage upon Polly. "I begin to despair of you, Miss Peach, for wherever you are, there also is trouble."

"One might say the same of you, sirrah!" she retorted indignantly.

"You are the cause, madam, not me," he replied, cradling the weeping Georgiana to his manly chest.

Polly was furious with him, and with herself for being so drawn to him. "Then please allow me to warrant your low opinion," she answered, and before she knew it was in her mind, she'd picked up the only glass of water to have remained upright on the counter. With a flourish she tossed the contents all over him, although in truth it was her own hot emotions she needed to douse.

Unfortunately she drenched Georgiana as well as him, and the lady in question screamed all the more. There were gasps all around, and Dominic looked as if he could cheerfully have choked his blond assailant, but before he could give in to any such urge, two burly footmen hurried over to eject Polly and her uncle, wheelchair and all.

Thus Polly's first—and only—visit to the Bath Pump Room came to a premature and rather undignified end.

Chapter 10

As Polly and Hordwell were politely but firmly ejected from the Pump Room, a bitterly angry Bodkin was busy searching 1 Royal Crescent. He was so dismayed by Polly's apparent betrayal that he could barely marshal his thoughts. His tail twirled resentfully, and as he combed the house for Nutmeg, he was plotting boggart revenge on his former friend.

His quest began in the basement, then gradually moved upward, but there was no sign of his lost sweetheart, not even a little brownie dustpan. Disheartenment was beginning to set in when he reached the third story, where the principal bedrooms were to be found, and opened the first door he came to. It was instantly identifiable as Hordwell's room, because of the old Turkish slippers placed neatly by the bed. A wicked smile creased the brownie's face. Hordwell always hid his valuables beneath his mattress, so the removal of said valuables—deeds, an important account book, a purse of gold coins, a fine pocket watch, jewelry, and various other items of importance—to a place where the miserable old curmudgeon would *never* find them, would cause a monumental fuss! Rubbing his hands with vengeful glee, Bodkin hurried toward the mattress.

Unfortunately for him, in his anger it had slipped his mind that there were other brownies in the world apart from Nutmeg and himself, and that they had charge of houses, just as he did of Horditall House. It was a cardinal rule that before entering a strange house, the resident brownie's permission must always be sought. The moment he entered 1 Royal Crescent, Bodkin had broken that rule, and he was about to be confronted in no uncertain fashion, because at that very moment the resident brownie, an elderly but very spry fellow by the name of Ragwort, happened to be clinging to the top of Hordwell's curtains, using a longhandled feather duster to clean the pelmet.

Ragwort had looked after the house ever since it had been built, and before that had been one of the select band of brownies looking after Bath Abbey. Like Bodkin, he only communicated with one human, in this case Giles, the footman. He was on good terms with all the other brownies on the crescent and had many friends in Bath itself, so when an impudent stranger entered unannounced, Ragwort wasn't at all pleased. Holding the feather duster aloft, he swung down the gold velvet curtains and dropped silently behind Bodkin, who was muttering impatiently under his breath as he felt beneath the mattress.

Ragwort's tail began to swish, and suddenly he jabbed at Bodkin's behind with the duster handle. "Hey, you! What are you up to? Trying your hand at a little thieving?"

Bodkin whirled about and gaped at the other brownie.

"Cat got your tongue?" cried Ragwort, prodding again with the duster.

Bodkin ran to a corner to grab one of Hordwell's spare walking sticks, then returned to confront his attacker, his tail lashing threateningly to and fro. "And who do you think *you* are? How dare you poke me like that!" he shouted, holding the walking stick like a sword, and assuming a fencing position he'd seen on one of Hordwell's sporting prints at Horditall House.

Ragwort did the same with the feather duster. "I'm the brownie of this house, and *you're* an intruder, that's what!" he declared, his tail matching Bodkin's lash for lash.

"How do I know *you're* not an intruder?" yelled Bodkin, lunging forward with his weapon.

Ragwort parried the thrust, and for several minutes the angry brownies fought a rather unlikely duel, which only ended when Bodkin tripped over Hordwell's slippers and fell. Ragwort immediately pressed the feather duster to his throat. "Identify yourself, thief!"

"I'm not a thief," protested Bodkin angrily, trying not to sneeze because the feathers were tickling his nose.

"You were looking under the mattress! That's not exactly innocent behavior!"

"I . . . I know I was, but I have good reason. I was going to hide old Hordwell's valuables to pay him back for what he's done to me. Oh, *please* can I get up?"

"Do I have your word you won't try to escape?" demanded Ragwort, and on receiving a compliant nod, he slowly removed the duster.

Bodkin scrambled to his feet, then kicked Hordwell's slippers petulantly. Stupid things, if they hadn't been there, he'd have won!

Ragwort eyed him. "Right, explain yourself, beginning with your name."

"I'm Bodkin, of Horditall House. At least, I *was* of Horditall House, but I've walked out."

"My name is Ragwort." The other brownie bowed politely.

Bodkin did the same. "I'm sorry I entered without your permission, Ragwort, but I was so angry I just didn't think." He explained all that had happened, then asked quickly. "Have you seen Nutmeg?" To his dismay, Ragwort shook his head.

"There hasn't been anyone like that on the crescent. I know all the brownies here, and if a new one had arrived, I'd be aware of it." Ragwort's brow darkened then. "Is it really true that Lord Benjamin and Mr. Horditall came to an agreement over her? What sort of agreement? A *financial* one?"

"I don't know exactly what form it took, but they certainly traded her in some way. She was brought here to look after Lord Benjamin's house, and the fact that she apparently went without protest must mean that either Hordwell or Lord Benjamin possesses her belt."

"No wonder you want to hide the old miser's valuables," Ragwort replied with feeling, then added, "I must say I'm surprised that Miss Polly is party to it. From what I've seen of her, she just doesn't seem to be like that."

"That's what I thought," Bodkin replied bitterly.

"Well, we'll punish all three of them, for it's no more than they deserve."

Bodkin looked urgently at him. "Are you *sure* Nutmeg can't be here?" He glanced around the room, almost as if expecting to see her.

Ragwort shook his head again. "I've already said so, haven't I? Besides, it probably wouldn't be this particular house anyway."

"Why? It's Lord Benjamin's, isn't it?"

"Not exactly. It belongs to his father, the Duke of Lawless. Lord Benjamin has only just moved here from his other house."

"What other house?" Bodkin asked swiftly.

"Further along the crescent. I forget the number, but I know which one it is. He resided there a year ago, when your Nutmeg disappeared, and it's still in his name, but he's let it to someone called Sir Dominic Fortune."

"So Nutmeg might be there?"

"Look, I keep telling you that I'd know if there was a stranger on the crescent. Ever since Caraway left, that house hasn't had a brownie. It's the only one that doesn't."

"Caraway?"

Ragwort colored a little. "A close lady brownie acquaintance. She and I had a terrible falling out, and she went off in a huff to stay with her family in Wells. That was before Lord Benjamin took the lease."

"Oh, what am I going to do?" wailed Bodkin, sitting on the floor and hiding his head in his hands.

Ragwort looked sadly down at him. "Well, to start with, I'll take you to meet the other brownies on the crescent. There's always an outside chance someone might know something. But before we go, let's find Hordwell's precious bits and pieces and hide them. What about the chimney, eh? There's a nice little ledge not far up. We can put some things there as well, his brush and comb, for instance! Come on!" Grabbing Bodkin by the arm, he made him get up again to continue with the examination of the mattress. Hordwell's little hoard soon came to light, and the brownies hid them all up the chimney, taking care to keep clear of the rather smoky fire in the hearth. Hordwell's brush and comb followed, then his two pairs of spare shoes, and his entire supply of monogrammed handkerchiefs.

Standing by the fender, Ragwort slipped a friendly arm around Bodkin. "Don't fret, for I'm sure we'll find her."

"I do hope so, for I love her very much," Bodkin replied.

"Cheer up. It's Halloween in a day or so, and just *think* of the fun we'll be able to have at these horrid humans' expense!"

Bodkin's face lit up a little as he remembered his pumpkin. "Oh, yes, Halloween . . ." he murmured. Ragwort then led him from the room, down through the house into the gardens at the rear.

By now, Polly and Hordwell were driving up along George Street on their way back to the house. Polly was still smarting from events at the Pump Room, and felt as if everyone they passed was whispering about it, which was impossible, of course. She could not believe she had tossed water over Sir Dominic Fortune. What on earth had possessed her? But then, if he hadn't been so impossible, it wouldn't have happened. And if Uncle Hordwell hadn't been so deliberately awkward and difficult . . . Her thoughts were interrupted as she realized the carriage was approaching Zuder's. She recalled the odd scene she'd witnessed earlier and hurriedly requested the coachman to halt.

Hordwell looked curiously at her. "Stop? Why?"

"Oh. I just wish to go to Zuder's."

"Not to spend *my* money, I trust," he said quickly.

"If I spend anything, it will be my allowance, which, incidentally, I used to pay for your wretched wheelchair a little earlier," she reminded him, and climbed down to the pavement.

He affected not to hear. "Just remember that we have to leave for the review in a short while," he said, clasping his hands on one of his walking sticks, and looking out of the other window.

Polly resisted the temptation to slam the carriage door on him. What a parsimonious old skinflint he was, she thought, wondering how on earth her dear sweet mother could have had such a brother.

The carriage drove on, and she went into the pastry cook's. The shop was very busy, and the babble of conversation was almost as great as that in the Pump Room. Waiters scurried between crowded tables, and everything smelled of coffee, sugar, and vanilla. Only one waiter wasn't serving, and he hovered in readiness near the counter, so she quickly made her way toward him. "May I have a word with you?" she asked, giving him one of her most dazzling smiles.

He was instantly her slave. "Oh, yes, madam."

"I know it's none of my business, but I was passing the shop earlier today, and saw Herr Zuder and all of you standing by that table over there." She pointed. "Could you possibly tell me what had happened?"

"Certainly, madam. It was all very strange. You see, when we opened up this morning, we found that someone had broken in overnight and helped himself to whatever took his fancy. It seems he climbed in through a broken skylight in the roof. It's been tied securely now, and will be properly repaired tomorrow." His brows drew together. "What we can't understand is how no one noticed anything from the street. There are always carriages driving by after dark, yet no one seems to have seen whoever it was, even though he sat right by the window!"

They didn't see because Bodkin is invisible, she thought, and a plate by itself would probably not attract attention. As the waiter hurried away to one of the tables, she thought about what she'd discovered. She knew the brownie's sweet tooth, and was sure that if he'd come here once, he'd come again. She must try to leave a message where he was bound to find it, and the obvious place was the skylight. There was a door at the rear of the shop, and after making sure no one was paying her particular attention, she slipped through into the hallway beyond, where it was much cooler and quieter. Her breath stood out a little as she hurried up the uncarpeted staircase. Four steep flights later she was in the attics, and it didn't take her long to find the offending skylight. It had indeed been very securely tied, but using the little scissors she'd always carried in her reticule since requiring to urgently cut the knotted lace of a friend's ankle boot due to a bad sprain, she poked and pried until she'd loosened the knots. The skylight immediately jerked slightly ajar, and the morning breeze swept coldly over her as she searched in her reticule for her notebook and pencil. She scrawled a swift message.

Bodkin, Uncle Hordwell swears the agreement in the ledger was meant to be a temporary thing with Nutmeg's comfort and well-being in mind. He intended to suggest to her that she might like to stay in Bath for a while until her house in Horditall had been refurbished, but she walked out before anything was put to her. I believe him, and so must you. Please come to me at 1 Royal Crescent, so we can talk. Polly.

After stretching out to tuck the note in a prominent position beneath one of the slates, she tied the skylight again, then hastened downstairs again. She passed unnoticed through the shop and out into the street. Just over five minutes later, she arrived at Royal Crescent, where she was greeted in the hallway by the sound of sobbing coming from the library. Puzzled, she went to see who it was, and found the entire staff facing her white-faced, furious uncle. It was the maids who were crying, their aprons raised to their eyes. Polly looked inquiringly at Hordwell. "Whatever is wrong, Uncle?" she asked.

"Well you may ask, well you may ask!" Hordwell cried. "My most precious belongings have been stolen, as well as my brush and comb, shoes and handkerchiefs."

Polly stared at him, Bodkin's name leaping into her mind. This was just the sort of thing a boggart-brownie would do!

Hordwell glared at the little gathering. "Who was it, eh? Who robbed me?" They all vehemently protested their innocence, but he wasn't convinced. "Don't think to gull me, you rascals! One of you, maybe more, entered my room and removed my property. Who was it? I *demand* to know!"

Polly looked at him in dismay. "Uncle, you can't make unsubstantiated accusations. If there has been a theft, then we must inform the relevant authorities, but I have to say that I do not believe any of the servants would do such a thing. My guess is that it was a burglar from outside." A certain brownie, to be precise . . . "Indeed, Uncle, I believe you should apologize to everyone for maligning them so."

Hordwell scowled. "Apologize? Now look, Polly, I'm not about to—"

She interrupted. "I'm convinced they are innocent, and that you must therefore make amends for your unjust accusations." She did not doubt she was right, for the servants' expressions of outrage were clearly sincere, and besides, she would lay odds upon Bodkin being the real culprit.

With ill grace, Hordwell did as she said, and after a moment the servants all shuffled out. As they went, Polly halted Giles. "Please see that someone reports this unfortunate incident to the authorities."

"Certainly, Miss Peach."

As the door closed behind them all, Polly looked at her uncle.

"I'm very sorry you've been robbed, but you really should not accuse people like that."

"Well, *someone* stole my things!" he pointed out angrily.

"Yes, and the authorities will be told."

"They won't do anything about it."

"Maybe, but at least you have the comfort of being wealthy enough not to suffer too much," she said.

"That's hardly the point! And I certainly can't replace my account book." He closed his eyes a little faintly. "Oh, my account book . . ."

She ushered him into his chair and poured him a glass of cognac. "Here, sip this and take some deep breaths. You'll feel a little better presently."

"I doubt it, oh, I doubt it," he muttered, taking the proffered glass and gulping the contents. "Another one, if you please, my dear."

"But, your gout—"

"To perdition with my gout!"

She poured a second glass. "What of the review?"

"Eh?" He looked blankly at her.

"The review, and the luncheon party that will be right next to the Duke and Duchess of York?"

His lower jaw jutted. "I am no longer in any mood for such frivolity," he grumbled, remaining firmly in his chair.

She was dismayed. "But, Uncle, you've already informed the Gotenuvs you'll be there, and you've presumed upon their hospitality by including me as well!"

"I know, but I now feel too fragile for such rigors. You will have to go without me!"

"Uncle Hordwell, I don't even know the Gotenuvs."

"Then you will have to introduce yourself. I will hear no more of it, Polly. You go on your own, and that is the end of it. I insist."

She didn't argue anymore, for he'd had a nasty shock, and she didn't wish to upset him more. But right now, the last thing she wished to do was go alone to an army review!

Chapter 11

When it was time to leave for Claverton Down, Polly emerged from the house in her best cream silk gown, gray velvet spencer, and pink straw hat. She carried a pink pagoda parasol, and there was a tiny posy of late pink dianthus pinned to her lapel. But as the carriage drove off, Bodkin hastened invisibly from the basement area of the house next door and jumped aboard. He and Ragwort had seen the carriage at the curb again, and Ragwort had asked his friend Giles, the footman, why it was needed. The brownie stowaway made himself as comfortable as he could in the luggage boot. Ragwort had now introduced him to the other brownies on Royal Crescent, but they didn't know anything about Nutmeg. Ragwort had promised to make a thorough search of Sir Dominic's house this afternoon, as it seemed the only place she might possibly be. Bodkin leaned forward to press his nose to the little window at the rear of the carriage. He could see Polly's pink hat, and scowled at it. He'd teach her a lesson for letting him down. Oh, the devilment he was going to get up to at the review!

Claverton Down lay a mile or so out of Bath, and the carriage was soon caught up in a throng of fashionable vehicles driving to the review. The jam of traffic became worse close to the down, for the presence of royalty was always a magnet second to none. Polly lowered the window glass and leaned out. The sound of a brass band drifted on the air, and she could also hear a particularly loud sergeant-major shouting orders. Rows of army tents adorned the open grassland, each one providing quarters for six soldiers. Six fine cavalry horses were tethered outside each tent, and hay bales and water troughs were all around. Soldiers were either putting the finishing touches to their spotless regimentals, or grooming their mounts. Sunlight flashed upon golden epaulettes, medals, and polished brass buttons. Plumes fluttered from bearskins, and banners streamed in the autumn breeze that swept pleasantly over the down.

Numerous stalls sold drinks, gingerbread, and pies, and among the many hawkers who'd converged on the lucrative scene was the enterprising Pump Room flower woman, this time selling posies of asters, the regiment's emblem. Apart from the drab army tents, there were a number of much larger, brighter private tents, culminating in the purple-and-gold splendor of the royal pavilion. Nearby, all the private carriages were drawing up in lines of military precision, and ladies and gentlemen strolled everywhere, waiting for the arrival of the Duke and Duchess of York.

Polly's carriage took its place among the others, and she climbed down to join the general perambulation that proceeded the review. Bodkin alighted as well, his presence detectable only by the imprint of his feet upon the grass. Keeping close to Polly, he looked around to begin his campaign. But as he did so, he was astonished to see numerous other brownies, some in groups, some alone, all intent upon enjoying the review as much as the humans. Some arrived the same way he did, seated in relative comfort at the back of carriages, but some walked, while others—mostly daring young males—chose to hang onto horses's tails, causing the riders or coachmen to wonder why their animals were so nervous and skittish today.

Bodkin hadn't realized that town brownies joined in human entertainments as much as their cousins in the country. At Horditall all the local brownies attended weddings, anniversaries, christenings, fairs, May Day, Christmas, and—of course!—Halloween. Now it was clear the same things went on in towns. His eyes began to gleam, for he had seen several notices regarding the Halloween festivities in Sydney Gardens. These other brownies were bound to be there, all of them indulging in a little friendly mischief, and he would be there too. But there would be nothing friendly about Bodkin of Horditall and his famous jack-o'-lantern! He and Ragwort were going to subject old Hordwell, clammy Lord Benjamin, and traitorous Polly to an unforgettable Halloween!

As Polly raised her pagoda parasol and walked slowly past the lines of carriages in search of the count and countess's pavilion, she sensed nothing of Bodkin close behind her, or of the other brownies all around. Her most immediate thoughts were of her Russian hosts, whose luncheon party she really did not wish to join; indeed she still felt it was an imposition, but she'd promised Uncle Hordwell, and she was a niece of her word. The purple-and-gold royal pavilion stood out from all the others, not only by its size and regal colors, but also by the gilt coronets surrounding its canopy, and of the elegant but lesser tents on either side, she couldn't guess which might be the one she sought. There was nothing for it but to ask at each entrance until she found the

Gotenuvs'. Hesitantly she folded her parasol and approached the first, where a number of guests were sipping champagne. The far end of the tent was taken up with white-clothed trestle tables that groaned beneath the weight of a very fine buffet luncheon, and by the shrillness of the guests' voices, she guessed they had been imbibing for some time.

She was about to discreetly ask one of the more matronly ladies if this was the Gotenuvs' party, when her dismayed glance fell upon two familiar faces by the buffet. Polly did not know their names, but recognized the couple from the Pump Room. The man's head was bandaged as a result of the blow from the falling glass, and it seemed to Polly that he still looked a little dazed. Or maybe such a vacant visage was customary. The woman wore a primrose gauze gown, and her sky blue pelisse was adorned with a knot of forget-me-nots. The wispy net scarf around her tall-crowned hat floated when she turned her pretty head, and she was all fluttering eyelashes and fascination as she leaned on the man's arm. Polly thought wryly that if anything, *he* should be leaning on *her* arm. He certainly looked wan enough after his unfortunate morning mishap!

Suddenly Georgiana looked directly at her. Recognition vanquished the flirtatious smile, and with a haughty toss of her head, she looked away again. Polly's heart sank, for if this was indeed the Gotenuvs' party, she would definitely be unwelcome in that particular quarter. Maybe in all quarters, for it was clear who would be regarded as the villains of the Pump Room! Discretion got the better part of valor, and Polly decided to withdraw from the tent. Promise or no promise, she wasn't going to run this particular gauntlet. She turned to leave, but had to pause because another group of guests was entering.

Bodkin had observed Polly's reaction to Lord Algernon and his love, and sensed the hostility of Georgiana's glance. In a trice he decided on his first attack. Jumping up, he snatched Polly's folded parasol from her hand and hurled it at the top of Georgiana's hat. Like a javelin, it pierced the modish net-swathed headgear and carried it into the heart of the huge raspberry-and-cream jelly that was the buffet's *pièce de résistance*. Georgiana gave a shriek of alarm, and as everyone stared, the jelly collapsed with a loud squish. Georgiana stared at her ruined hat for a moment, then, not knowing that the thrower of the parasol had an accuracy that was quite infallible, and that she had therefore never been in a moment's danger, she fell hysterically into the marquess's arms.

Polly was stunned, but then her glance fell upon the group of guests who had just arrived. They were mostly gentlemen who'd ridden from Bath, but among them was none other than Sir Dominic Fortune. Carrying his hat under his arm and dressed in the pine green coat and cream breeches that were *de rigueur* for riding, he was gazing at the jelly with apparently as much surprise as everyone else, but she felt certain he was the one who'd grabbed the parasol. So he wished to be avenged for this morning, did he? Well, she would see about *that*! Her eyes flashed, and she faced him furiously. "How dare you, sirrah!" she cried.

Dominic's startled gaze swung toward her, for that was the first he'd noticed her. Then his eyes' expression darkened as he realized he was being accused. "Are you accusing *me*, madam?"

"I am indeed, for who else would do such a thing?"

The jelly—and Georgiana's hysterics—suddenly took second place as all eyes swung to the new disturbance at the tent entrance.

Dominic was furious. "I have neither reason nor inclination to perpetrate such a dangerous act, Miss Peach, but since you have already attacked me once today, I presume this is yet another example of your questionable conduct!"

"*My* questionable conduct? Sirrah, you seized my parasol and threw it!"

"Oh? And did you see me do it?"

"I did not need to, for you are right here!"

"So are a number of others. Why do you not accuse *them*?"

Polly was so upset that she could have struck him. "I do not accuse them because I do not know of any motive they could have, but you, sirrah, have motive enough, as witness *your* conduct this morning! Your interest in a certain lady was so marked that I can only presume when you threw my parasol just now, her escort was your intended target!" The awful accusation was out before she could prevent it, and it was clear that everyone knew of whom she spoke, even though no names had been mentioned. She closed her eyes faintly. She shouldn't have said it, she really shouldn't . . .

Lord Algernon went even more pale, and stared at Dominic as if at the devil himself. Appalled gasps spread through the tent, and Georgiana screeched all the more, stamping her foot like a spoilt child. "Oh, monstrous creature! Monstrous creature!" she sobbed.

Dominic was incensed. "Miss Peach, I find your suggestion most offensive, for you denigrate not only my character, but Lady Georgiana's as well!"

Polly's fists were clenched as she stood up to him. "I *didn't* throw the parasol!"

"Nor did I!"

As they gazed brightly at each other, both so incandescent with anger that further words failed them both, Bodkin rubbed his hands with glee and gave a low chuckle. Polly heard him, and her lips parted on a gasp of realization. She glanced around, but saw nothing. She still knew he was there, though, and was deeply hurt that he could be so vindictive. She was his friend—she'd even come to Bath to help him, and this was the thanks she got!

Dominic watched her curiously. What was wrong with her? Had she been allowed too soon from a Bedlam? Yes, that increasingly seemed the likelihood! "Are you feeling unwell, Miss Peach?" he asked then.

Her eyes flew guiltily to his face. She'd accused him of a dreadful thing, of which she now knew him to be innocent. What on earth was she going to say to him? "I . . . I, er . . ."

She was spared the need to say more because at that moment there came from outside the sound of a resounding *feu de joie*, then hearty cheers as the Duke and Duchess of York arrived with their entourage. As the regimental band began to play "God Save the King," the need to see royalty at close hand got the better of the gathering in the tent. The incident with the jelly was forgotten as everyone surged out through the entrance, forcing Polly and Dominic to step hastily out of the way. Lord Algernon dashed out as well, for he had duties to perform in the review, but Georgiana had to remain behind, because it would be a social disaster to appear before royalty without a hat. Sniffing pathetically and dabbing her eyes with her handkerchief, she stared at her once jaunty hat and the devastation of jelly and parasol. Gingerly she reached out, took the parasol between her thumb and first finger, and dropped it contemptuously to the grass. Then she rescued the hat and tried to mop up what she could.

Polly found the jelly of infinitely more interest than Georgiana, for it was shaking most suspiciously, as if someone—or something—were eating it. *Bodkin!* Without a second thought she hastened forward, and at her approach Georgiana fled from the tent, not observing Dominic, who had withdrawn into the shadows to watch Polly's peculiar conduct.

Chapter 12

Polly reached the shivering jelly and whispered urgently. "Bodkin? I know you're there! Why have you done this?" she hissed angrily, but there was no response.

Dominic heard her low voice, but could not make out what she was saying. All he knew was that she seemed to be addressing the jelly, and his conviction increased that she should be under lock and key.

Polly spoke again, but there was still no answer, even though she *knew* the brownie was there by the way the jelly continued to tremble. Now that she was close she could see small pieces of jelly being grasped by invisible fingers and shoved indecorously into an invisible mouth. Hoping to catch him unaware, she suddenly darted forward, snatching at the air where she knew he would be. She caught his arm, and with a squeal he squirmed so frantically that he wrenched himself free almost immediately.

Dominic's eyes widened. What on earth was she doing? And why did she squeal like that? Oh, heavens, she was becoming violent!

A whiff of cloves drifted briefly over Polly, then the buffet was knocked in all directions as Bodkin fled along the trestles. She followed, trying to snatch him again. "For heaven's sake listen to me!" she breathed.

"Traitor!" he hissed from the end of the last table, then jumped down, and she saw his footprints on the grass as he ran to the side of the tent.

She called after him a last time, still keeping her voice low, for fear someone might be just outside the tent. "I'm not a traitor, I'm your friend, Bodkin. Please go to Zuder's. I've left a message for you!" But the side of the tent was wrenched up as he wriggled beneath it, then he'd gone.

Knowing there was no point in trying to find him once he was outside, she picked up her parasol from the grass where Georgiana had dropped it, glanced in dismay at the mess of jelly and cream all over it, then turned to leave the tent. She immediately halted in dismay, for Dominic barred the entrance. His arms were folded, and his eyebrow raised quizzically. He was now convinced beyond all doubt that she belonged in a Bedlam.

Polly found it hard to meet his eyes. "Please stand aside, sir."

"Why have you taken it upon yourself to hound poor Lady Georgiana?" he demanded, thinking that was as good a place as any to commence a probe into her sanity.

"Hound her? I'm not hounding anyone, sir. To be sure, her ladyship is a very silly creature who seems quite capable of all manner of hysterics without any help from me."

"Miss Peach, you have quite clearly set out to pick on her, and—"

Polly interrupted. "Even if I were, what business would it be of yours? Are you the lady's husband? Her beau, maybe?"

"I happen to be her very close friend."

"Clearly not as close as you'd like," Polly observed with stinging accuracy.

He colored. "Improper remarks seem to flow from your lips, Miss Peach."

"And ungentlemanly conduct appears to come equally as easily to you! How dare you accuse me of making improper remarks, when your own comments haven't exactly been agreeable for the past minute or so!"

"When it comes to manners, may I remind you that you not only consigned me to that cursed farmer's yard yesterday, but you also threw a glass of water over me earlier today!"

"Both actions being the direct result of your rudeness, sir!"

"And I suppose you also threw your parasol at Lady Georgiana because *I* was at fault?" he inquired icily.

"I didn't throw it."

"Which presumably means you are about to accuse me again?" She lowered her glance. "No."

"Well, that is something, at least." He searched her face. "In your questionable opinion, who is the guilty party? The Duke of York? The Duchess, maybe? Perhaps you think the man in the moon came down on the off chance?"

Fresh anger sparked in her lavender eyes. "I don't know who did it, but I *do* know that you are one of the most obnoxious men in England!"

"No, madam, not obnoxious, merely unfortunate for ever having crossed your path!"

"Oh, believe me, I feel unfortunate for the very same reason!"

For a moment they glared at each other, then he glanced at the ruined buffet. "Why were you talking to the jelly?" he demanded. "You do know you were talking to it?"

She was acutely embarrassed. Could she risk telling him the truth? No, for he didn't seem the sort of person who would ever believe in brownies, and he clearly already believed her to be quite mad.

"I'm awaiting an explanation, Miss Peach."

"I wasn't talking to the jelly, sir, but to a small boy, a street urchin, behind the trestles. You probably couldn't see him, but he was stealing food. I challenged him, and he scrambled under the side of the tent. Surely you saw the canvas move?"

"No, I saw nothing."

"Nevertheless, that is what happened." She met his gaze without flinching. "Look, Sir Dominic, I'd be grateful never to see you again, and I will dance a jig if I am spared any more of Lady Georgiana's studied hysterics, so if you will let me pass now, we can forget each other's existence."

He hesitated, ran his fingers through his dark hair, then remained where he was. "Miss Peach, street urchin or not, I have to say that I find aspects of your conduct quite disturbing."

"What exactly are you implying, sir?" she asked stiffly.

He didn't quite like to go so far as to say he thought she was utterly mad. "Just that maybe you aren't quite as, er, hale as you might be."

"Meaning you think I am an escaped lunatic?"

"Er, no, of course not . . ."

"Don't lie, sirrah, for that is *exactly* what you think!" she cried.

His patience snapped. "Very well, yes, that *is* what I think! In fact, I believe you to be the most unhinged creature I have ever encountered!"

"Excepting only Lady Georgiana!" she fired back. "Be honest, sir. The only reason you're attacking me like this is because you wish to curry favor with the most monstrously insincere female in society!"

"Don't presume to criticize her!"

"I'll criticize her if I wish, Sir Dominic." Polly was becoming increasingly upset by the argument, although he could not have told that from her spirited stance.

He looked away. "I think perhaps we should call a truce, Miss

Peach, otherwise this unedifying contretemps will keep us here until the review is over."

"I asked you to let me pass some time ago, but you would not."

"So again it is my fault?"

"Yes, on this occasion most definitely."

He stood aside and swept her a bow. "Then pass, by all means," he said sarcastically.

She stalked out of the tent without another word, then hurried back to her carriage. Inside, she leaned her head back against the upholstery and closed her eyes. What was it about Sir Dominic Fortune that so set her at sixes and sevens? If she wasn't furious with him, she was pondering how it might be to surrender to his kisses! She determined to remain in the carriage until the review was well under way, then slip directly back to Bath, but she remembered the Gotenuvs. She'd given her word to Uncle Hordwell, and so had at least to seek them out for a while. *Then* she could leave. With a sigh, she alighted from the carriage again.

The review was just commencing. The immaculately turned out cavalry regiment was lined up in readiness, and as the necessary orders were given, the band struck up. Drums and brass thundered to "The British Grenadiers," and the magnificent cavalcade moved forward to pass before the royal pavilion, where the Duke and Duchess of York and their entourage sipped champagne.

The thirty-seven-year-old second son of King George was splendid in the uniform of commander-in-chief at Horse Guards, the army headquarters in London, with immense plumes streaming from his *chapeau-bras*. The duchess, a German princess, was dressed in blue and white, also with vast plumes, and she carried the ribboned basket of asters that had been presented to her on arrival. She was a small, vivacious, rather eccentric woman who kept over a hundred dogs, which had caused so much dissent in the marriage that she and her husband now lived separately. There had been an argument that very morning, but while her face was stony, his bore the vague smile of someone who had been overindulging in champagne since breakfast. On an occasion like this, it would have become him much more to take the salute properly on a horse, without any sign of champagne within fifty yards, but he was too dissipated and pleasure-loving to bother with such niceties. He found the delights of the officers' mess infinitely preferable to those of the parade ground, much to the overt anger and disapproval of many of the officers present.

Polly observed Georgiana in the royal pavilion. She had acquired a square of silver brocade from somewhere, and with a little deft folding and pinning had turned it into a commendable hat. She had also managed to position herself so close to the royal pair that she seemed of their personal party. The business of the parasol was clearly behind her as she wallowed in a condescending word from the duchess.

Polly eyed Dominic's love with dislike. What an outwardly vapid but inwardly designing witch the woman was. And what a fool Sir Dominic was for so clearly adoring her to distraction. But then, given his superior opinion of himself, he probably warranted such a creature. As Polly watched, Dominic entered the pavilion and discreetly drew Georgiana aside. His appearance on the scene did not please the lady at all, for she shook her head angrily when he whispered something to her. He was insistent, and with a very bad grace she allowed him to lead her away from the royal pavilion. Polly couldn't help following them, for the thought of eavesdropping was too great a temptation.

She was to be disappointed, however, for the conversation was over almost before it began. Georgiana so resented being removed from such a coveted position beside the duke and duchess that she dealt Dominic a sharp slap, then hurried away again, leaving him to rub the angry mark on his cheek.

Polly felt a little sorry for him, but her sympathy was short-lived. Let him suffer, she thought, and turned away to resume her search for the Gotenuvs.

Chapter 13

Polly did not immediately find the Gotenuvs, but she soon detected Bodkin again, for just as she reached the royal pavilion, there was a telltale disturbance. It happened at the precise moment the Marquess of Hightower's company rode past. Georgiana's duke-to-be seldom looked impressive, but at that moment he did.

His regimentals were dazzling in the October sunshine, his upright sword, drawn in salute, could not have glittered more, and his fine black horse moved in perfect time to the band. But suddenly there came a strange warbling whistle that Polly recognized only too well, for it was the sound Bodkin made when he summoned his bees. He certainly couldn't be summoning the Horditall bees from this distance, but perhaps *any* nearby bees would respond! Knowing the power the brownie had over the insects, she expected to hear a loud buzzing at any second, but there was nothing. Then Lord Algernon's horse went quite berserk. With a neigh of pain, it began to rear and buck, and Polly saw a single bee flying away from its neck.

The marquess was caught quite unawares, lost his seat, and was deposited in an undignified heap in front of the Duke of York. His sword was jerked from his gauntleted hand, and its point pierced the grass between the duke's feet. Horrified gasps buzzed as the stunned duke stared at the shuddering weapon, then stepped back in alarm. The horse bolted across the downs, and several gentlemen from the royal party hurried to attend to the unfortunate marquess. The rest of the regiment displayed commendable discipline, not faltering by so much as a step as the review continued. It all happened within ten feet of Polly, who was the only person present to know what had really happened. But why Bodkin should choose Lord Algernon, she could not imagine.

As soon as Lord Algernon fell, Georgiana rushed forward with such exclamations of alarm and concern that the duchess felt obliged to comfort her. The gentlemen conveyed the marquess into the pavilion and laid him upon a sofa, where Georgiana ministered to him with a scented, jelly-stained handkerchief. Lord Algernon hardly seemed to know what had happened to him. His face bore a confused expression, as if he could not imagine how he had gotten into the pavilion, but then, Polly thought uncharitably, from what she'd seen of him, he probably didn't!

Her thoughts returned to the matter of Bodkin's whereabouts. She looked intently all around for any further sign of him, but all seem quiet. The duke had recovered sufficiently to resume his rather haphazard inspection of the regiment. Rank after rank of mounted men passed by in rigid formation, and His Royal Highness gazed blandly at them, snapping his fingers to one of his gentlemen for another glass of champagne.

As Polly stood there, it suddenly dawned on her that the marquess's unseating had been another attempt by Bodkin to point an incriminating finger at her! The horrid little boggart had tried first with the parasol, and had now chosen to coincide her arrival at the pavilion with Lord Algernon's mishap. Exactly how she was meant to be implicated in what happened to the horse, she didn't know, but nevertheless she was certain that had been the brownie's intention. An unsettling sense of foreboding began to pass through her, for if the second attempt had failed to cause trouble for her, she guessed it wouldn't be long before Bodkin tried again. Where was the wretch? If only she could speak to him long enough to tell him the truth!

Suddenly her reticule was snatched from her, just as the parasol had been earlier. She gasped with alarm. Was she the victim of a thief, or was Bodkin at work again? There was no sign of a fleeing miscreant, no angry protests as people were elbowed aside to clear the way. It *must* have been Bodkin! Gazing frantically around, she was horrified to find herself suddenly looking into Dominic's eyes again.

He was standing about ten feet away from her, and his gaze was suspicious to say the least. A mixture of indignation and anger spurted through her, for it was clear he believed she had something to do with what had happened to the marquess. Then he looked away as something in the review proved temporarily more interesting than mad Miss Peach. In fact it was Harry Dashington's company riding by, although Polly was not to know that as her gaze followed Dominic's to the gallant major. As they both watched, Polly's heart plummeted as she saw her reticule fly through the air to strike the flank of Harry's horse. The animal gave a nervous whinny, then ceased its collected trot to caper around. Harry strove to keep his mount under control, but it was too unnerved, and he was soon obliged to jump down from the saddle or be flung at the duke's feet like Lord Algernon. As he grabbed the reins to prevent the horse from making off, a strangely raucous voice yelled out a command. "Company, halt!"

The light dragoons reined in immediately, looking around in amazement to see why they'd been ordered to do so. Harry gestured wildly for them to ride on, but before they had the wit to do so, the ranks behind collided with them. Instant chaos ensued, and the openmouthed Duke of York stared in utter fascination as the proud review descended into pantomime.

Polly slipped hastily away into the crowds before Dominic

could publicly accuse her. Her thoughts were savage. *Oh, Bodkin, if I lay hands upon you, I'll tie your tail in a knot!* As soon as she'd gotten well away from the pavilion, she gathered her skirts to run to her carriage. Her reticule wasn't of importance, for it contained nothing of value, and besides, she could hardly risk being seen retrieving it! To her dismay she heard footsteps in pursuit, and knew it would be Dominic. She didn't halt until her hand was on the carriage door, but then she turned reluctantly to face him.

He held up her reticule angrily. "You left this behind, I believe, madam!" he snapped.

"I admit it's mine, Sir Dominic, but someone stole it just before it was thrown at the horse," she said defensively.

"Oh, of course! I suppose it was the same villain who made free with your parasol!"

"Yes, probably," she replied, reaching out for the reticule, but he snatched it back.

"Miss Peach, it was bad enough that you threw your reticule, but why did you have to go so far as to shout that order? And what did you do to Hightower? I didn't see exactly what happened, but I *know* you were behind it!"

"I wasn't behind anything, I didn't throw my reticule, and I certainly didn't shout that order!"

"Your capacity for lying is astounding! Of course you did it all!"

"And your capacity for not listening to the truth is equally astounding!" she cried. "I haven't done any of these things, yet you accuse me as if you have proof and this were a court of law!"

"I don't need proof to know you are guilty. Madam, have you any idea of the damage you've caused?" He gestured behind at the confusion of horses and riders. "As it is, you've made a mockery of the entire occasion, but you might easily have killed Hightower and Harry."

"Harry?"

"Major Harry Dashington, your unfortunate victim, and my best friend!"

"I'm very sorry for what happened to both of them, but I wasn't responsible for either occurrence. In fact the first incident was caused by a bee. I saw it fly away from the horse's neck. Be sensible, Sir Dominic. You know where I was standing, so how could I possibly have thrown the reticule from that angle? And how could I shout without everyone around me knowing?"

"Miss Peach, where you're concerned, anything is possible." He thrust the reticule into her hand, deciding she was too impossible for further argument.

"Very well, if that's to be your attitude, perhaps I should point out that *you* were present on all three occasions today, and so just as likely to be guilty as I."

He was outraged at such a suggestion. "That's totally ridiculous! I was once an officer in the Duke of York's Own Light Dragoons, so the last thing I'd do is heap ridicule upon such a distinguished regiment, *or* endanger the lives of fellow officers!"

"I have only your word for that. You seem quite as mad to me as I clearly seem to you."

"Indeed? Well, if you're so innocent, why are you running away like this?"

"It was in the vain hope of avoiding another disagreeable confrontation with you. Unfortunately, I didn't run quickly enough, for here you are."

"*Please* don't let me detain you a moment more, Miss Peach, for this conversation is clearly an exercise in futility."

His tone was condescending, but before she could issue a suitable devastating response, something happened that rendered them both speechless. A number of riderless horses suddenly bolted from the down in the direction of Bath. The runaways weren't army horses, but belonged to some of the gentlemen who'd ridden from Bath, and Dominic's thoroughbred was at the head of them. Polly watched, too, for although Dominic's horse was riderless, it seemed being urged for all it was worth. *Bodkin*, she thought with an inward sigh.

Cries of dismay resounded from people who'd witnessed this fresh disturbance, and several gentlemen ran pointlessly after their fleeing property, but stood no chance of catching up. A group of ladies in the carriage next to Polly's were so alarmed that they were obliged to resort to *sal volatile*, and a number of children in the crowds began to cry.

Polly glanced at Dominic, who had wisely chosen not to chase after his mount. "I trust you do not mean to accuse me of *this* as well? Mayhap my arm is long enough for me to have untied them while standing here talking to you?"

"No, Miss Peach, I have to judge you totally innocent this time," he murmured as the little herd disappeared toward Bath.

"Fortune smiles upon me at last," she replied drily.

The review had now become such a shambles that the Duke of York decided it was advisable to lower a timely curtain. He issued the orders, and highly embarrassed officers went about the business of calling off the long-rehearsed parade. People began to return to their carriages, offering seats to those whose horses had now gone, and Polly felt obliged to offer similar assistance to Dominic. She didn't *want* to extend any assistance to him, not only because he was so disagreeable, but also because such an act would infringe upon propriety, but circumstances seemed to require it.

She looked a little awkwardly at him. "I . . . I know it may not be quite the thing, and that you would prefer to travel with Beelzebub himself, but under the circumstances I feel it right to offer you a seat in my carriage for the return to Royal Crescent." She didn't want him to accept; indeed she was convinced he'd decline in no uncertain manner, but to her horror he nodded.

"I would be most grateful, Miss Peach," he murmured.

"You . . . you would?"

"Certainly. Are you leaving now?"

"Well, I . . ." What of the Gotenuvs? she thought. Was there any point now in trying to find them? She thought not. "Yes, I think it best, don't you?"

"There is little to stay here for," he replied, opening the carriage door to hand her inside, then he clambered in as well and sat opposite her. As the carriage drove off from the scene of the virtual annihilation of the Duke of York's Own Light Dragoons, Polly was aware of a most unwanted flutter of excitement because she was alone and private with Dominic. In spite of everything, she couldn't help being drawn to him. Oh, if only they could be more amiable toward each other. If only a lot of things, come to that . . .

Chapter 14

The return to Bath was at first conducted in a rather awkward atmosphere, for once they were alone together, Polly grew more and more conscious of how flagrant a breach of etiquette and propriety the short journey *à deux* was. What Dominic thought, she did not know, but she wished with all her heart that she hadn't given in to the urge to ask him to accompany her. But it was too late now.

"Will you be long in Bath, Miss Peach?" he asked, clearly just to break the silence.

"I trust not."

"So it isn't a pleasure visit?"

"Far from it."

He looked inquiringly at her. "I'm sorry to hear that."

She met his gaze. "Are you? I would have thought you'd exult in the knowledge that I am here under disagreeable circumstances."

"You wrong me, Miss Peach, for I am not the monster you seem to think."

"And I am not the lunatic *you* seem to think," she replied.

He gave her a sheepish grin. "You have me there, for I confess I *did* wonder."

"Past tense? Come now, sir, be honest. You *still* harbor doubts concerning my sanity."

He laughed. "No, Miss Peach, I no longer harbor doubts."

"Presumably because you now *know* me to be mad," she murmured.

"I crave your pardon for any thoughts I may have had, for your innocence regarding the runaway horses rather put everything into perspective."

"Even though you believe I throw parasols at innocent bystanders, talk to jellies, lay waste to buffets, and throw reticules at horses?"

"You embarrass me, Miss Peach, for I now accept that I was guilty of leaping to conclusions because of your coincidental presence. I crave your forgiveness."

"And I crave yours, sir, for I have said some monstrous things as well."

"Then we will begin again, mm?" He smiled.

She flushed, then fidgeted with her reticule for a moment. How pleasant it was to converse with him like this. And how much he improved when he smiled.

"Have you been to Bath before, Miss Peach?" he asked.

"Yes, occasionally. I'm actually from London, and have only lived in the country for about eighteen months."

"I don't recollect ever encountering you in London."

She smiled a little ruefully. "Perhaps because I didn't move in your exalted circles, Sir Dominic. My father was the banker, Mr. Septimus Peach, and I fear he wished to save me from wicked aristocrats."

Dominic's eyes lightened. "So you're *that* Miss Peach! As it happens, your father was my banker, and I'm pleased to say that my title did not prevent us from enjoying an excellent association. I was deeply saddened to hear of his demise. And his wife's, of course. I . . . I mean, your mother . . ."

Polly bit her lip. "I will never drive over Westminster Bridge again, for to be sure it is the most cruel place on earth as far as I am concerned."

"I had no idea you were the Peach's Bank heiress."

"You make me sound like a lady's novel, sir."

"Not intentionally, I assure you. What possessed you to live out in the wild sticks of Somerset?"

"I am my uncle's ward, and he decreed I must live with him. I'm obliged to obey him until I'm twenty-three, when according to my parents' will, I can set up a household of my own, provided I find a suitable lady companion to keep watch over me. I'm only twenty now, so there is some time to go."

"But at twenty-three you'll secure the necessary companion and flee back to the delights of the capital?"

"Unless I have been dragged in manacles to the altar before then," she said with feeling.

Dominic was increasingly intrigued. "Am I to understand your uncle has put forward a bridegroom for whom you do not care?"

"Yes. Lord Benjamin Beddem, for whose temporary absence in London I am duly grateful."

Dominic had to smother a smile. "Lady Georgiana's brother, eh?" he murmured a little mischievously.

Polly stared at him. "Are you jesting?"

"I fear not."

"That shallow, designing creature is a *Beddem*?" Georgiana as a sister-in-law was almost as unpalatable a prospect as Lord Benjamin as a husband!

"Please do not criticize her, Miss Peach."

She searched his face, inexplicably hurt to realize how deep his affections for Lady Georgiana went. "But how can you possibly like her, Sir Dominic?" she asked a trifle too candidly. "She's quite the most blatant schemer I've encountered! Everything she does is with an eye to her own personal advancement."

"I would prefer not to hear any more of your opinion, Miss Peach," he said warningly.

Polly bit her lip, then looked quickly out of the window. He was right to reprimand her, for she really didn't know Lady Georgiana well enough to presume to speak out. But that didn't mean she was wrong about the lady! Lord Benjamin's sister had a character that was odious in the extreme, and her clearly indicated ambitions showed her to be little more than a highborn adventuress!

After a moment Dominic resumed the conversation as if Georgiana had never been mentioned. "You and Lord Benjamin, eh? A marriage truly made in heaven."

"I'm glad you think so," she replied, more than a little miffed that he should find it amusing.

"Forgive me, it's just that Beddem's search for a fortune is very well known in society, and if he snaps you up, he'll undoubtedly solve his problems, but at the same time he'll acquire a far from meek wife."

She looked crossly at him. "Is that all you can say of me? That I'll be a far from meek wife?"

He studied her. "No, I can also say that you have a sharp tongue, to say nothing of a hot temper and inclination to mulishness. On the brighter side, I have to admit that you are also refreshingly spirited, and very pretty indeed."

He was twitting her, and she knew it, but she couldn't help being needled by his criticism. "Now let us consider you, Sir Dominic. When I look at you, I see someone who possesses a sharp tongue and hot temper to match mine, who considers himself of better breeding than almost everyone except the royal family—probably of them as well, come to think of it—and who flatters himself that he is one of the most stylish men of his generation. On the brighter side, I think you are very handsome, and can probably be exceedingly charming when you choose."

He smiled. "Remind me never to repeat the mistake of seeming to criticize you, Miss Peach. Tell me, will you be attending any of the other social occasions arranged for the period of the Duke and Duchess of York's stay in Bath? The Halloween festivities at Sydney Gardens Vauxhall, for instance?"

"My uncle and Lord Benjamin will be attending, but I will not." *I hope I will have left Bath by then!*

"At least you must be attending the ball tomorrow night?"

"Yes."

"Then I trust you will reserve a measure for me?"

The request took her by surprise. "You are prepared to risk partnering me? Are you not afraid my reticule will come to life and strike you? Or that my wrist favor may untie itself and fix prettily in your hair?"

He laughed. "I am more than prepared for such possible hazards."

"Then I will gladly reserve a measure for you."

"A *ländler* would be most agreeable."

"If that is what you wish, then of course."

He changed the subject to something a little more thorny. "What do you think really happened with your parasol? We know that neither of us committed the crime, so who did?"

"I've already said I don't know," she replied uncomfortably.

"Yes, you do know, Miss Peach. It's written all over you," he said quietly.

"I assure you you're wrong," she replied, meeting his eyes squarely. She wasn't about to confess to knowing a brownie! If she did, he'd revise his opinion concerning her sanity.

Another heavy silence fell. By now the carriage had almost reached Bath, and in the crowded streets it was possible to detect the riotous passage of the runaway horses. Sedan chairs had been abandoned by their carriers, sometimes with unfortunate passengers still inside; the display outside a fishmonger's shop had been knocked over; and carriages and carts had been damaged against the high pavements as they tried to avoid the oncoming stampede.

Polly gazed at it all with renewed dismay. Bodkin had certainly given vent to his fury today, for he'd left a trail of devastation wherever he went. Oh, how she prayed his need for sweet comfort would take him to Zuder's skylight tonight, so that he'd see her note. Surely *then* he'd give her a chance to explain both her innocence and that of Uncle Hordwell? It wouldn't help him to find Nutmeg again, but at least he'd stop being angry, and might come home, where he belonged.

While she was pondering this hope, Bodkin and his equine team had just arrived on the sloping common in front of Royal Crescent, where the horses lost interest in flight and halted to graze. Gratified to have caused such a huge amount of trouble at the review, the brownie jumped down, then hastened up toward Dominic's house, at the door of which Ragwort was beckoning excitedly.

"Come quickly, Bodkin, for I think I may have happened upon something."

"Have you found Nutmeg?" Bodkin cried, seizing his arms excitedly.

"Not exactly. Oh, come on inside and you'll see for yourself." The door opened as a footman came out, having recognized Dominic's horse on the common, and the two brownies slipped inside.

Minutes later, Polly's carriage halted outside 1 Royal Crescent. She wasn't at all surprised to see the horses; indeed she half expected it, for Bodkin was bound to ride back here. Where had the mischievous little scoundrel gone now? Oh, once she found him, she was going to give him a piece of her mind second to none! His conveniently long tail wouldn't only be tied in one knot, but in as many as she could manage!

The carriage halted, and as Dominic alighted, he saw the footman leading his horse off the grass. "Thank goodness for that—I thought I'd never see my best mount again," he said.

Polly smiled. "Well, that's one blessing."

"So it seems." He turned to her. "Thank you for being bold enough to offer to convey me."

"I trust for your sake that Lady Georgiana doesn't find out."

"I hardly think she will believe us to be embarking on a liaison."

"I was alluding to her dislike for me," Polly replied, then gave him a slightly indignant look. "Anyway, why shouldn't she suspect us of a liaison? What makes it so impossible a thought?"

"I meant only that I've made my love for her so very clear that she would think it unlikely that I'd seek consolation elsewhere just yet."

"It would do the horrid *chienne* good, maybe it would even make her as jealous of me as you are of Lord Algernon. I don't know what she sees in him, unless it be his title and expectations."

Dominic gave her a thoughtful look. "Maybe you're right, and she would benefit from a little such food for thought. And maybe Lord Benjamin would be a little deterred if he thought you were bestowing favorable smiles upon me."

"Unfortunately, no one has witnessed our escapade, except my coachman and your footman, and I doubt if either Lady Georgiana or Lord Benjamin would pay heed to a mere servant."

"No, but they'd pay heed to an incorrigible old gossip like the Marquis de Torkalotte."

"Who?"

"The elderly French gentleman strolling along the pavement behind you. He's a close family friend of the entire Beddem family, including the duke himself."

She glanced around and saw an elderly gentleman of flamboyant but rather old-fashioned appearance. Powdered, patched, and bewigged, he was returning from an afternoon perambulation to his elegant house in the Circus. Polly was puzzled. "But what is there for him to tell anyone? All we're doing is standing here in civil conversation. He doesn't know we traveled together in the carriage. We could simply have met as I alighted on my own."

"Oh, I think we can give him something to broadcast," Dominic said, and before Polly realized what was happening, he'd pulled her into his arms. He pressed her close, his parted lips upon hers in a kiss that was really quite shocking. His fingers wound warmly into the hair at the nape of her neck, and his mouth teased hers in a way she'd never experienced before. The kiss continued as the Marquis de Torkalotte strolled past, his head pulled on a string as he goggled at the astonishing scene.

As soon as the Frenchman was out of earshot, Dominic drew back. "There, I fancy that was scandalous enough to spread all over town, don't you?"

Polly's face was crimson with mortification and with aroused emotions she would have preferred had remained asleep. "How dare you!" she breathed, and dealt him a slap on the other cheek to the one Georgiana had struck earlier. "There, a matching pair, I believe!" she declared, then turned to hurry into the house.

Dominic gazed after her, his expression hard to decipher, then he walked quickly toward his own house. Polly peeped out around the dining room curtain, and as he vanished from sight, she leaned back against the wall, her eyes closed. Her lips still seemed to burn from his kiss, and she knew that in spite of the circumstances, she had found those few intimate seconds quite the most exciting imaginable. Strange new feelings now whirled unstoppably through her, and she was conscious of a delicious ache she knew only he could soothe. *Oh, Devil take him!* He was arrogant, presumptuous, selfish, and unkind, but oh, how easy it would be to love him!

Chapter 15

Bodkin and Ragwort knew nothing of the startling developments on the pavement outside 1 Royal Crescent. Ragwort had led Bodkin up to Dominic's bedroom, where he pointed out something wedged between the carpet and the dado. It was something that was visible only to brownies, the buckle from a brownie's belt. Ragwort prodded it with his foot. "That doesn't belong to anyone *I* know," he declared.

Bodkin gazed at it. Was it Nutmeg's? He didn't know! For the life of him, he suddenly couldn't remember what her belt had been like.

Ragwort glanced at him. "Well? Do you recognize it?"

"No," Bodkin replied sorrowfully. "It might be hers, but then again it might not. My mind is a blank."

Ragwort sighed. "Well, it's the only clue of any sort that one of our kind has been here. I've even asked Giles if he knows anything."

"Giles?"

"My footman friend at number one. I wondered if he'd overheard anything strange between Mr. Horditall and Lord Benjamin, but he hasn't. If it weren't for you, no one here would know a brownie named Nutmeg even existed."

"Oh, she exists. She's wonderful, and I love her with all my heart." Bodkin sighed, then inspected the buckle again. "Maybe it belonged to the last brownie who looked after the house. Caraway, wasn't that her name?"

Ragwort nodded and colored a little. "Yes, it was her name, but this isn't her buckle."

Bodkin raised an eyebrow. "You seem very sure of that."

"I am."

"What happened between you and Caraway?"

Ragwort's face was now the color of beetroot. "It's none of your business, Bodkin, *Nutmeg's* the one we're concerned with now." He poked the buckle again with his foot. "So you can't tell if this is hers?"

Bodkin picked it up and turned it over carefully in his hand. "It *might* be, Ragwort. Oh, I'm in such a state over her that I can't remember anything."

"Well, let's assume it's hers. Its presence means she's been here, and if that's so, maybe she still is. Although where, I really don't know. I hunted high and low while you were at Claverton Down. By the way, did you get up to some good mischief?"

"Oh, yes." Bodkin relayed his pranks.

"You actually brought the review to a standstill?" Ragwort was impressed.

"Yes, although I wasn't able to make as much trouble for Miss Polly as I'd hoped."

"I still can't believe she's part of it," Ragwort said.

"Oh, she is. Why else would she be all smiles with Hordwell? Look, I don't want to talk about Miss Polly. Let's get back to Nutmeg. Have you tried calling her?"

Ragwort was indignant. "Of course! What manner of dumb-cluck do you take me for?"

"All right, all right, I only asked," Bodkin said quickly.

"Anyway, calling her is actually quite pointless, and I don't really know why I bothered."

"What do you mean?"

"If someone's holding her captive through her belt, she won't be able to speak or communicate in any other way with anyone trying to rescue her."

Bodkin stared at him. "Of *course* she can speak!"

"Not if someone has her belt," Ragwort repeated patiently. "For the same reason, she can safely be left anywhere her captor chooses. It doesn't matter where he goes—she cannot run away, because she's completely in his power. That's why, if it *is* Lord Benjamin, he doesn't have to give her a second thought until he has the page from Nostradamus. He can put her entirely from his mind. It's like buying a new handkerchief, then folding it away in a drawer until it's needed."

Dismayed, Bodkin sat on the floor and gazed tearfully at the buckle. "We country brownies must be very naive, because I didn't know any of that," he confessed miserably. "Oh, Ragwort, how on earth am I going to rescue her?"

"I don't know, and that's fact. Unless . . ."

"Yes?"

"Well, if we could find the rest of her belt and steal it back, then we—" He broke off with an irritated snort. "Come to think of it, that won't do any good, because *you* can't remember what her belt looks like!"

Bodkin lowered his eyes glumly. He felt so utterly foolish. Why couldn't he recall Nutmeg's belt? He'd seen her wearing it every single day for months.

Ragwort leaned against the dado, his arms folded and his tail swishing idly. "This is most perplexing. Which of them has the belt? Hordwell or Lord Benjamin?"

"Or Sir Dominic Fortune. Maybe he's part of it all, too." Bodkin glanced around the room. It was the principal bedchamber, and Dominic's possessions were everywhere, including the book he was reading, a small box containing his neckcloth pins, seals, and rings, a tortoiseshell hairbrush and comb, and his gray paisley dressing gown draped casually over the foot of the vast green velvet four-poster. The walls and dado were cream and gold, and a fine chandelier chinked gently in the breeze from the open window.

Bodkin's face was thoughtful. If Dominic had the belt, maybe it was here in this room right now. "Ragwort, are you sure you've searched *everywhere* in here?"

"Until I'm blue in the face," Ragwort replied flatly. "You can search again if you like, but I've had enough."

Footsteps approached the bedroom door, and the brownies fell silent as Dominic came in. He was tugging off his neckcloth, which he tossed onto the bed, then he stepped to the window and looked down at the sloping hillside, where most of the runaway horses had now been rounded up. He recognized one of the animals, a fine colt named Golden Pear, which had almost won the Derby that summer. An old nursery rhyme came to him, and he murmured the first line aloud. "I had a little nut tree, nothing it would bear, but a silver nutmeg, and a golden pear."

Bodkin and Ragwort exchanged glances. Surely this was no coincidence! He knew about Nutmeg, and must have the belt! Bodkin got angrily to his feet, his tail beginning to twirl, but Ragwort put a restraining hand on his shoulder and shook his head. Then he pulled Bodkin toward the door and only ventured to whisper when they were in the passage.

"Leave him for the time being."

"I want to run him through!" cried Bodkin with a little more vehemence than was wise.

Dominic heard and called out. "Is someone there?"

Ragwort clamped a hand over Bodkin's mouth. "You really are a country bumpkin, aren't you?" he breathed, watching as Dominic looked curiously out into the apparently deserted passage.

The moment Dominic's door had closed again, Ragwort took his hand away from Bodkin's mouth. "Come on—it's not the end of the world yet. Let's go back to my house and share a dish of sweet tea."

"Or maybe some mead? I've brought some with me from Horditall, and if I say so myself, it's very fine." This was by way of a peace offering, for Bodkin knew he'd been less than helpful or sensible over the past few minutes.

Ragwort flushed a little and cleared his throat. "Er, no, thank you all the same. Alcohol doesn't agree with me."

Bodkin looked curiously at him. "What do you mean?"

"Tea will do me nicely right now," Ragwort replied, ignoring the question.

Bodkin didn't press further, and together they scampered down through the house to the entrance hall. A maid was just coming in through the front door with two baskets of produce she'd purchased in the town for the cook, and as she put them down and turned to close the door again, the brownies slipped outside.

In his room Dominic took off his coat and boots, then undid his shirt before lying on the bed, his hands behind his head. He stared thoughtfully at the bed hangings. He'd come here to find a bride and forget Georgiana, but now she was in Bath, too, and he found it very painful indeed; indeed was in half a mind to return to London. Still, there was tomorrow night's ball at the Assembly Rooms, where he'd be able to inspect the likely contenders in his own private marriage mart. Please let them be an improvement on Miss Polly Peach, the only young lady—apart from Georgiana— he'd encountered since arriving. He thought of Polly for a moment. What an aggravating creature she was, so much so that it had been a positive pleasure to confound her with a kiss. Oh, yes, he'd stopped her breath for a moment *then*! He smiled a little. "You stopped your own breath a little too, Dominic Fortune," he murmured, for he wasn't usually given to such public displays. Memories of the kiss washed over him with unexpected warmth. Plague take it, he'd *enjoyed* kissing her, in fact if he was strictly honest, he'd enjoyed it too much for comfort. His body stirred a little, and he closed his eyes. If he didn't dislike her so, he could almost swear he desired her . . .

Downstairs, the tired maid carried the baskets to the basement kitchens, where the cook, a plump woman whose rosy cheeks and good-natured smile were an excellent advertisement for the quality of her cooking, examined the purchases with great care. She went over the cooking apples in particular, then frowned at the maid.

"Were these the best you could find?"

The maid was crestfallen. "Yes, Mrs. Matthews."

"But it's autumn, the best time for apples, and these aren't even very large. Oh, dear, I'd much prefer them to be better quality. Sir Dominic is very fond of my apple pie, and he has Major Dashington coming to dine tonight."

"I really couldn't find any better, Mrs. Matthews," the maid insisted.

The cook nodded. "Oh, very well, but mark my words, Jinny Carter, if I go to town tomorrow and find there *are* better apples, it will be the worst for you."

Jinny's eyes filled with tears. "But that's not fair, Mrs. Matthews, they might put out better ones by tomorrow!"

Mrs. Matthews beckoned another maid. "Get to work peeling these, Anne."

"Yes, Mrs. Matthews."

"And you, Jinny, go out in the garden and see if there's any fresh mint for the leg of lamb. I think you'll find some beneath the mulberry tree, where last week's frost didn't reach." The cook shook her head and tutted. "Lamb indeed, such a washy meat compared with mutton, but Sir Dominic will insist he prefers it."

Jinny hurried thankfully out of the back door and up the steps to the garden, where George, the gardener, was raking up autumn leaves. She paused to greet him for a moment and remarked that this was one of the finest falls she could remember, so warm that by this time of year the fine potted orange trees adorning the rooftop terrace above the kitchens had usually been taken in. George grunted in response, for he was a man of few words, so Jinny hurried on about her business.

As she neared the mulberry tree, which was right at the bottom of the garden, next to the door in the high wall that bordered the lane behind, she noticed that the door's catch had worked loose. Left as it was, anyone who felt like it could just walk in. She'd have to tell George, for such things were his task. Reaching the tree, she began to gather a large handful of the mint, but then she heard an ominous buzzing sound from the branches overhead. She glanced up, and her eyes widened as she saw a seething swarm of honeybees against a fork in the tree trunk.

With a gasp, she grabbed the last of the mint, then stepped hastily away. Now there were two jobs for old George to deal with, she thought, and hurried toward him, but he gave her such a glower that she changed her mind. Let him find out for himself, and serve him right if Sir Dominic got to hear that he'd neglected his work. Tossing her head again, she stalked past him without a word.

Chapter 16

It rained heavily that evening. Polly stood at the library window, looking along Brock Street, where the cobbles shone in the light from the lamps. She wore the ivory woolen gown in which she'd traveled from Horditall, now with a fringed crimson-and-gold shawl around her shoulders. Her blond hair was brushed loose because she'd had a headache before dinner, and her face was pensive as she gazed at her reflection in the rain-spotted window.

She was worried about the kiss on the pavement, and how far and wide the Marquis de Torkalotte might already have spread the juicy tidbit. Right now, how many Bath dinner parties were being far more amused by his tittle-tattling than by the debacle on Claverton Down? Was the Peach's Bank heiress being sniggered at over the mulligatawny? Were her morals—or lack of them—under discussion as the red mullet was served? She glanced at her uncle, who'd fallen asleep in his fireside chair. He hadn't heard the lurid tale yet, but was sure to be regaled with it when he arrived at the King's Baths in the morning. He was still in a bad mood anyway, for there was no sign of his valuables, and he was still convinced that the servants were dishonest, every man Jack and woman Jill of them! One thing was certain, she wasn't going to accompany him anywhere tomorrow, not even the Assembly Room ball. Her gown and accessories had been brought from Horditall, but she hadn't tried anything on, nor would she after that kiss. She'd spare her blushes by claiming another headache that incapacitated her all day and into the night! She closed her eyes, wishing she could dislike Sir Dominic Fortune as much as he deserved, but instead she was in peril of falling head over heels in love with him!

A carriage was splashing along Brock Street, preceded by a soaking wet link boy with a smoking torch. She watched it idly, her thoughts still upon Dominic, but then a face looked out as the vehicle passed by, and she recognized Dominic's friend, Major Dashington, who'd suffered Bodkin's attentions at the review. Was he going to see Dominic? Curiosity got the better of her, and she hurried to the dining room, from where she could look along the sweep of the crescent. The carriage drew up at Dominic's door, and the major climbed down. His uniform shone in the light from the lamps as he quickly crossed the pavement to the door, which opened immediately to admit him.

Polly drew her shawl more closely around her shoulders and returned to the library. There she sat on the sofa opposite her uncle and picked up her volume of *The Castle of Otranto*. At last she was able to put her worries aside, and was soon lost in the tale of gothic horror. Several hours passed, broken only by Hordwell's snores and Giles's bringing her the tray of tea she rang for. She was just about to pour herself a cup when she became aware of a faint noise from the sugar bowl. A sugar lump rose into the air, then disappeared as someone ate it. As a second lump followed suit, she sat forward urgently.

"Bodkin?"

The second lump was hastily dropped, and she heard footsteps pattering toward the door. In a trice she got up to follow. "Bodkin!" she called. "Please stop, for I must speak to you! Didn't you go to Zuder's? Haven't you seen my note?"

But the footsteps ran down the stairs toward the kitchen basement. Polly followed, paying no heed to the startled servants as she pursued the invisible brownie to the back door, the handle of which rattled as he tried to get out. For a moment she thought she had him trapped, but then the door opened, and he dashed out into the rainswept night. Without hesitation, Polly ran out as well. "Bodkin, come back! I have to talk to you!" she called, following the wet squelch of his footsteps on the flagstone path. The wind stirred through the trees, and she lost the sounds he made in the rustle of leaves. "Bodkin!" She glanced around, hardly aware of the rain.

Suddenly the door in the garden wall banged, and she knew he'd gone out into the lane. Impulsively she gave chase again, even though her hem and shoes were already soaked. Lamps shone above each garden door along the seeming deserted lane, and raindrops flashed their pale arcs of light. Puddles filled the deep ruts that grooved the way, and water poured from the eaves of some sheds. She listened carefully, trying to hear the brownie above the loud patter the rain made on the ivy against the wall. Then she saw one of the puddles splashing quite violently as Bodkin stumbled and fell.

The brownie scrambled to his feet and fled toward the nearest door, which happened to be that of Dominic's house, although he didn't realize it. George the gardener hadn't noticed the broken catch, so Bodkin slipped into the garden beyond, then set off toward the kitchens, where a little shelter seemed likely. But he hadn't gone more than a few yards when a familiar droning sound caught his attention. He looked quickly at the mulberry tree in the corner. *Bees! A swarm of them!* His eyes lit up for a moment, but then Polly called again, and he ran on to the basement, where he hid behind an enormous rainwater butt that stood against the wall, directly below the rooftop terrace.

Polly had seen the door to Dominic's garden being pushed open, and knew where Bodkin had gone. That particular garden was the very last in the crescent that she would have chosen to enter, but having come this far in pursuit of her prey, she didn't intend to give up now. After a tentative glance inside, she followed the brownie. By now she was so wet right through that her woolen gown clung to her like a second skin, her hair hung in rats' tails around her shoulders, and the fringe of her shawl was dripping as if it had just been hauled out of the washtub. She, too, heard the sound of bees coming from the tree in the corner, but she hardly gave them a thought as she advanced slowly through the icy downpour. Then a slight sound drew her attention to the house.

There were lights in the kitchens, and another in the dining room above, where she guessed Dominic and Major Dashington were now enjoying postprandial cognac, mayhap smiling about the lesson that had been taught the Peach's Bank heiress! The sound came again, like a slight shuffling on gravel, and this time it seemed it came from the terrace on the kitchen roof, where she could see a line of orange trees in large pots. If Bodkin was there, he was right outside the French windows of the dining room, only a thickness of glass away from Dominic and his friend. Dismay struck her, for the likelihood of those gentlemen being alerted was rather too great for her peace of mind. She gazed intently at the orange trees, then became certain she could make out a telltale shudder of leaves on the one that stood above the large water butt by the kitchen door. Dominic and Major Dashington or not, she had to reason with the infuriatingly obstinate brownie. Reluctantly, she approached the steps that led up from the garden to the terrace.

Harry Dashington had just left the house because he was duty officer at midnight. As his carriage followed a link boy into the murk of rain and darkness, Dominic returned to the candlelit blue-and-gold dining room to collect his glass of cognac, intending to adjourn to the drawing room. As he reached across the table for it, he heard a low voice from beyond the window. Puzzled, he straightened, but there was only silence. Thinking it was a trick of the rain, he reached for the glass again, only to pause once more as he distinctly heard a female voice speaking in a low, urgent undertone.

"Bodkin! If you don't listen to me, so help me I'll . . ." Whoever it was refrained from describing the intended punishment.

Wondering what on earth was going on outside, Dominic went to the heavily draped indigo velvet curtains and peeped through the crack between them. The window ran with rain, so he couldn't see anything, but he heard the voice more clearly now.

"Bodkin, I think you are the most aggravating, awkward, unfair, judgmental thing in all creation, and I'm beginning to be sorry I ever thought you my friend!"

Dominic's eyes cleared a little, for although he couldn't see the owner of the voice, he suddenly knew who she was—Miss Peach, if he wasn't mistaken! *Now* what was the astonishing creature up to? Turning back, he extinguished the candles on the table, then stepped behind the curtains and waited until his eyes were accustomed to the dark before softly undoing the window catch. He flung the windows open without warning and stepped out into the rain. "What's afoot here?" he demanded loudly.

Polly, who had just realized it was only a cat hiding by the orange trees, was so startled that she tottered against the pot and knocked it over with a crash. The terrified cat erupted from hiding with a yowl like that of the Devil himself, and poor Polly lost her balance completely. With a scream, she fell over the edge of the terrace and landed with a huge splash in the water butt below. Now it was Bodkin's turn to get a fright, for the butt rocked to and fro, threatening to topple backward against the wall, crushing him in the process, so he fled down the garden, then out into the lane again.

Appalled, Dominic ran down the steps to rescue Polly, who was splashing and choking in the water butt. The servants rushed out to see what was going on, and two of them helped him to pull her safely out. He gathered her strongly into his arms and carried her into the warm kitchens, where Mrs. Matthews quickly wrapped her in a warm blanket.

Dominic waited as the cook pressed a glass of hot milk into the trembling hands of the bedraggled intruder; then he spoke. "Miss Peach, as soon as Mrs. Matthews has something dry for you to put on, I wish to receive your explanation for this latest escapade. I will await you in the drawing room." Without waiting for her reply, he left the kitchens.

Polly sipped the hot milk. She was freezing cold, but her cheeks were on fire with humiliation. What on earth was she going to say in her defense? There simply weren't any mitigating circumstances to offer for her having trespassed as she had. He must think she'd been eavesdropping at the window upon his conversation with Major Dashington, but then she realized the major had been nowhere in evidence. Clearly he'd already departed, for which she was thankful, as it meant she had only Dominic himself to confront. As if that were not bad enough!

Perceiving that Polly and the maid Jinny were more or less the same size, Mrs. Matthews dispatched the latter to get her best dress and shawl from her attic room, and then the menservants were banished from the kitchens as Polly received a second soaking, this time a warm soapy one in front of the fire. Half an hour later, her wet hair clean again, but still left loose, she was as ready as she was ever likely to be to face Dominic. After thanking Jinny most sincerely for the loan of the simple pink dimity gown, and promising to more than recompense her and the kind cook for their trouble, she reluctantly ascended to the drawing room on the second floor.

Chapter 17

The drawing room was splendid, with gray brocade walls and a gold-and-white ceiling. Portraits gazed down from every wall, and firelight danced on gilded French furniture. A single candle illuminated the mantelpiece, and Dominic stood beside it, the light burnishing his dark hair copper. He wore the formal attire he'd donned for dinner, and the diamond pin at his throat flashed as he turned when she entered.

"Ah, here you are at last," he murmured.

"You should not have ordered me here at all," she replied, having decided that the best form of defense was attack. "I admit to having trespassed *outside* your property, but it ill becomes you to oblige me to be alone with yóu. Perhaps you intend to humiliate me again?"

"You seem to do that very well by yourself," he replied. "Besides, we were alone in your carriage earlier today," he reminded her a little tersely.

"That was different. It would have been wrong *not* to offer you the use of my vehicle."

"How very selective a way of approaching such an important item of etiquette."

"Are you surprised? You behaved very badly indeed when we last parted." She drew Jinny's shawl closer about her shoulders. "I trust you mean to be a gentleman this time, Sir Dominic?"

"Since there are no witnesses, there would be little to gain from pressing unwelcome attentions upon you now, so you are quite safe."

"I notice you express no regret for having conducted yourself so monstrously."

"I apologize."

"Would that you meant it."

He smiled a little. "From which acid tone I can tell you have now fully recovered from your unfortunate drenching."

"A drenching that could easily have been avoided if you had not leaped out at me like that," she retorted.

"Leaped out at you? Oh, come now, the fault was yours for

being there in the first place, for I certainly have not given you carte blanche to enter my property as and when it pleases you. By the way, what *were* you doing there?" he added.

"I . . . I was looking for the cat," she said, relieved to have thought of a reasonable explanation. "I thought I'd found her, but it seems it was yours."

"It's Mrs. Matthews's cat, not mine," he replied, swirling the glass of cognac he'd now successfully retrieved from the dining room.

"Yes, well I suppose cats aren't really the usual choice for gentlemen."

He searched her face in the moving glow of soft light from the candle and the fire. "You intrigue me, Miss Peach."

"The feeling is not mutual, I assure you." *Oh, liar!* He intrigues you so much you want to know *everything* about him!

"I'm neglecting my duties as host. Please be seated." He gestured toward a chair that was close to the hearth, and she sat down rather unwillingly, for by accepting the invitation, she felt she was allowing him a point of some sort. Another faint smile played upon his lips. "It is mere politeness, Miss Peach, nothing more."

She forbore to reply.

"Bodkin is rather a strange name for a cat, don't you think?" he said then.

"I . . . I suppose it is."

"How even more strange that I've just recalled hearing you call the same beast at the review, just before the buffet was obliterated."

"Before you accuse me again, *I* didn't obliterate it!" she said defensively.

"No, it was a street urchin, was it not? To return to the mysterious Bodkin. Am I to presume you took a *cat* to Claverton Down?"

Her cheeks were uncomfortably warm again. "You are mistaken to think I called for Bodkin on that occasion, Sir Dominic."

"I think not, Miss Peach, for I definitely remember the name."

"You misheard," she insisted then looked stonily at the fire in an effort to bring the subject to a close.

He raised an eyebrow. "So it's to be petulant noncooperation now, is it?"

Polly's lavender eyes were angrily bright as they swung toward him. "Sir Dominic, I would much prefer to be allowed to go home than to stay here and be treated like this by you!"

"Oh, I'm sure you would, but I have yet to receive a proper explanation for your intrusion upon my property!" he replied with equal rancor.

"I've already told you, it was—"

"I know, it was Bodkin the cat," he interrupted in a long-suffering tone. "Miss Peach, I do not believe in the existence of any such feline!"

"That is your prerogative, sir."

"I would dearly like to shake you," he murmured conversationally.

"Lay one hand upon me, and I will scream the house down!"

"Yes, I rather think you would."

"It would be no more than you deserve after your conduct earlier."

He gave a wry laugh. "I rather enjoyed that, actually."

Polly's cheeks flamed to crimson. "Was that supposed to be a compliment?"

He became more serious. "Yes, I suppose it was," he said quietly.

She drew back. "Don't even think of repeating the exercise, for I've already warned you I will scream."

"And I have already promised to conduct myself with all suitable restraint," he reminded her. Then he smiled again. "Can we resume the truce we enjoyed in your carriage? It would make life very much easier, I fancy."

"By all means, although in my opinion it will not last any longer than its predecessor."

"Why? Because we are incapable of conducting ourselves graciously? Come now, Miss Peach, we're both civilized people, so I'm sure we can manage to be agreeable toward each other."

Polly shivered suddenly as a slight draft chilled her shoulders, which were damp from her wet hair. She was about to pull the shawl closer once more, when something pulled it up for her, flicking her hair deftly aside in the process. Polly froze with surprise. *Bodkin?* No, he was still in a towering huff with her, so who could it be? *Nutmeg?* Almost immediately she felt guilty for even thinking the latter thought, for she had accepted her uncle's explanation regarding Bodkin's beloved. No, the explanation was obvious. The house's resident brownie was attending to her needs.

"Is something wrong, Miss Peach?" Dominic inquired.

"No, I . . . I was just a little cold," she replied, still glancing around. She knew the signs to look for, the faint chink of invisible keys, imprints on the carpet, the occasional patter of bare feet on floorboards, and the faint fragrance of cloves. All but the chink of the keys were present now. She wondered if the brownie knew of Bodkin.

"Please allow me to draw your chair closer to the fire," Dominic said, stepping toward her.

"That won't be necessary," she said quickly, "for I'm sure the heat will do Lord Benjamin's fine French walnut no good." She'd looked away for a second, and when she looked back, there were no imprints on the carpet, and the scent of cloves had gone. She saw the door swinging slowly to.

He looked at her. "I'll warrant that at Horditall House you are accustomed to sitting on the rug before the fire," he observed suddenly.

She met his eyes in surprise. "Yes, I am. How did you guess?"

"Put it down to my great intellect. Please feel at liberty, if you wish."

She hesitated, longing to do it, but afraid that if she did, what was left of propriety would fly out of the very window.

He knew what she was thinking. "There isn't anyone to know, and as we are already guilty of heinous offense, you may as well compound the felony."

"I prefer to remain as I am," she said.

"As you wish, but *I* intend to make myself comfortable." To her surprise, he sat on the floor and leaned back against the chair opposite her, his one leg bent, the other stretched out.

She was suddenly suspicious, for even if she stayed where she was, anyone who entered the room now would find a very cozy scene. "Is my name in fresh peril from your trickery, Sir Dominic? Have you perhaps sent a footman for the Marquis de Torkalotte?"

"How swiftly you've perceived my plot, Miss Peach," he replied, meeting her eyes with cool steadiness.

Chapter 18

Polly's heart lurched with horror. "You monster!" she breathed, starting to get up.

Suddenly he began to laugh. "Be easy, Miss Peach, for no one is about to arrive."

"But you said—"

"Yes, I did, and it was no more than you deserved for suggesting I'd stoop to such an act."

She hesitated. "I already know the sort of act to which you will stoop, sir. Besides, the Marquis de Torkalotte might just as well be here to record this, for he will have seen to it that this afternoon's escapade is all over Bath by now."

"No, he won't."

"How can you be sure?"

"Because I have called upon Torkalotte, threatening to expose a certain dark secret of his if he says so much as a word."

She stared at him. "But, why? I thought you *wanted* the story to get out, so that Lady Georgiana would be made jealous."

He rested his right wrist on his raised knee and swirled his almost empty glass. "Do you really think I would do that?"

"As far as I was concerned, you *did* do it," she replied.

"I knew Torkalotte was the only witness, and that he could easily be silenced."

"Windows have eyes, too, sir, and there are thirty-three houses in this crescent."

"I would be very surprised if anyone was watching us, for to be sure most of the crescent was at the review, and those who remained would have been more intent upon the strange business of the runaway horses. Rest easy, Miss Peach, for your good name is safe."

"Then why did you do it in the first place?"

He met her eyes. "I don't really know," he confessed.

"You have an easy charm, sir. Too easy by far, in fact."

"Meaning that you think me a practiced seducer?"

She colored. "I . . . I wouldn't know about that . . ."

"It's what you think, nevertheless."

"Are you such a person?" She made herself look at him again.

"I've had my triumphs, Miss Peach, but I'm certainly not a womanizer." He smiled into her eyes. "May I know your first name?" he asked suddenly.

She stiffened. "Why do you want to know that?"

"Certainly not for an improper reason. It was merely a polite question."

She hesitated, then relaxed again. "My name is Polly."

"Margaret, surely?"

"No, I was named just Polly."

"Polly Peach? It reminds me of—"

"Mr. Gay's *Beggar's Opera*?" she interrupted.

"Yes."

"It's no accident. *The Beggar's Opera* was my parents' favorite, and it amused them to name me after the heroine, Polly Peachum."

"What better reason to choose a name," he murmured, giving her a smile.

Her heart tightened treacherously, for when he was like this, she found him irresistible. She made herself speak of something that would break the spell. "Do you think you will ever win Lady Georgiana from the Marquess of Hightower?" she asked.

His glass became still. "That is a rather personal question, Miss Peach."

"Such inquiries are not your sole prerogative, sir. Besides, perhaps you intrigue me after all," she replied, being as disarming as she could because she really wanted to know.

He smiled. "Now whose charm is too easy by far?" he murmured. "Very well, I will indulge you. I do not know if I can win her back, but I rather fear not."

"Then you will have had a lucky escape," Polly said bluntly.

"I've asked you before not to speak ill of Lady Georgiana—" he began, but Polly broke in quickly.

"We have a truce, Sir Dominic, and believe me, I speak ill of her with good cause."

"Perhaps I should point out that you are hardly acquainted with her, and cannot therefore be any real judge of her character."

"I do not need to know her to understand her. My guess is that her sole interest in Lord Algernon is the fact that he will one day become Duke of Grandcastle. Unless you have expectations of suddenly becoming elevated to a similar rank, you will never win her. Not that she's worth winning anyway; indeed I think she would make you a very bad wife."

"Do you indeed?"

"Yes." As their eyes met, an additional observation ran silently through her head. *I'd make a far better wife for you, the finest of wives, in fact . . .* The moment the startling thought entered her head, she became filled with confusion, and rose agitatedly to her feet. "I . . . I think I should return to my uncle, Sir Dominic."

Startled, Dominic got up as well. "Why, is something wrong?"

"No, of course not." Somehow she managed a smile. "I will return Jinny's clothes in the morning, with a purse for both her and Mrs. Matthews for their kindness to me."

Dominic raised an eyebrow. "And what of *my* kindness?" he inquired with aggravating humor. "Doesn't that warrant a suitable reward, too? After all, I did rescue you from the terrors of the water butt."

"Yes, you did, after causing me to fall into it in the first place," she said tartly.

"I will apologize and set aside all claim to a reward if you tell me why you really came here tonight."

"I've already explained I was looking for the cat."

"Hmm, if that is still to be your story, I fear I must withhold my apology."

"You are free to withhold as you wish, Sir Dominic."

"I'm grateful for your understanding, Miss Peach," he murmured, reaching for the bellpull, and then instructing the footman who came to bring two hooded cloaks.

As the footman hurried away, Polly looked at Dominic. "Do you mean to walk me to the door again?"

"Certainly."

"I wish you would not."

"Then you wish in vain. Miss Peach, I will escort you from door to door even if you are kicking and screaming in protest, so you might as well accept graciously."

A minute later, enveloped in cloaks to keep off the rain, they stepped out into the wet darkness, but almost immediately Polly halted in dismay, for a mud-spattered traveling carriage was drawn up outside the door of 1 Royal Crescent. Two footmen were carrying luggage into the house, and another was pressing coins into the hand of the link boy who'd conducted the vehicle through the town. Lord Benjamin had returned early from London!

"Oh, no!" Polly breathed in horror, for her absence was bound to have been noted by now. What possible story could she give that would satisfy her uncle?

Dominic saw the carriage as well. "Beddem has come home earlier than expected?"

"Yes, he wasn't supposed to be back until the day after tomorrow."

"Halloween? How appropriate."

"What am I going to say? How on earth am I going to explain not only being out like this, but wearing someone else's gown? A maid's, at that!" She drew back into the doorway as cloaked footmen emerged from number one with lanterns, clearly about to start to search for her. Polly felt apprehensive. "My uncle would have slept on if Lord Benjamin hadn't returned. Now he must be very anxious about me. I . . . I can't let them search. Please let me go through your house so I can slip in through the kitchens."

"That won't do." Dominic suddenly caught her and began to usher her along the pavement. "Leave the talking to me," he instructed.

"But—"

"Trust me, Polly."

"Trust *you*? I would as soon—"

"Trust Old Nick? Yes, I know, but this happens to be one scrape with which I think I can be of assistance."

They'd almost reached number one now, and the first footman, who happened to be Giles, caught a glimpse of Polly's face in the light from his lantern. "Miss Peach?" he cried relievedly, for he hadn't relished the prospect of combing the streets of Bath on a night like this. However, his glad smile faltered a little when he saw she was alone with a gentleman. "Is all well, miss?" he asked quickly.

"Yes, yes, of course," she replied, feeling quite out of control of the situation. What on earth did Dominic have in mind? Indeed, what could he say to alleviate the situation for her?

As Giles turned to tell his fellow footmen the search was no longer necessary, Dominic again ushered Polly toward 1 Royal Crescent. They were just ascending the small flight of steps at the door, when it swung open for another footman to emerge to join the search. His lantern illuminated their faces, and as he gasped and stood aside for them, Polly saw her uncle and Lord Benjamin standing in the hall in earnest conversation. They saw her at the same moment and turned openmouthed as Dominic almost propelled her into the house. What no one saw was Ragwort seated at the top of the staircase, listening and watching.

Giles hastened to relieve Polly and Dominic of their cloaks, but although Dominic surrendered his, Polly wasn't similarly willing. If she could hide Jinny's pink dimity, she would, for this situation was bad enough already without her uncle and Lord Benjamin discovering she had changed her clothes as well!

Lord Benjamin's face was a study of suspicion as he unfastened his own traveling cloak, then tossed it on the table next to his top hat and gloves. He was corseted in such a way that his rear end protruded and his chest was puffed out like that of an angry cockerel. Beneath the cloak he wore a biscuit-colored coat, dark brown waistcoat, and cream breeches, with a green silk neckcloth of such intricate yet voluminous proportions that he had to raise his chin in order to look over it. The second son of the Duke of Lawless was as pudgy, soft, and pink as ever, and his thinning brown curls were in such neat rows that they must have taken his coiffeur a positive age to achieve. His brown eyes were swift and calculating as he gauged Dominic, clearly wondering if he was another challenger for the hand of the Peach's Bank heiress.

Hordwell shuffled awkwardly forward on his walking sticks. "Polly, m'dear? Are you all right? I've been quite frantic since it was realized you weren't in the house," he asked in genuine concern.

"Yes, Uncle, I'm quite all right." She hurried to hug him, praying that Dominic had suffered a stroke of absolute genius to extricate her from *this* fix.

Hordwell looked a little guardedly at Dominic. "What is the meaning of this, sir?"

Lord Benjamin spoke before Dominic could reply. "I'm sure there is a reasonable explanation. Is that not so, Fortune?"

"Of course there is a reasonable explanation, Beddem. Do you imagine I would willingly allow anything to jeopardize Miss Peach's reputation?" As he said this, he steadfastly avoided looking in Polly's direction, for the specter of the pavement kiss loomed rather large. Then he swayed a little and passed a hand over his forehead. "Forgive me, I . . . I still feel a little shaken. The footpads . . ."

Polly's lips parted in astonishment. *Footpads?* Hordwell and Lord Benjamin were taken aback, then the latter cleared his throat. "Well, if you're in some distress, Fortune, perhaps it would be better if we adjourned to the drawing room. Er, no, to the library, it's a little less formal." Clearing his throat again, he moved toward the door in question, and everyone followed.

Chapter 19

As they all went into the library, Ragwort hastened downstairs to slip inside as well. He cast around for somewhere suitable to sit, and his glance fell upon a cozy spot between the sofa and the hearth. As he hurried over to it, a tantalizing smell wafted to his nostrils. It came from the glass of cognac on the table by Hord-well's favorite chair. When Ragwort had told Bodkin that he and alcohol did not agree, what he'd really meant was that after as lit-tle as two small glasses of wine, he became carefree to the point of recklessness. After one glass of cognac he was liable to do any-thing! Therein lay the reason why Caraway had left him. The brownie hesitated longingly, but then conquered his desire and went to sit in the place he'd selected.

He was dismayed at what appeared to be further evidence of Polly's involvement with Bodkin's enemies. Hordwell and Lord Benjamin were the instigators of Nutmeg's disappearance, and Dominic seemed to be in present possession of Nutmeg's belt. As for Polly herself . . . The brownie glowered darkly as she sat on the sofa, almost close enough for him to touch. Pretty and golden-haired she may be, he decided darkly, but she was also a snake in the grass. He had observed her chasing poor Bodkin from the house earlier on, and had put the wrong interpretation upon it. He knew she hadn't caught his new friend, because Bodkin had re-turned briefly to reassure him about his escape, before hurrying away through the rain to cosset himself at Zuder's. Now, under very questionable circumstances, Polly had come back with Dom-inic, whom he, Ragwort, was beginning to strongly suspect of being her lover, because the undercurrents between them were so strong as to be almost tangible. Miss Polly Peach was no friend of Bodkin's, no friend at all!

Hordwell eased himself painfully into his chair, picked up the glass of cognac, then fixed Dominic with a look that showed he would be hard to convince with a story of footpads. Polly fidgeted nervously as she tried in vain to conceal the clothes she wore be-neath her cloak. She looked anywhere and everywhere, except at Dominic.

Lord Benjamin took up a commanding position with his back to the fire. "Now then, what's all this about footpads? And how can it possibly involve Miss Peach?" he inquired, glancing curiously at the quality of Polly's pink dress.

Dominic had remained standing by the sofa. "With all due re-spect, Beddem, I don't think it's rightly any of your business. What I have to say is for Mr. Horditall and his niece alone." He passed a hand over his forehead, as if still a little overcome.

Lord Benjamin flushed. "If it concerns my guests, sir, it concerns me," he said pompously, but was nevertheless rendered a little uneasy by Dominic's act. "Oh, do sit down, man!"

"Thank you." Dominic took his place next to Polly, much to Lord Benjamin's ill-concealed resentment. Dominic ignored him, and addressed Hordwell. "Sir, allow me to introduce myself. Sir Dominic Fortune of Bellevue Castle in the county of Hertfordshire. You may have heard of it?"

Hordwell certainly had, as indeed had Polly, for Bellevue Castle was one of the most splendid medieval fortresses in the south of England. Refurbished and improved until it was now the last word in fashionable luxury, it boasted gardens that were said to contain more roses than any other estate in the realm. Such an address could only find favor in Hordwell's eyes. "Oh, yes, indeed, sir. You are very fortunate to be master of such a magnificent estate."

"I am, sir." Dominic paused. "Mr. Horditall, are you willing for me to speak of my dealings with Miss Peach in front of a third party?" he asked, knowing such an inquiry would annoy Lord Benjamin intensely.

Hordwell was in a cleft stick. He didn't want to offend his host and prospective nephew-in-law, but neither did he wish to risk exposing anything scandalous or embarrassing where Polly's last hour or so was concerned. He flushed, then decided to put his trust in fate. "By all means speak in front of Lord Benjamin," he said, crossing his fingers in the concealment of his chair.

"As you wish." Speaking only to Polly's uncle, Dominic embarked upon his explanation. "If it were not for Miss Peach, I would now be lying . . . possibly dead . . . in the gutter of Royal Crescent."

"Mercy on us," whispered Hordwell.

Dominic went on. "I fear that as I walked home earlier this evening, I was set upon by footpads not long after I had passed this house. Miss Peach happened to be looking out of a window, and in the heat of the moment came hurrying out into the rain to drive them off."

Hordwell gasped. "Oh, Polly, you rash child!"

A perverse bubble of laughter rose in the rash child's throat, and she had to bow her head to hide the fact.

Dominic proceeded. "Hearing her raising the alarm, the villains took fright and ran away, and Miss Peach was able to keep me sufficiently conscious to help me to my own house. In the process, we both stumbled considerably, and I fear Miss Peach's gown was not only wet through but also torn. So noble a heart has she, that nothing would do except she saw me safely inside, then she ordered a footman to bring a doctor. She remained there until she was sure I was well again. All I was able to do for my fair rescuer in return was to instruct one of my maids to provide a dry gown, and then escort her safely home when I had sufficiently recovered." With this, Dominic took one of Polly's hands, and drew it solemnly to his lips, his gray eyes admiring and grateful.

Ragwort glowered from the floor by the sofa. He'd wager the last pot of honey in Bath they were lovers.

Lord Benjamin was dumbfounded by Dominic's tale, and Hordwell looked fit to faint clear away. Polly felt she would explode with suppressed mirth, for—unlike the truth—the picture he painted didn't have a rainwater butt in sight! Lord Benjamin recovered first, his astonishment beginning to turn to suspicion that all was not as it should be. "Well, Fortune, I must say that for someone who has been attacked by footpads, you are remarkably free of bruises."

"Miss Peach's timely appearance spared me," Dominic replied, as if butter would not melt in his mouth.

Lord Benjamin's eyes narrowed. "Why was no word sent here? Miss Peach's uncle has been most anxious since her absence was discovered."

Dominic turned to Hordwell. "I realize we were remiss in not advising you of the situation, sir, but in the heat of the moment, I fear it slipped both our minds. May I say, sir, that you have a most splendid lady for a niece. I doubt if a more admirable heart exists in the whole of England." He looked at Polly as he said this, and when he saw she could barely contain herself, he earnestly pressed a handkerchief upon her. "Don't cry, Miss Peach, for all is well now, thanks to you."

Polly took the handkerchief and dabbed her eyes in order to hide her face. If Dominic said much more, she knew she would positively curl up! To her relief, he rose to his feet. "I trust this is explanation enough for you, Mr. Horditall?" he inquired, still looking all innocence, and then swaying again for good measure.

Hordwell nodded. "Yes, yes, of course, sir."

"Sir, I gather you and Miss Peach are attending the ball tomorrow night?"

"Eh? Well, yes . . ."

Polly glanced toward the fire, where a small blue flame danced above its golden fellows. She now wanted to attend the ball after all . . .

Dominic spoke again. "Mr. Horditall, it would please me greatly if you would kindly regard tonight as a formal introduction, for I would very much like to pay my respects at the ball."

Hordwell glanced at Lord Benjamin, whose face resembled a thundercloud. "Er, yes, of course, Sir Dominic."

Dominic turned to Polly a last time. "I still cannot thank you enough for all you did tonight, Miss Peach, and if there is ever anything I can do for you, please do not hesitate to ask."

Somehow she managed to meet his eyes without bursting. "I will bear that in mind, Sir Dominic."

He raised her hand to his lips, then whispered so that only she could hear. "Until we meet again, Polly." For a moment his fingers tightened over hers, then he turned to bow to the two men. A moment later he had left the house.

Polly sat where she was, feeling Lord Benjamin's gaze upon her. She sensed he was about to probe more into what had happened, and before he could start, she suddenly got up. "I . . . I feel very tired now, Uncle, so with your leave I will retire."

Hordwell was startled. "Eh? But, Polly, you haven't had time to greet Lord Benjamin properly!"

She gave the latter a briskly apologetic smile. "Please forgive me, Lord Benjamin, but under the circumstances, I'm sure you'll understand." Without waiting to find out whether he understood or not, she gathered her skirts and hurried relieved from the room.

Ragwort watched her leave. He didn't believe a word of the footpad story. She and Dominic had commenced an affair—it was as simple as that. Oh, just *wait* until he told Bodkin how far her treachery had gone! Just wait! The brownie decided not to follow her, but remained where he was, hoping to hear the two men mention Nutmeg when they were alone. He was disappointed, for their conversation centered solely upon whether or not Dominic had just told them the whole truth, a question of intense concern to them both.

Before going upstairs, Polly slipped into the dining room to watch Dominic return to his house. She saw him walk along the wet pavement, being sure to pause occasionally as if weak, in case either Hordwell or Lord Benjamin should be spying. Polly smiled, watching until he disappeared through his front door, then she turned away from the window. A stark and irrefutable fact now was clear; she had stepped beyond the point of no return into love. But how did he feel about her? Did she dare to hope that after tonight he regarded her in a new, more favorable light, and that Georgiana was no longer quite so precious in his eyes? A wave of excitement washed over her, but it was tinged with more than a soupçon of apprehension.

Gathering her skirts, she made her way upstairs to her room.

Chapter 20

Polly was too restless to go immediately to sleep, which was hardly surprising after all that had happened. She undressed, washed, and put on her frilled nightgown, but as she sat before the mirror to brush her hair, listening to the rain dashing against the window, her thoughts returned to the ball. She was apprehensive about that too. Was her gown really suitable for such a grand occasion? What if her accessories were too fussy, too plain, or even too old-fashioned? Oh, there was nothing for it but to try everything on now!

Twisting her hair up on top of her head, and fixing it with a single pin, she stepped out of her nightgown and went to the wardrobe to take out her ball gown. It was made of spangled lavender silk exactly the same shade as her eyes, and she always wore it with her mother's amethyst necklace and earrings. There was a spray of artificial lily-of-the-valley for her hair and a silver-spangled reticule and ivory fan for her wrist. The final touch was a delicate silver lace shawl. But when she had put everything on, she was unhappy with her reflection. It didn't feel right. But why didn't it? She had always been pleased with everything before, and it was all still in pristine condition, even the little flowers in her hair, although she suddenly didn't particularly like either them or the way her hair was piled on top of her head. She wanted something new, something different . . .

The flowers were swiftly unpinned and tossed on to the dressing table. Then she studied herself again. Were the amethysts too old-fashioned? No, she was sure not; they were very fine indeed. Was it the gown's sleeves? They were perhaps a little plain, for it was all the rage to wear bows on them. She would purchase some suitable satin ribbon tomorrow and make some bows, but that still wouldn't quite achieve what she wanted. There was something else. She continued to look at her reflection, twisting this way and then that, and suddenly she had one of those flashes of inspiration that every woman knows now and then. The necklace would make an excellent circlet! Yes, that was it! Deftly, she took the necklace from her throat and arranged it around her forehead. A delighted smile lit her face. It looked splendid, and once she'd made the bows for the sleeves, she would feel more than ready to face the Duke and Duchess of York. And she would hold her own with the likes of Lady Georgiana Mersenrie!

A yawn overtook her, and she knew it was time to sleep. She changed back into her nightgown, extinguished the candles, and was just about to climb into bed when she heard a solitary carriage drive into the crescent from Brock Street. The coachman flicked his whip and called out to his team, but Polly didn't give the vehicle a second thought. She certainly would have if she'd known who was in it, and where it was going.

A little earlier, when Dominic returned to his house, he had also been too restless to sleep. Polly was on his mind, both for herself, and her insistence that there was a cat called Bodkin. Was it wrong to disbelieve her? What if there really was such a creature, and it was locked in a cupboard? This was possible, he decided, so he took a candlestick and went from room to room, calling softly. "Bodkin? Are you here? Answer me, you dratted feline!"

He had almost completed his inspection of the third floor when he heard a shuffling sound. He froze, glancing around as the candle shadows leaped over the walls of the empty bedroom he happened to be in. "Bodkin?" he said again.

There was silence, then the sound of running footsteps retreating along the passage to the landing. It certainly wasn't a cat! The hairs on the back of Dominic's neck prickled, and he followed cautiously. "Who's there?" he called, so intent upon the mystery that as he stood at the top of the staircase, wondering if his quarry had gone down, up, or into one of the other rooms on the same floor, he didn't hear the carriage draw up outside. As a consequence, when someone knocked loudly at the front door, he gave such a start that he almost dropped the candlestick.

A footman hastened from the kitchens, still buttoning his braided coat as he opened the door. He had to step quickly aside as Georgiana swept in, her midnight blue cloak parting to reveal an exceedingly décolleté damson satin gown beneath. She flung her hood back from shining dark curls to which she had again fixed a false white braid. "I must see Sir Dominic immediately," she declared, beginning to tease off her long white evening gloves.

The footman wasn't sure what to do, then decided it was best to bow to her wishes. "Er, who shall I say, madam?" he inquired, helping with her cloak.

"Lady Georgiana Mersenrie, you numbskull," she replied in a short, irritated tone.

Dominic went down the staircase. "What an unexpected honor," he said, nodding at the footman, who withdrew thankfully.

Georgiana's eyes filled with tears, and before Dominic knew it, she'd flung her arms around his neck and buried her face against his shoulder. "Oh, Dominic, I'm so utterly wretched!" she cried, clinging to him.

He put his hands on her little waist. "What is it? What's happened?" he asked.

She raised her head and stretched up to put her lips briefly to his, then she drew away, her eyes lowered unhappily. "I . . . I feel so confused, Dominic. Seeing you again like this has put me in such a dilemma . . ."

He searched her face in the candlelight. "Have you and dear Algie fallen out?" he inquired shrewdly.

She flushed. "Is *that* why you think I've come?"

"Yes," he replied frankly, then took her hand and led her into the library. He closed the door, placed the candlestick on the mantelpiece, and faced her. "Have you and Hightower quarreled?" he asked.

She couldn't meet his eyes. "We did have a small disagreement," she admitted.

"Not so small, if you've come running to me."

"He was very mean."

"In what way?"

She bit her lip a little sheepishly. "To be truthful, it was all something and nothing; indeed. It was mostly my fault."

"So, he wasn't the mean one," Dominic observed dryly.

"Not really. I picked on him a little."

"You do surprise me."

She flushed again. "Don't be horrid."

"Georgiana, I'm merely pointing out that you and he aren't in the least compatible. You want his title, but unfortunately the man comes with it!"

"I know; indeed I know it so well that all I could think of was you." She subjected him to the full force of her wonderful dark eyes. "And now that I'm with you, I think choosing Algie was the most foolish thing I've ever done."

Dominic's feelings were mixed. She was saying the very thing he wished to hear, and yet . . . She was exquisitely beautiful, and just to look at her made his body ache, but could he believe anything she said? Could he even *like* her? For weeks she'd been making it painfully plain she'd settle for nothing less than a duke, and even today at the Pump Room she had taken spiteful pleasure in taunting him, yet now she was so wide-eyed and earnest that she all but displayed wings and a halo! Polly had called her shallow and designing, as well as the most monstrously insincere female in society, and . . . He paused as he realized he'd thought of the Peach's Bank heiress by her first name. Devil take it, if he remembered correctly, he'd even *addressed* her thus!

Georgiana was perplexed by his silence. "Don't you love me anymore?" she whispered, her voice like a warm velvet caress.

He saw tears shimmering on her lashes, and the moment of truth slid back into the mists of desire. "Oh, my dearest Georgiana . . ." His hands stretched toward her, and she gave another little sob as she came into his arms.

"Make love to me again, for I need you so," she begged, pressing her wonderful body to his.

He felt control slipping away. "My darling," he whispered, and his lips found hers in a kiss that smoldered with passion.

Someone—or something—sneezed behind them, and Dominic broke away to turn sharply, thinking a footman had entered for some reason, but no one was there—at least, no one *visible*. "Who's there?" he demanded, feeling certain that eyes were upon him from somewhere by the door.

Having heard nothing, Georgiana looked at him in confusion. "Why are you asking that? We're quite alone, Dominic."

He remained intent upon the door. "Bodkin?" he called suddenly.

Georgiana blinked. *"Bodkin?"* she repeated. "Dominic, are you feeling quite well?"

"Perfectly," he replied. To Hades with Polly Peach and her wretched cat!

Georgiana took his face in her hands and stood on tiptoe to put her parted lips to his.

He forgot the sneeze, forgot Bodkin, forgot Polly . . .

Much earlier in the evening, when Bodkin had shinned up the drainpipe to Zuder's skylight, he'd immediately seen Polly's note. But the rain had done its worst, and as he took the square of paper to read, it fell apart in his fingers. Tossing the soggy fragments aside without another thought, the brownie tried to open the skylight, but instead of opening easily as it had before, it refused to budge. He gritted his teeth to tug and push, then in a fury jumped up and down so violently that he almost tumbled back down the slippery slates. Pulling himself together, he applied himself sensibly to the problem. He didn't intend to allow a mere roof window to keep him away from the sweet things he craved.

As luck would have it, his knife was tucked into his belt, so he used it to attack the skylight, hacking and slicing, carving and stabbing, until at last the unfortunate window gave up the struggle. The triumphant brownie gave a whoop of delight, dropped into the attic, then scampered down through the building to fall ravenously upon the goodies below. For the next hour he indulged in an orgy of gobbling. Sugary footprints, crumbs, cream, jelly, and custard soon littered everything, and there wasn't a single dish in the shop that hadn't been decimated in one way or another, whether by being sampled, or trodden on as the greedy brownie scrambled over the glass shelves behind the once pristine counter. It was a disgraceful exhibition by a brownie who had once been one of the most mild, tidy, agreeable of creatures, but a boggart is a boggart, and that is that.

Having gorged to the point of bursting, he staggered back up to the roof, and with some difficulty hauled himself out through the skylight onto the slates. It was still raining heavily, and this time he did lose his balance. With a yell he rolled down to the gutter, which he grabbed to save himself, but it came away from the roof, swinging him out above the alley below. He wrapped his arms and legs tightly around it, and gazed down in dread, waiting for the inevitable. It came soon enough. With a mournful groan, the gutter detached itself completely and plunged down, brownie and all. It pierced the muddy ground like Lord Algernon's sword at the review, and juddered to and fro so fiercely that Bodkin felt quite dizzy, but at last it became quite still, and he was able to slide down to terra firma.

Thanking the powers that be for his lucky escape, he began to run back to the Royal Crescent mews. Once in the haven of his hayloft, the excitement of having decimated Zuder's a second time began to fade. The drumming of the rain on the roof made him feel quite low, and his thoughts turned to Nutmeg. Where was she? Was she well? Did she miss him? Oh, how he'd punish the wicked humans for what they'd done! He glanced at the pumpkin, and his eyes flashed with bitter fire. Halloween was only a day or so away, so it was time to make a start. Taking his knife again, he set about creating the largest, most horrible jack-o'-lantern that ever was.

Much later, in the small hours, when even Bodkin had finally gone to sleep, Polly awoke with a start as something disturbed her. Puzzled, she got out of bed and went to the window. The rain had stopped, and all was quiet, but just as she was about to turn away, she heard a carriage driving out of the crescent into Brock Street. She saw a link boy running past, followed by an elegant scarlet vehicle drawn by a team of two cream horses. The coachman shouted encouragement to the team, then flicked his whip. It was the same shout she'd heard earlier, she thought, looking more closely as the carriage swept by. A flawless profile was visible inside. *Georgiana!*

Polly's heart twisted, for where else could Lord Benjamin's sister have been in the intervening hours, except with Dominic? Her eyes stinging with tears, Polly hurried back to bed, where she cried into her pillow as if her heart would break.

Chapter 21

The day of the ball dawned bright and sunny; indeed it could not have been better than the previous evening had it tried, but Polly awoke feeling wretched, with red eyes and a wan face. All she could think of was how foolish she'd been to think fondly of

Sir Dominic Fortune. As to wondering if he felt the same way about her . . . How could she have been so naive? Lady Georgiana Mersenrie was the one he wanted, and probably the one he deserved.

She did what she could to make her eyes look less swollen and tearstained, but not even her Chinese box of cosmetic papers could really disguise the truth. All she could do was pretend to have gotten dust in both eyes, and then brazen it out. Once again the ball was out of the question, so new bows and so on were no longer of any consequence. All in all, Nutmeg notwithstanding, she felt so out of sorts that she thought of returning to Horditall, indeed of *skulking* back there.

But as this cowardly thought registered, she drew herself up sharply. "Where's your pride, Polly Peach?" she demanded of her reflection in the mirror. "You've got to snap your fingers at them, show you don't care what they get up to." She'd have to go to the ball after all, just to look down her nose at Dominic and his precious *chienne*. Yes, that was what she had to do. *Then* she could skulk back to Horditall to nurse her misery in private.

She got up to select the second of the two morning gowns she'd brought with her from Horditall. It was a peppermint-and-white striped muslin, with which she always twisted her hair into a knot that was intertwined with matching striped ribbons. At least, she didn't usually do the twisting, for that was her maid's task, but this morning she had to labor upon it herself. Some time passed before she felt she'd achieved something remotely acceptable, then she inspected her reflection again. "Well, that's the best you'll look today, my girl," she murmured resignedly, then went down to endure breakfast with her uncle and Lord Benjamin.

They were already seated at the table, each with a newspaper and a gargantuan plate of food. Their chairs scraped hastily as she entered, and as she smiled and murmured a greeting, she was disagreeably conscious of how Lord Benjamin's eyes moved over every inch of her. He had the ability to make her feel virtually naked! Giles drew out a chair for her, brought her the breakfast she requested, and then withdrew from the room.

Hordwell immediately commented upon her pallor. "What's this? Have you been crying, m'dear?" he inquired solicitously.

She gave a light laugh. "Dear me, no, although thank you for being concerned. The truth is that I spilled my cosmetic powder, and it went into my eyes."

"Ah." He proceeded with his breakfast.

Lord Benjamin studied her, for she had rather unwisely sat directly opposite him. "May I say how very charming you look this morning, Miss Peach?"

"Thank you, Lord Benjamin," she murmured, avoiding his gaze.

"Your uncle informs me you'll be attending the ball tonight. I trust you'll keep a measure for me?"

She managed to give a weak smile. "Yes, of course."

Hordwell looked up from his newspaper. "Hm, it seems the review turned into a shambles yesterday. Why didn't you mention any of this, Polly?"

"It slipped my mind, what with the business of your valuables."

His brow darkened. "Some fiend has them, and I'll get them back if it's the last thing I do!" he growled, and began to regale Lord Benjamin with the sorry tale.

As she hoped, the apparent theft took up most of the subsequent conversation, and she stayed out of it by steadily eating her breakfast and keeping her eyes lowered. The ball would be her grand gesture, when she would have an opportunity to snub Dominic. She would then leave for Horditall first thing tomorrow morning. After all, what point was there in staying? Bodkin was determined to be quite impossible, and Nutmeg seemed to have vanished into thin air, so Polly Peach might just as well return to the wonderful isolation of Horditall.

She was so lost in thought that she didn't notice her uncle suddenly wink at Lord Benjamin, although she did look up when his chair scraped as he rose to his feet. "You must both forgive me," he said, "but it's time for me to adjourn to the Pump Room for the water." Taking up his walking sticks, he hobbled out, and Polly's heart sank as she realized he'd deliberately left her alone with her loathed host and suitor.

As the door closed, Lord Benjamin gave her a warm smile. "Well, my dear, how very agreeable it is that you are here beneath my roof."

"I shall be returning to Horditall in the morning," she replied, determined to snuff any encouragement he might perceive in the situation.

"Indeed? I was under the impression from your uncle that you would stay on a little longer."

"Then I fear he gave you the wrong notion, sir."

"May I inquire why you came here?"

"Oh, it was just female foolishness. I dreamed my uncle was unwell, and so had to rush here to be certain he was all right. He persuaded me to stay a few days. That's all." She looked quickly at him. "I did not wish to presume upon your hospitality, but my uncle insisted. I would have preferred to stay at an inn or hotel."

"That would not have done at all, my dear; indeed, you are most welcome to lengthen your sojourn if you wish," he said softly.

She colored. "I must decline, sir, for I have many things to do at home," she replied.

He got up suddenly and came around the table to stand behind her. "You will soon be here for always, Miss Peach—Polly—for you will be my wife." He placed his soft pink hands upon her shoulders.

She leaped up from her seat as if scalded. "Don't presume, my lord!" she cried, moving away.

"It is no presumption, madam, for the match has been agreed upon."

"Not by me!"

"Nevertheless, it is settled. Your uncle wishes the contract to be signed, and—"

"Then let him marry you, for I vow you and he would make a handsome pair!" she answered acidly.

He flushed. "You *will* marry me, Polly, for I am set upon it."

"I gave you no leave to address me so familiarly, sirrah. As for marriage, all you want is my fortune, and I would as soon give it to Old Nick as hand it to you!"

His eyes cooled. "I'm prepared to overlook this little unpleasantness and give you another chance. Maybe after the ball, when you see how agreeable it is to be linked with me and viewed as the future Lady Beddem, you'll see sense." With that he turned on his heel and walked from the room.

Polly rested her hands on the back of a chair and closed her eyes. Oh, this was unendurable, but she'd brought it on herself by staying in this odious house! She'd known from the outset that it was a mistake, but for Bodkin and Nutmeg's sakes, she'd allowed her uncle to inveigle her into staying. Now look what had happened. She drew a long breath, trying to think what to do next. Her uncle and Lord Benjamin were going to an exhibition of watercolors this afternoon, which would give her an opportunity to leave for Horditall before they knew anything about it. She would present her uncle with a fait accompli. Yes, that was for the best. She had to forget putting a metaphorical tongue out at Dominic, and quit Bath without further ado.

Suddenly she became aware of a fragrance that had nothing to do with breakfast. *Cloves!* She glanced quickly around. "Bodkin? Is that you?"

It was Ragwort. He'd witnessed her scene with Lord Benjamin, and had now moved quite close to her, wondering if things weren't quite as he'd concluded after all. Polly sensed where he was and reached out so suddenly that he was obliged to step hastily aside. His tail swished uneasily, for she was only the second human he'd come across who was so sensitive to brownies, Giles being the first.

Polly spoke urgently. "Please listen to me, Bodkin, for I've only come here to Bath to help you. I'm your friend, truly I am! My uncle promises me there was no agreement with Lord Benjamin about Nutmeg. They merely wished to offer her a chance to come to Bath to stay while her house at Horditall was refurbished. But they didn't have a chance to ask her about it, because she walked out. I'm afraid that's what happened—she really did leave of her own accord. I'm very sorry. Oh, Bodkin, at least make yourself visible to me again, for I do hate talking to thin air."

Ragwort realized she believed everything she said, but he knew things couldn't have happened that way, not if the belt buckle found in Dominic's house did indeed belong to Nutmeg, which he was convinced it did. He wanted to tell Polly that he'd relay her words to Bodkin, but he couldn't bring himself to speak to her. Giles was the only human he'd ever conversed with, and then only infrequently. Such contact was something of a taboo for him, and so he held his tongue.

Polly gave up crossly. "Oh, I wash my hands of you, Bodkin. Be a horrid boggart if you must, but you're in the wrong. I'm going back to Horditall this afternoon, so you can get on with it by yourself!" Catching up her skirts, she swept from the room in a rustle of peppermint-and-white stripes. She wouldn't stay in the house; instead she'd soothe her anger, injured pride, and offended feelings by doing a little shopping in the fashionable shops of Milsom Street. And tonight she'd sleep in her own bed, listening to the owls in the beech trees at Horditall!

*   *   *

Bodkin had slept on a little longer than he intended and stirred as a couple of grooms entered the stable to clean some harnesses. The brownie opened his eyes slowly, then gave a start, for about a foot away was a large, leering, orange-yellow face, with jagged teeth and staring eyes. Bodkin scrambled away, his tail bolt upright with shock, but almost immediately he felt utterly foolish, for it was his jack-o'-lantern. He breathed out with relief, then rubbed his hands gleefully, for if it had frightened *him*, just think what it would do to humans on Halloween!

Feeling infinitely better than he had on going to sleep, he made himself comfortable and applied himself to a breakfast of honey from his jar. Afterward he rubbed some clove balm into his fur, brushed it until it shone, then climbed down the ladder to investigate the bees in the mulberry tree. After that he intended to search Dominic's house again if he could, because he too was now convinced that the buckle belonged to Nutmeg.

He inhaled deeply of the morning air. How fresh everything smelled after the rain, and how bright and autumnal the leaves were in the sunlight. Oh, how he loved the fall, especially when the sky was so very very blue. He'd met Nutmeg on a day like this. His smile faded and a tear rolled down his cheek. Apart from the belt buckle, he was no nearer finding his adored one than he had been on first arriving! Maybe he'd never find her.

He pushed open the door into Dominic's garden and went inside, where he found Mrs. Matthews's large marmalade cat strolling down the path toward him. Cats could see brownies, and she arched her back, spat like water in hot fat, and fled back toward the house. Bodkin took no notice as he inspected the tree. The familiar drone of the bees was pleasing to his ears as he scaled the trunk, but as he examined the swarm, his jaw dropped in astonishment, for they were the Horditall bees! "My friends, my dear, dear friends . . ." he murmured, sinking his hand deep into their seething depths. The bees began to hum, buzzing all over him until he was covered, even to the tip of his tail. He chuckled as he leaned back against the tree trunk. "Oh, how good it is to see you again," he declared, and as the bees tingled deliciously in his fur, he began to ponder how excellent a weapon they would be for Halloween. Oh, yes, with them *and* his ferocious jack-o'-lantern he would be the very king of mischief!

Polly had long since set off for the shops of Milsom Street when Bodkin at last tore himself away from his busy little friends. After promising to return soon, he jumped down from the tree and hurried toward the house. The French windows of the dining room were open, and inside he saw Dominic lingering over a leisurely breakfast. The brownie slipped in and took great pleasure in knocking a dish of damson preserve onto Dominic's spotless white riding breeches. Dominic jumped up with a curse that would have done credit to the entire army of fishwives at Billingsgate, and Bodkin grinned evilly to himself as he set off to search yet again for Nutmeg.

But although he went over every inch of the house with a fine toothcomb, he found nothing. Glumly he left again, going out through the front door just as Dominic—clad in fresh breeches— left to ride with Harry Dashington in Sydney Gardens, it being as much the thing for gentlemen to show off their superb mounts at the Bath Vauxhall, as it was in Hyde Park itself. As Dominic rode off on his mettlesome bay, Bodkin strolled dejectedly across to the common, wondering where to search next. Oh, it seemed an impossible task, for he didn't know where to begin, and even if he got close, Nutmeg wouldn't be able to communicate with him because someone had her belt. His tail began to swish as he glanced darkly back at the crescent. Hordwell and Lord Benjamin knew where she was, and so did Dominic and Polly. They would pay, oh, how they would pay! The swish became an angry twirl as he went down the sloping grass to see what was what, which in boggart terms meant what trouble he could cause.

It wasn't long before the peaceful common was peaceful no more. Two dogs that hated the sight of each other had their leads tied together, some children were robbed of their ball, two young mothers had their hats snatched off, and a temperamental artist, who was painting a delightful view of Bath, suddenly found that a thick black line had appeared across his little masterpiece. With a cry of anguish, the unfortunate painter shot to his feet, in the process knocking over his easel, paints, brushes, and other paraphernalia.

Bodkin the Boggart couldn't have cared less as he strolled smugly back to the crescent, tail still atwirl. His need to be naughty pacified for the time being, he was now in the mood for some hot sweet coffee, a sticky bun, and a chat with his new crony, Ragwort. It was during this chat that at long last he learned Polly wasn't disloyal to him after all, even if the discovery of Nutmeg's belt buckle suggested she was wrong to trust her uncle. Bodkin was delighted to know he'd wronged her, and his spirits soared, although he was a little ashamed of his recent misbehavior. He eagerly awaited her return from shopping so he could make himself visible to her again.

Chapter 22

Polly's route to Milsom Street took her past Zuder's, where the atmosphere of concern and outrage told her Bodkin had paid another overnight visit. He must have seen her note, she thought, yet he hadn't sought her. It had clearly made no difference at all. He was now quite beyond redemption, she decided, and walked on by, determined to never again bother with a brownie.

Milsom Street sloped downhill from George Street toward the abbey and Pump Room, and was lined with shops that were temples of fashion. The pavements were crowded, carriages rattled on the cobbles, and sedan chairs bobbed hither and thither. Street traders called their wares, albeit discreetly, for to bellow the qualities of hot meat pies or the season's first roast chestnuts would have been most unseemly in such gracious surroundings.

Polly browsed along the shop windows, her mood gradually lightening, but it wasn't until she came to Miss Pennyfeather's haberdashery, its doorway draped with stylish English and French tulles, that she espied something she simply had to purchase. The display of fripperies was astounding, but in the midst of it all she espied a small lace day bonnet that was made of exactly the same lace as the collar of one of her gowns. She knew her regret would be eternal if she did not snap it up.

The shop bell tinkled agreeably, and the pleasant smell of leather, cloth, and perfume enveloped her. Miss Pennyfeather's establishment bulged at the seams with shawls, handkerchiefs, lappets, ribbons, artificial flowers, buttons, buckles, gloves, and parasols; indeed there was said to be a greater choice here than in Piccadilly. A number of other customers were already queuing, because Miss Pennyfeather's two assistants were ill, and there was only the owner herself to serve. So Polly took up a position at the end of the oak counter and waited patiently for her turn. Her attention was upon the heavily laden shelves and neat little drawers lining the wall behind the counter, so she did not at first recognize anyone else in the shop. It wasn't until a loud, affected female voice complained about the unendurable wait that Polly glanced along in dismay to see Georgiana and her marquess standing only six feet from her.

Lord Algernon was in his uniform, and Georgiana was superb in a turquoise silk pelisse and matching gown. She wore a wide-brimmed, dark blue hat, around the crown of which a gauze scarf trailed almost to the floor, and the inevitable white curl fell elegantly to her shoulder. A dark blue folded parasol was clasped in her gloved hands, and she resembled one of those serene illustrations from *La Belle Assemblée*, except there was nothing at all serene about her mood. Dominic's disagreeable love was clearly more disagreeable than ever this morning, for her lips were turned down pettishly, and she fidgeted with an impatience that was completely out of proportion to the situation. Clearly her overnight hours of stolen passion had not improved her temper, Polly thought, wondering what the unfortunate marquess would have said if he knew of her infidelity. It didn't occur to Polly that Georgiana might not have been unfaithful; indeed such a possibility was out of the question, for the nighttime visit to Royal Crescent indicated only too glaringly what she'd been up to. Polly drew back toward the door, deciding that not even the lace bonnet was worth the risk of coming face-to-face with Lord Benjamin's termagant of a sister.

But Georgiana turned and recognized her immediately. "Well, if it isn't Little Miss Parasol," she declared acidly.

Everyone else turned as Polly reluctantly responded. "Good morning, Lady Georgiana."

"It is a relief you have no javelin to hurl at me this time."

"I did not hurl anything at you, Lady Georgiana. Besides, you would appear to be the one with such a weapon today."

Miss Pennyfeather became a little flustered, realizing a scene was imminent. She was a plump little woman, with her gray hair in a bun, and spectacles perched on the end of her snub nose. She smoothed her starched apron, then tried to carry on dealing with the lady she had been serving. "Now then, that was two yards of the pink ribbon, wasn't it?" she said, trying to keep her hand steady as she picked up the scissors.

"No, three yards of the blue," the lady replied, her attention more on what was happening behind her than upon her intended purchase.

Georgiana tilted her head a little haughtily, her disparaging glance taking in Polly's peppermint-and-white gown and green velvet spencer. "I did not know that green stripes were in this year," she murmured, every word clearly audible because of the hush that had descended over the shop.

"And I did not think anyone with such a sallow complexion would wear that particular shade of turquoise," Polly retorted, never one to back down when provoked.

There were gasps, and Miss Pennyfeather's hand trembled violently. "Oh, dear," she muttered, cutting three yards of the pink and realizing her error. She reached for the blue, and promptly cut two yards of it. "Oh, dear," she exclaimed again, and paused to take a huge breath to steady her nerves as she saw Polly and Georgiana drawing themselves up for more, like angry cats.

Georgiana's dark eyes flashed with loathing. "You are very presumptuous, Miss Peach," she observed coldly, her knowledge of Polly's surname revealing that she'd gone to the trouble to find out.

"I'm merely following your example, Lady Georgiana," Polly responded. More gasps greeted this, but when she glanced at the marquess, to her astonishment, he gave her a slight smile, although he took care that Georgiana didn't see.

Georgiana flushed. "You clearly have no idea how to go on, Miss Peach," she said scathingly.

"If you are anything by which to judge, Lady Georgiana, I'm relieved not to know," Polly retorted, standing her ground like a bantam cock. The marquess smiled again, and she felt quite awkward.

By now Georgiana had realized Polly wasn't quite the easy victim she'd thought, so she brought the confrontation to a close. "Come, Algie, we'll go where the company is more gracious," she declared airily, then caught him in the act of a third sly smile. She struck his arm sharply with her parasol. "Algie!" she breathed, then marched from the shop. He grabbed his gloves and helmet from the counter, then hurried after her. The bell jangled, and then there was silence.

"Oh, dear," sighed Miss Pennyfeather, thinking of the customer she had just lost.

All eyes were upon Polly, who did not quite know what to do. Her instinct was to scuttle out and have done with it, but then her spirit rebelled against such a craven act. She still wanted that day bonnet, and she was going to purchase it! Holding her chin up, she resumed her place at the end of the counter, and as she gazed steadfastly at the shelves once more, the other customers gradually returned to their own business, although there was a great deal of whispering.

Ten minutes later, Polly emerged in triumph. The lace bonnet was wrapped in brown paper in her reticule, and she'd found some very pretty buttons that would go very well on another gown she had at Horditall House. But anger with Georgiana still simmered beneath the surface, and Polly knew that the best way to deal with it would be to go for a long walk. Seeing a notice advertising the Halloween attractions at Sydney Gardens, she decided to see what the Bath Vauxhall was like, for although she'd been to the town before, she had never actually been to the gardens.

To get there, she had to cross the Avon by beautiful Pulteney Bridge, which was lined on either side with little shops. From there she traversed Laura Place to proceed down residential Great Pulteney Street, the long prospect of which was closed by the handsome facade of the Sydney Hotel. Behind the hotel stood the autumn trees of the Vauxhall, which was laid out on rising land at the extreme eastern boundary of the town. The hexagonal gardens were enclosed by high walls, beyond which there was open countryside.

Admittance was through the hotel itself, the entrance to which was beneath a lofty portico supported by four fine Corinthian columns. The hotel was much frequented by Bath society, and the coffee room was consequently very full. The refined surroundings and undoubted dignity of the establishment made her think how excellent it would be if for any reason she was unable to leave Bath today. No sooner had the thought occurred, then she wisely decided to see if a room was available. She was in luck, for a gentleman had canceled his booking barely five minutes before. Apart from this one room, the hotel was completely full because of the expected presence of royalty at the Halloween celebrations, so without further ado she booked and paid for the room—just in case.

Chapter 23

From the double doors at the rear of the hotel, Polly emerged beneath an orchestra balcony into a wide semicircular area, framed by private alcoves where meals could be enjoyed. A broad walk, crowded with people, ascended up an undulating slope toward a classical temple. The walk was flanked by bowling greens, shrubberies, flower beds, groves, and waterfalls, and apart from the temple there was a sham castle and a labyrinth. Directly adjacent to the perimeter walls were broad rides, where many ladies and gentlemen exercised their fine mounts. Preparations were in hand for the Halloween bonfire and fireworks display, and from the size of the bonfire it was clear it would be a very elaborate affair indeed.

She strolled up the walk, enjoying the surroundings. Autumn leaves rustled underfoot, a blackbird sang its heart out in a silver birch tree, and the contretemps in the haberdashery now seemed a trivial affair that had ended most satisfactorily in Georgiana's defeat. She even managed to banish Dominic to the far extremity of thought.

On reaching the top of the walk, she came upon the new cut of the Kennet and Avon canal, which sliced through the gardens by way of a conveniently steep dip in the land. The cut had only been built that summer, and there was a paved path along the water's edge, then a retaining wall to hold back the sharp incline of the land. Two gleaming wrought iron bridges spanned the water, and little canopied pleasure boats could be hired, in which it was possible not only to row into the heart of the town, but also right out into the countryside toward the village of Bathampton.

Polly leaned over one of the bridge parapets for a while, watching the ripples and reflections on the water, then she turned to go, because she wanted to give herself enough time to prepare for her surreptitious departure for Horditall. But as she descended the walk close to the temple and heard voices and giggles coming from the labyrinth behind it, a chance glance across at the nearest ride revealed the unwelcome sight of Dominic and Harry Dashington coming her way.

She froze, wondering if they'd seen her, or if the direction they took was mere coincidence. To her relief, they reined near the edge of the ride to take leave of each other, then Harry rode down toward the gateway provided for riders. Dominic remained where he was, but although his attention was upon his departing friend, Polly knew that at any moment he might turn toward her. Knowing she wasn't ready to speak to him, she glanced around. The temple and labyrinth offered shelter. Which should she choose? She decided on the labyrinth, and ran toward it without further ado.

After going some way in, she paused by a wrought iron seat, sat down, and toyed restlessly with her reticule, wishing she'd never heard of brownies or set eyes upon Sir Dominic Fortune. She would wait about ten minutes, then slip out. He would surely have gone by that time.

"I have the strangest feeling you're trying to avoid me, Polly," a voice said suddenly. Dominic was standing a few feet away, his riding crop tapping the back of his gleaming top boots.

Her heart tightened, and she could only stare mutely at him.

He came a little closer, his expression quizzical. "I'm right, aren't I? You *are* hoping to avoid me?"

She found her tongue. "What makes you think that, sir?"

He could not mistake the deliberate formality. "I would appear to be in your bad books for some reason. May I know why?"

"You aren't in my bad books, sir; indeed you aren't in any book at all."

"I see." He glanced at the empty space beside her. "May I?"

"By all means," she replied, but as he sat, she rose to leave.

His fingers immediately shot out to restrain her. "Tell me what I've done, Polly," he repeated.

"Unhand me," she said coldly, trying to pull free.

His grip was firm. "Tell me," he insisted.

Reluctantly, she sat again. "You haven't done anything of which I am aware."

"I know an untruth when I hear it," he said. "I'm clearly in the kennel for something or other, because when we parted last night, I seem to recall you were most amiable toward me."

His words presented her with an excuse, and she seized it. "That's the point, sir, I fear I may have been a little forward, and today I'm rectifying the lapse."

"Indeed? Well, that could easily have been done without the extreme of running away to hide! All you had to do was accord me a civil nod as you continued to walk by."

"I . . . I didn't think."

"No, because you're still not telling me the truth." He put a gloved hand to her chin, forcing her to look at him. "What's happened, Polly? Why were we friends yesterday, but not today?" As her lips pressed mutinously together, he tweaked her chin. "Don't I deserve your honesty?"

She pulled away from him, deciding to tell him a little of the truth. "Very well, it concerns Lady Georgiana," she said. That was the true bit.

"Georgiana? In what way?"

Now for the diversion from the real truth. "I had a very disagreeable encounter with her this morning in Milsom Street, and since she is clearly your *raison d'être*, I thought it best to give you a wide berth from now on. I wouldn't wish to give her any further excuse for proving what a *chienne* she is." It was a secondary reason, not the main one at all.

"Georgiana doesn't choose my friends, Polly. *I* do."

"Mayhap you should tell *her* that."

He smiled and leaned an arm on the back of the seat, so that his hand rested directly behind her. "Polly, I assure you that Lady Georgiana Mersenrie and I are a thing of the past."

It was such a monstrous lie that Polly laughed aloud. "You don't really expect me to believe that, do you?"

"Well, I suppose it doesn't really matter whether you do or not; indeed it is none of your concern at all, but nevertheless I wish you to understand that I am no longer intent upon winning Georgiana."

She couldn't help a disbelieving laugh. "Well, untruths slip easily from your tongue, I'll grant you that."

"Meaning what, exactly?" he inquired, a cooler light entering his eyes.

"Meaning that I don't believe you—indeed I know you to be lying!"

His expression was now quite chill. "I'm not in the habit of lying, Miss Peach," he said in a rather clipped tone.

"Nor am I, sir. Oh, have done with pretense, Sir Dominic. I heard her carriage arrive at your door last night, and in the middle of the night I saw her leaving. She may cling to the Marquess of Hightower's arm in public, but *you* are the one she visits in private!"

He tapped his riding crop rather irritably against his boots. "So that's it—the Peach's Bank heiress is jealous!"

Outraged color suffused Polly's cheeks, and she leaped to her feet. "How *dare* you!" she cried, then looked quickly away as some people went by on their way out of the labyrinth. The argument by the bench could not be mistaken, and they hurried on past, some of them stifling embarrassed giggles.

Dominic waited until they'd gone, then got up as well. "I dare because it's so! You're jealous. Why else would you be behaving like this?"

"Perhaps because you are endeavoring to gull me, sirrah!"

"Gull you? And why, pray, would I do that?"

She didn't answer; indeed she didn't know what to say, for there seemed no reason for him to attempt to draw the wool over her eyes. She just knew he was.

A lady and gentleman passed by, and again Dominic waited until they'd gone before replying. "You really are an aggravating creature, aren't you? One day you're excellent and witty company, the next you have solid bone between the ears!"

"Don't speak to me like this!" she cried.

"I'll speak to you however I choose!" he answered angrily.

She struck him. It was an action so bitter and instinctive that she hardly knew she'd done it until he caught her wrist to prevent her from repeating the process.

He looked furiously into her eyes. "That's twice you've presumed to strike me, Miss Peach. Pray do not let there be a third time, or I may forget I'm a gentleman," he breathed.

"A gentleman is something you are not, sirrah!" she replied, close to tears.

"Since you've given this dog such a bad name, you may as well see what happens when he lives up to it," he said, suddenly taking her by the waist and pulling her toward him.

There was nothing she could do to prevent him from subjecting her to the most intimate kisses and caresses she'd ever known. His lips moved over hers with relentless passion, and his hands roamed her body as if they were both in a feather bed, not the maze at Sydney Garden Vauxhall! Her anger dissolved into new confusion, and her skin felt warm and tingling as the blood quickened through her veins. To her dismay she began to submit to him. There was nothing she could do—or wished to do—to prevent her body from sinking against his, or to stop her lips becoming soft and pliable.

For a long moment he pressed her to him, but then released her. His face was flushed and his eyes dark. "Now what madam? Do you still deny jealousy? Do you think my kisses are false? Or could they be true? Mm? I will leave you to ponder the puzzle, the answer to which I may or may not choose to unveil to you tonight at the ball." Turning on his heel, he left her.

Polly was so shaken that she had to sit down. A maelstrom of emotion still whirled within, and she was trembling from head to toe. Her lips seemed bruised yet wonderfully warm, her breasts felt as if his fingers still cradled them, and her whole being felt enriched. She was truly alive for the first time ever.

It was some time before she was able to leave the labyrinth. She saw no sign of Dominic, for which she did not know whether to be thankful or not. She was hardly aware of the long walk back to Royal Crescent; indeed she was in something of a daze. People, streets, traffic, all passed in a blur. Common sense told her that she must make herself remember how long Georgiana had been with him during the night, and leave Bath today as planned; but wild abandon told her to stay, to go to the ball, to pray Dominic would give her the answer she craved . . .

Victory went to wild abandon. After all, she now had a room at the hotel and didn't have to stay beneath Lord Benjamin's roof another night. She could attend the ball with her uncle and him, then return to the hotel afterward. *Please let Dominic's kisses have been true. Please . . .*

Dominic had already ridden back to the crescent. He was seated at his writing desk, quill poised above a fresh sheet of paper. Polly's fragrance still seemed to cling to him, and myriad emotions crossed his face as he thought what to put in a letter he knew he must write. He couldn't believe he'd behaved as he had in the labyrinth, nor could he believe how aroused he'd become. He dipped the quill in the ink, and began to write.

October 30th, 1800. Royal Crescent. My dearest Georgiana . . .

Chapter 24

Bodkin made himself visible to Polly the moment she entered 1 Royal Crescent, and the footman—not Giles—had retreated below stairs again. Ragwort was with Bodkin, but he did not appear to her because he was too shy, as well as too set in his ways.

Polly was so astonished to see Bodkin that she dropped her reticule. He ran to pick it up and hand it back to her a little sheepishly. "I've been a very silly brownie, Miss Polly," he confessed. "You *were* my friend all along. I know that now."

"Silly? I prefer to describe you as boneheaded and downright wicked," she declared, thinking of his antics, especially at the review.

Both his head and his tail hung low. "But I really did think you'd betrayed me, Miss Polly," he explained, shuffling his feet.

"You should have known me better than that."

"Yes, Miss Polly."

She softened a little. "I suppose this change of heart means you found my note?"

"Well, I found it, but I couldn't read it because the rain had ruined the paper."

"Then, why didn't you ask me what—?"

He interrupted, gesturing toward the empty air beside him. "My friend Ragwort told me. He's the brownie of this house."

She was startled to realize there was someone else present. "Er, how do you do, Ragwort," she said.

"How do you do, Miss Polly," replied Ragwort's disembodied voice.

Bodkin explained. "It was Ragwort in the dining room this morning, not me, and he told me what you said. I'm sorry I turned against you, Miss Polly, but when I saw you leaving here with your uncle yesterday, I really did think you supported what he'd done."

"I would never do that. Anyway, he didn't do anything to Nutmeg, Bodkin, nor did Lord Benjamin."

"That's where we think you're wrong," Bodkin replied, but at that moment a footman emerged from the kitchen stairs with a tray, upon which was a newly replenished decanter of cognac for Hordwell in the library. Bodkin promptly disappeared, and Polly pretended to be searching for something in her reticule.

As the footman went into the library, she whispered to the brownies. "We can't talk here—let's go to my room. We'll be more private there." Without waiting for them to reply, she hurried up the staircase.

A minute later, they were all three seated on her bed, although Ragwort's presence was shown only as a dent in the coverlet. Polly told them what her uncle had told her, and then she looked at them. "Now then, that's my uncle's version of events. Why do you think I'm wrong to believe him?"

The brownies produced the belt buckle, but didn't immediately say where they'd found it. "I wasn't sure if it was Nutmeg's at first, but I'm certain now," Bodkin finished.

Polly examined it by touch, for she couldn't see it. "So it *could* belong to someone else?" she ventured hopefully, for that would mean her uncle hadn't lied to her.

"If it isn't hers, whose is it? All the brownies on the crescent will vouch that they don't recognize it."

All the brownies on the crescent. Were the situation not so serious, Polly would have smiled. The moment of reflective humor faded. "Bodkin, even if it *is* Nutmeg's buckle, where is she now? On your own admission you haven't found any other trace of her." She paused. "You haven't said where you found it."

Bodkin glanced unhappily at Ragwort, for neither of them wished to divulge something they were sure would upset her.

"Well?" Polly prompted.

Bodkin cleared his throat. "We, er, we found it in Sir Dominic's bedroom, and there isn't supposed to be a brownie in that house. The last one was Ragwort's sweetheart, Caraway."

"She wasn't my sweetheart!" cried Ragwort indignantly.

"Oh, yes, she *was*, and I'd hazard you wish she *still* was," Bodkin retorted.

Polly hardly heard them arguing. A pang of dismay had struck her on learning where the buckle had been found. "Does that mean you think that Dominic, I . . . I mean Sir Dominic, has control of Nutmeg?"

Ragwort answered. "Forgive me, Miss Polly, for I know you and he are lovers, but—"

"Sir Dominic Fortune and I are *not* lovers!" she interrupted hotly.

He flinched at her vehemence. "All right, please forget I said it, but last night, I really did think . . . Put it this way. I was by the library sofa last night, and I watched you both very closely. You certainly seemed like lovers."

"Well, we aren't, nor will we ever be." She colored nevertheless.

There had been a sweethearts' tiff, Ragwort thought. "As you say, Miss Polly," he murmured, catching Bodkin's eye and pulling a disbelieving face.

Bodkin looked at Polly. "Anyway, the fact that we found the buckle in Sir Dominic's bedroom may or may not implicate him. It could have lain there since Lord Benjamin occupied the room, but it has to be said that we know Nutmeg isn't in *this* house, and if her buckle was in Sir Dominic's bedroom . . ." He spread his hands sadly.

"I really don't think Sir Dominic would be involved in something like this," Polly said, aware of leaping to his defense.

Bodkin tactfully changed the subject. "Ragwort told me what Lord Benjamin did and said at breakfast."

She bit her lip and gazed steadfastly at the foot of the bed. "I wish Lord Benjamin would accept that I will never marry him. I don't care if my uncle is my guardian or not. I simply refuse to become Lady Beddem!"

"Lord Benjamin will never back down while the duns press him at every turn. He needs your fortune, Miss Polly. You really shouldn't be staying in his house, you know," Bodkin added.

"I was foolish enough to let my uncle prevail, but then Lord Benjamin came back earlier than expected. Anyway, I intend to go to the ball tonight, and that's the only reason I haven't already left for Horditall. I saw no point in remaining in Bath while you were being so obstinate, but I'll stay on if you wish, to help you look for Nutmeg."

"You can't stay beneath Lord Benjamin's roof!" the brownies cried together.

Polly smiled. "No. I've taken a room at the Sydney Hotel for tonight, and will go there after the ball. I may be able to secure it for longer." Oh, how glad she was that she'd taken that room. She didn't want to leave Bath until her dealings with Dominic had been resolved, nor—now that she and Bodkin were friends again—did she want to go until the search for Nutmeg was either successful or called off.

Bodkin looked intently at her. "If you wish to avoid Lord Benjamin's wandering hands, Miss Polly, I think it's best if you return to Horditall without delay. Don't even go to the ball tonight, just leave now. I have Ragwort to help me find Nutmeg."

"I must go to the ball, and anyway, I'd feel dreadful at Horditall, knowing you were searching for Nutmeg."

"No ball is worth it, Miss Polly. Ragwort and I could help you pack your things, and as soon as Hordwell and Lord Benjamin have gone to the art exhibition, you could be on your way. It would be done with before either of them has a chance to protest."

"I know, and that was indeed my original intention, but I really must go to the Assembly Rooms."

"Why is the ball so important?" Bodkin was curious, guessing there was more to it.

"I have a very good reason, but I don't intend to tell you what it is, for to admit it would make me feel a little foolish."

"Why?"

"Because I fear I may be pinning my hopes upon the impossible."

Ragwort's thoughtful gaze hadn't wandered from her face, and now he got straight to the point. "It's Sir Dominic, isn't it?" he guessed shrewdly.

She went a little pink. "No, of course not," she fibbed.

He caught Bodkin's eye again and pulled another disbelieving face.

Polly smoothed her skirts self-consciously, but then a thought struck her. "Look, I've just recalled something odd that happened last night in Sir Dominic's drawing room. I don't know why I didn't think of it before, especially as there isn't supposed to be a brownie there." She related the incident with her shawl, then added. "And I saw imprints in the carpet, and smelled clove balm, to say nothing of seeing the door closing behind someone."

Bodkin's eyes brightened joyously. "It *was* her, I know it was!"

Polly was anxious to prevent any leaping to conclusion. "I still don't think Sir Dominic has anything to do with it." She remembered how mystified Dominic had been by her story of a cat called Bodkin. Surely if he knew about brownies and had one in his house, he would have hazarded a guess what sort of being she might really be seeking. Instead, he'd been very convincingly puzzled. She had to defend him again. "I really don't think Sir Dominic has any idea that such things as brownies really exist."

Ragwort and Bodkin exchanged glances, not able to quite believe that the master of a great house like Bellevue Castle, which would warrant the attention of many brownies, would not know of such things.

Polly detected their disbelief. "Look, I know you have doubts, and maybe they're justified, but I know what I think." She looked intently at Bodkin. "Anyway, if it *was* her, why didn't she reply when I spoke?"

Ragwort replied, "If someone has her belt, she can't utter a word."

"All right, but if you've searched that house from top to bottom, why haven't you been able to detect her? Why hasn't she knocked something over, rattled something, shaken a curtain? Anything to let you know she was there."

"Because she has to keep well out of our way. That's how it is when a brownie is held captive. Our hope was that we'd hear something and be able to catch hold of her—that way we'd know for certain," Ragwort answered. "If we could only find her belt, all would be well."

"And the belt is as invisible as she is," Polly murmured, closing her fingers over the little buckle.

"Yes."

Polly handed the buckle back to Bodkin, then got up suddenly. "I'm going to tackle Uncle Hordwell again," she declared, and before they could say anything, she went downstairs to the library.

Chapter 25

When Polly had gone, Ragwort leaned back against the bed's finely carved footboard. "She won't learn anything new, except that he's guilty," he mused.

Bodkin nodded, then grabbed his tail as it began to twirl. Oh, how he loathed Hordwell Horditall and Lord Benjamin Beddem! And how suspicious he still was about Sir Dominic Fortune!

Ragwort observed him and nodded approvingly. "That's right,

my friend, you keep yourself under control, for you're a pest when you're a boggart. Now look, I've been thinking about this ball tonight. Shall we go as well?"

"To a grand ball?" Bodkin's eyes brightened, and his tail stopped twirling.

"Every brownie in Bath will be there. It will be great fun."

Bodkin's excitement died. "It wouldn't be right for me to have fun when poor Nutmeg may be—"

"We can use the occasion to enlist help," Ragwort interrupted. "If the whole brownie population of Bath is on the lookout, there's more chance of finding something out. Well, isn't there?"

Bodkin hesitated. "Yes, I suppose there is."

"It's settled then. We're going."

Downstairs in the library meanwhile, Hordwell was again browsing through the morning newspaper. He looked up with a smile as Polly entered. "Ah, there you are, my dear. I trust you did not overspend in Milsom Street?"

"If I did, it would have been from my own purse," she replied.

He caught the intonation, correctly gauged her mood as confrontational, and leaped to the wrong conclusion. "I trust you do not mean to argue again about the match with Lord Benjamin?" Wards were supposed to obey their guardian's commands, yet he was defied at every turn!

"There is nothing to argue about, for I will *never* be his wife."

Hordwell's lips pressed together, but he said no more.

Polly faced him. "Uncle, about Nutmeg . . ."

"Oh, not that again!" He folded the newspaper crossly and slammed it down upon the table by his chair, almost knocking over the decanter of cognac.

"Yes, that again. Do you swear upon everything you hold dear that you and Lord Benjamin had nothing to do with her disappearance?"

"Yes."

"Please look at me when you say that, Uncle."

He obliged, meeting her gaze full square. "Yes, I swear it. Now that's enough, Polly, is that clear?"

"Oh, yes, very clear," she replied. His reaction told her beyond all shadow of doubt that he was lying. Disappointment swung unhappily through her, for although she knew him to be a rascally old miser, she really had hoped he was innocent of this.

Hordwell snatched up the newspaper and made a great fuss

about reopening it. "I trust all is well with your ball gown for tonight?" he said then, banishing the subject of brownies in no uncertain manner.

"Yes," she replied shortly, then turned to leave the room.

"See that you look well for Lord Benjamin," he called after her.

She slammed the door and hurried back upstairs, but was immediately forced to stop because Lord Benjamin barred her way.

"Why the hurry, Polly?" he murmured, his eyes lingering on the curve of her breasts.

"Miss Peach, sir," she corrected coldly.

"What a stickler you are for the rules, and yet you deign to accept my hospitality. To my mind that is the act of a coquette."

She gasped. "It certainly is not, sirrah! How dare you say such a thing!"

"You play ice with me, but your actions speak very differently. If that is not the sign of a coquette, I know not what," he murmured, coming down the steps toward her.

She shrank back a few steps, then held her ground again. "And what of your actions, sir? You keep forcing your attentions upon me when you know they are not welcome!"

"I know no such thing."

"You cannot possibly imagine I would wish to marry a man who stoops so low as to hold a brownie captive," she said then, watching his face closely.

He paused, his eyes suddenly wary. "Brownie? I don't know what you're talking about."

"Oh, yes, you do." she breathed, loathing him more by the second. "Where is she? Where's Nutmeg?"

His left hand, the scar on the little finger catching the light, moved rather oddly toward his coat pocket, but then he drew it away again. "I fear you must be unwell, my dear. Everyone knows that brownies are figments of the imagination," he said softly, descending another few steps and reaching out toward her.

"What of the page by Nostradamus?"

He halted. "How do you know—?" He broke off, and his gaze became coldly veiled.

There was no longer any room for doubt. He was indeed the Englishman who was purchasing the page in question. She was about to say as much when little footsteps suddenly pattered down the stairs behind him. He turned and saw no one, but he certainly felt the fierce shove of four small hands. With a cry of alarm he teetered on the brink of falling downstairs, but managed to stretch a pudgy hand to the banister. His eyes swung accusingly to Polly. "You pushed me!" he cried.

She drew back. "Don't be foolish, Lord Benjamin. I was in front of you, remember?"

"Someone pushed me."

She met his gaze. "Someone invisible, it seems," she said softly. "Nutmeg isn't the only brownie in creation, Lord Benjamin. They are everywhere, even in this house."

As his haunted gaze scanned uneasily around, she seized her opportunity to hasten on up the stairs. The two unseen brownies were close at her heels, and once in the safety of her bedroom again, with the door firmly bolted, they all three resumed their positions on the bed. Bodkin reappeared to her, but Ragwort remained invisible.

Bodkin spoke first. "I hope you've now seen sense about going to the ball?"

"No." She had to go, because of Dominic.

"Miss Polly—"

She interrupted with a change of subject. "Thank you both for saving me from Lord Benjamin."

"We enjoyed it," Ragwort replied frankly. "I'd have made sure he went to the bottom, but Bodkin held me back."

"Yes," declared Bodkin firmly, "because if he'd fallen that far, Miss Polly would have been accused. One of us has to think, Ragwort."

"And usually it's me," retorted Ragwort indignantly.

Polly held up her hands. "Please don't quarrel, for we have important things to discuss."

They subsided, and Ragwort looked at her. "Your uncle's guilty, isn't he, Miss Polly?"

She sighed sadly. "I fear so. Oh, he still denies everything, but I can tell he's fibbing. He and Lord Benjamin made a captive of Nutmeg, and I think she's in Sir Dominic's house."

Bodkin's tail began to twirl again, and he kept it under control by sitting on it. Again Ragwort showed approval of his restraint. "A wise move, my friend, for you don't want to be a boggart again just yet. Halloween is nigh, remember?"

Polly remembered the pumpkin. "What are you going to do that night?" she asked Bodkin, and when he declined to reply, she became uneasy. "I shudder to think how far you may go for revenge,

Bodkin, but please promise you won't harm my uncle. I know he's done some wicked things, and that he can be a most stingy, bad-tempered, disagreeable old man, but he's still my uncle, and in spite of his sins I do love him."

"I promise not to lay a finger on him." Bodkin was all innocence as he replied, but visions of the monstrous jack-o'-lantern hovered in his mind's eye. With such a weapon, he wouldn't need to *touch* his victims, just terrorize them!

Chapter 26

As the hour of the ball drew near, a thick mist rose from the Avon. The air was very cold, smoke hung low over Bath, and the light from carriage lamps and link boys' torches was muted as society arrived at the Assembly Rooms. But there was nothing muted about the military band that played with gusto outside the main entrance, ready to launch into the national anthem as soon as the Duke and Duchess of York's cavalcade was in the offing. Not that the royal party's approach would be unhindered, for the press of people and vehicles that had gathered in this one small corner of Bath had to be seen to be believed. In Polly's opinion, a snail's pace would be more swift!

She sat in Lord Benjamin's carriage, keeping as far into the corner of the seat as she could, because his lordship had plumped himself right next to her, his thigh almost touching hers. Her uncle seemed blissfully unaware of the situation; indeed if she was not mistaken he was doing his utmost to ignore it! She fiddled with her fan and reticule and tried to think of something more agreeable than Lord Benjamin Beddem. Did she look her best? She could just see her reflection in the window glass. The amethyst necklace certainly looked fine around her forehead, and for once she'd achieved a very creditable coiffure. Her lavender silk gown was as it always had been, and she was glad now that she hadn't over-adorned it with bows on the sleeves. In spite of her cloak, she was beginning to feel cold. The short journey to the rooms should only have taken a minute or so; instead they'd been caught up in this horrid jam for over half an hour. Lord Benjamin's leg pressed briefly against her thigh, and she shuddered, although not with the cold.

Foot by foot the carriage edged closer to the rooms, but then there came shouts for the way to be cleared, and everything came to a complete standstill. The band began to play "God Save the King," and Polly looked out as the royal carriage threaded its way past, preceded by pages with flambeaux. A detachment of light dragoons brought up the rear, and the townspeople who thronged the pavements began to cheer at the top of their lungs.

Hordwell scowled and huddled more deeply into the shawls and rugs with which he'd wisely enveloped himself. "Now I suppose it will take us lesser folk even longer to get to the door," he grumbled, his slavish reverence for royalty taking second place for once.

Lord Benjamin grunted agreement, but his hand slid secretly toward Polly's leg. She realized what he was up to and struck his knuckles with her closed fan. As he snatched his hand away with a smothered oath, she hissed at him too low for her uncle to hear. "Remember the staircase, sir. We may not be the only three in this carriage."

Lord Benjamin glanced nervously at the seemingly unoccupied seat next to Hordwell. He wasn't to know, as Polly did, that Bodkin and Ragwort were tucked in the luggage boot at the rear of the vehicle.

The cheers at the entrance redoubled as the royal party alighted, but it seemed an age before all the other carriages began to move again. At last Polly could see the Assembly Rooms ahead. They were contained in a very austere building that gave little hint of the splendors within. Lanterns shone along the walls, and fan-shaped arrangements of Union Jacks and regimental standards had been placed on either side of the entrance, their golden fringes and braid glinting in the flickering light of torches carried by the footmen who greeted each new arrival. Flowers and moss had been scattered over the steps that led to the vestibule, and the light inside was dazzling.

As the carriage from 1 Royal Crescent arrived, two of the footmen hurried to open its doors, lower the rungs, then present supportive elbows for those inside to alight. Smoke from their torches swept into the vehicle, as did the raw cold of the night and the racket of the band, which was now playing a rousing march. Polly was assisted down first, and as she paused to shake out her skirts, she glanced into the vestibule. The royal party had progressed farther into the building, and above the band she could just hear as the ballroom orchestra began to play the national anthem. She turned as her uncle alighted next. He was very awkward because of his gouty foot, and he grumbled a great deal as the footmen did their best to ease him down gently. Polly quickly positioned herself next to him and linked her arm lightly at one of his elbows in order to prevent Lord Benjamin offering to escort her.

Bodkin and Ragwort had climbed out of the luggage boot, and saw numerous chattering groups of brownies converging excitedly on the entrance. They were all laughing and giggling as they prepared to enjoy the night ahead, and many of them waved at Ragwort before disappearing into the building. Ragwort grinned at Bodkin. "You see? *Everyone's* here! Come on."

"I must speak to Miss Polly first," Bodkin replied, hastening over to tug at her skirt. "We're going straight inside, Miss Polly," he whispered so that Hordwell would not hear.

"Just behave," she whispered back, recalling only too well what had happened at the review.

"I will," Bodkin promised, then he and Ragwort threaded their way inside.

At last Polly and her uncle, followed by Lord Benjamin, were able to enter the warmth and brilliance of the vestibule, where a chandelier tinkled gently in the draft from the constantly opening doors. Flags and flowers were everywhere, and the babble of conversation was quite deafening. More footmen waited to relieve new arrivals of their cloaks and other outdoor items, and although the heat in the vestibule was quite considerable, Polly shivered as she stood in just her gown and silver lace shawl.

Everyone was edging slowly toward the octagon in the heart of the building, from whence opened the three main rooms, the tea and supper room to the right, the card room straight ahead, and the ballroom itself to the left. The crush and heat were quite oppressive, and already several ladies had been carried in a faint to the various chairs and sofas against the walls. Elderly chaperones, whose territory the octagon usually was, were obliged to stand displeasedly wherever they could, and footmen with trays of iced drinks found it virtually impossible to cross from the tea room on one side, to the ballroom on the other. The occasion was an intolerable press—and therefore assured of being a resounding success.

Polly glanced around for Dominic, but couldn't see him anywhere. Nor could she see any brownies, although she knew them to be present. But because she was more accustomed and sensitive to them, she did occasionally hear their voices and feel them brush gently past. Indeed most people heard and felt them, but in a jam like this, such incidents were put down to the close proximity of other people, not to brownies!

Now that she was here, Polly was so nervous and apprehensive about what Dominic might say or do when they eventually came face-to-face, that she almost felt sick. She resorted frequently to her fan and tweaked her shawl so many times that she began to fear she would pull threads in it. At last the octagon was reached, but to her dismay her uncle and Lord Benjamin made for the card room. "But, Uncle, aren't we going to the ballroom?" she asked.

Hordwell waved her away. "Go there if you choose, for I know you look forward to its frivolities. At present Lord Benjamin and I prefer the green baize."

She seized the chance of escape before he changed his mind, and entered the ballroom to stand beside the red velvet sofas that were arranged in three tiers around the edge of the hundred-foot-long, blue-and-gold room. From here she could see everything.

The ballroom walls were very plain at the bottom, punctuated only by chimneypieces, where fires roared, and doors that led into a single-story passage that enclosed the outside of the building. However, the top half of the walls, too high for anyone to look in or out, was lined with fine windows that were flanked by Corinthian columns. The ceiling was deeply coved, and from it hung five magnificent chandeliers. There was an orchestra apse set high in the wall behind her, but the musicians were actually on a special dais at the far end of the room. The royal party had by now settled in a fine box that was so overhung with leaves that it resembled a bower. In his uniform, the Duke of York stood out against such a background, but his wife was lost in the foliage, for she wore clinging green silk and matching green plumes that undulated like water whenever she moved.

Uniforms were all around, of course, together with the formal black velvet that was otherwise *de rigueur* for gentlemen at such occasions. For the ladies, plumes were very much in evidence, many of them ridiculously tall, but there were also tiaras, hair slides, jeweled combs, and artificial flowers. Circlets were few in number, and no one else appeared to have had the happy notion of wearing a necklace around her forehead. Fans fluttered in the intense heat, ringlets bobbed against bare shoulders, and rich gowns of rainbow colors swung to the steps of the polonaise that was in progress. Incongruously, Polly found herself wondering if there were brownies dancing as well. What a comical sight it would be, all those little brown-furred creatures moving among the high and mighty of Bath society!

The polonaise ended, and as the master of ceremonies announced the next dance, a *ländler*, she moved a little closer to the floor. This was the measure Dominic had asked her to reserve for him, and she wondered if he had seen her yet. Was he coming toward her right now? Her heart quickened hopefully, but as she glanced around again, she didn't see him anywhere.

Without warning, Lord Benjamin stepped before her. "May I have this dance, Miss Peach?" he inquired in a tone that was more statement than request.

She gave a start of dismay. "Lord Benjamin? But I . . . I thought you and my uncle were—"

"I could not permit you to come in here on your own," he replied, and without further ado he took her by the arm and steered her firmly onto the floor.

She had to let him command her, for it would hardly have done to make any protest in the presence of royalty. But, oh, how she wished to tell him to unhand her, to leave her alone, to go to a very hot place! The orchestra struck up, and she could hardly conceal her revulsion as Lord Benjamin twined his arms in hers to dance. He was all smiles as they moved around the floor; indeed he bestowed such gushing beams upon her that she began to wonder if the moon was full. When at last, after what seemed an age, the *ländler* ended, he caught her hand and kissed it so profusely that it was almost as if he were hungry. Her cheeks flamed at such an unwarranted display, but when she tried to pull her fingers away, his grip tightened, holding her a few seconds more, before, to her relief, he left her. What on earth was the matter with him? It *must* be the moon, she decided, surreptitiously wiping the back of her hand against her skirt to remove all trace of him.

She returned to the edge of the floor to watch the next dance, a minuet. It had been in progress for some time before she saw Georgiana among the dancers. Lord Benjamin's sister was resplendent

in a cream taffeta tunic over a nasturtium undergown, with a nasturtium turban from which sprang one of the tallest plumes in the
room. Her dark eyes were warm and laughing, and her beautiful
profile much displayed as she turned her head flirtatiously one way
and then the other. Her lashes fluttered, and the glances she bestowed upon her partner were very inviting indeed. Polly's heart
twisted with pain, for her partner wasn't the Marquess of Hightower, but Dominic.

He looked superb in a tight-fitting corded black silk coat and
clinging white breeches, and his waistcoat was a rich white brocade. A solitaire diamond sparkled in his lace-trimmed neckcloth,
his dark hair was tousled, and there was a smile on his lips as he
looked at Georgiana. Suddenly, as if he sensed Polly's gaze, he
turned his head. He met her eyes for a long moment without ac-
knowledging her at all, then he looked at Georgiana again.

Polly felt the snub as if it were a slap. In no uncertain terms he
had provided the answer to the puzzle of the labyrinth; those kisses
had meant nothing at all, *she* meant nothing at all. Fighting back
tears, she turned on her heel to leave the ball.

Chapter 27

But as Polly turned to hurry away, she came face-to-face with
the tall, skinny figure of the Marquess of Hightower. He
bowed. "Why, Miss Peach, what a very agreeable surprise."

"My lord." As she sank dismayed into a curtsy, Polly couldn't
help noticing that in spite of his incredibly thin physique, Lord Algernon was wearing a corset! This was in a vain attempt to achieve
the puffed-out chest that was considered so desirable in certain circles, but it only succeeded in making him look strangulated as well
as gangling. That he was in uniform made his strange shape all the
more noticeable.

"May I say you're looking most delightful?" he declared, smiling.

"Thank you, sir," she replied, avoiding his eyes because she wasn't too sure of him. First he'd smiled at Miss Pennyfeather's, now he was smiling again. Was *he* moonstruck as well?

"I trust you will honor me with the next dance?" he said, as the minuet came to an end, and the master of ceremonies announced a cotillion.

She was about to politely decline, when she suddenly realized he was presenting her with a heaven-sent opportunity to get even with Dominic, to show her indifference. To scuttle away from the ball would be to let him see how hurt she was, but to stay and dance with Georgiana's duke-to-be . . . ! Oh, how excellent a riposte! So she smiled. "That would be most agreeable, sir," she said.

The floor filled rapidly with sets for the cotillion, and she prayed Dominic and Georgiana were observing her actions, but although she surreptitiously inspected the bystanders and tiers of sofas, they were nowhere to be seen. The cotillion commenced, and the marquess proved a surprisingly graceful partner—provided one kept one's eyes on his feet, not on the rest of him. To be truthful, she still did not dare meet his eyes too often, for he kept smiling at her in the same way he had in the haberdashery. The last thing she wished to do was encourage him, although she realized that in her desire to snap her fingers at Dominic, she might already have done so.

Polly knew that a number of her recent actions had been foolish. First she stayed at Lord Benjamin's house, then she allowed Dominic some monstrous liberties, now she danced with the Marquess of Hightower, who seemed to have formed some sort of penchant for her! "You've been very silly over the past few days, Polly Peach," she murmured to herself, deciding that the moment the dance ended, she would have nothing more to do with Lord Algernon. Or with Sir Dominic Fortune. Or with Lord Benjamin Beddem. Least of all with the latter!

The cotillion proceeded, the sequences obliging couple after couple to pay and receive forfeits, and it wasn't until it was almost her turn that she realized with a shock that Dominic and Georgiana were not only in the next set, but had observed her with the marquess. Dominic's expression was unfathomable, but Georgiana's was thunderous. It seemed that it was all very well for her to flirt outrageously—and more, if last night's little visit was any sign!—with Dominic, but quite out of the question for the Marquess of

Hightower to show even mild interest in someone else. Polly's propensity for foolishness surged irrepressibly to the fore again, and as Lord Algernon bent toward her for the forfeit, which providently happened to be a kiss, at the last moment she turned her head slightly, so that instead of kissing her cheek, he kissed her lips. Her eyes remained open, and she saw him blink with surprise, but then the dance carried them apart once more. She didn't look at him again, nor did she glance toward the adjacent set, but she could feel Georgiana's eyes boring into her. Whether Dominic looked or not, she could not tell, but she was satisfied that her bruised pride had been soothed. A little, anyway.

The cotillion ended, and she hastened from the floor before the marquess could fix himself to her side again. In her haste to avoid him, she virtually dove into the onlookers standing almost four deep at the side, then made her way quickly toward the door into the octagon. It was now her definite intention to leave the ball, so she had to find her uncle, plead one of her headaches, then flee to her haven at the Sydney Hotel!

She soon found Hordwell and Lord Benjamin in the card room, and Hordwell was so inordinately pleased to see her that she should have guessed something was afoot. But all she could think of was getting away in order to pack her things to go to the Sydney Hotel, so she didn't even wonder why her appearance in the room caused a stir of interest among nearby tables. Hordwell seemed disappointed that she wished to leave so quickly, but was immediately wreathed in smiles when Lord Benjamin offered to escort her safely home. The prospect of Lord Benjamin seeing her back to the crescent was too horrible, so she quickly protested that there was no need for him to tear himself away from the green baize, but to no avail. He rose to offer her his arm, and short of creating a scene, there was nothing she could do but accept. However, she had every intention of giving him his *congé* before they reached the vestibule!

The murmurs at the other tables at last communicated themselves, and she looked back curiously as Lord Benjamin led her into the octagon. What was going on? she wondered. But Lord Benjamin was steering her as quickly as possible through the squash in the octagon, but as they reached the vestibule, and she prepared to rid herself of him, he suddenly dragged her aside into a corner between a fine arrangement of tall, luxuriant ferns and the draped regimental standard of the Duke of York's Own Light Dragoons. "What are you doing? Why are—?" Her voice dried, and she became alarmed as he forced her against the wall, then leaned a hand beside her head. His face was only inches from hers, and his manner was threatening, although no one else knew because of the concealment afforded by the ferns and the standard. Conversation and laughter echoed all around, but in this secret little place, all she could hear was the pounding of her heart.

Lord Benjamin gave a mirthless smile. "You've been outmaneuvered, my dear, and not just here. I've informed your uncle that you accepted me during the *ländler* we shared so fondly; indeed I've seen to it that every table in the card room knows you are to be Lady Beddem."

She stared at him. So that was what had lain behind his lunatic smiles! "But I haven't accepted you, and you know it!"

"Yes, but they don't."

"I'll deny it."

"And I'll make a very public fuss; indeed I'll blacken your character, Polly. I'll say you received me in your bedroom, and that I stayed until dawn. I'll let the world know we anticipated our vows."

She was speechless with shock and dismay. Never for a moment had she imagined he would descend to such disgraceful depths! But then to her immeasurable relief, someone addressed her tormentor from behind.

"Methinks your threats and conduct are monstrous, Beddem," Dominic said as he put a very firm hand upon Lord Benjamin's shoulder, forcing him to turn around and face him.

Lord Benjamin's face paled. "A private discussion between a man and his fiancée is none of your business, Fortune!" he breathed, shaking angrily free.

"It is when said fiancée clearly isn't willing, nor even a fiancée, come to that," Dominic replied, his glance moving quickly to Polly. "Are you all right?" She nodded, so hugely glad of his presence that she could have burst into tears. He looked at Lord Benjamin again. "My seconds will call, Beddem, for this cannot be permitted to pass unchallenged."

Lord Benjamin's eyes widened with dread. "Seconds? Fortune, I—"

Polly interrupted quickly. "Dominic, I would rather leave it, for whether a lady is innocent or not, she always acquires a certain notoriety if duels are fought over her."

Dominic hesitated, then nodded. "If that is what you wish, Polly."

Lord Benjamin's relief was almost palpable.

Dominic looked at him in disgust. "You are a shabby excuse for a man, Beddem, and if I ever catch you forcing your disgusting attentions on Miss Peach again, I will make you sorry you were born. Remember, there is more than one way to skin a cat, even one as portly as you! Now, I suggest you return to the card room and right the wrong you've done this lady."

"Go to hell, Fortune!" Lord Benjamin was momentarily defiant again.

"Either do as I say, or my seconds will call after all, whether or not Miss Peach desires to leave matters to settle," Dominic said quietly, his voice almost lost in the general babble of the vestibule.

Lord Benjamin swallowed. "You wouldn't go that far."

"You think not?"

"If you imagine I'm going to make a fool of myself by taking back all I've said—"

"You'll look a bigger fool with my shot in your blubber."

Lord Benjamin's quick little eyes searched his face. "You want her for yourself! I knew it last night!"

"Beddem, the day you *know* anything, will be the day it rains elephants." Dominic toyed with the lace at his cuff. "Now then, what's it to be? A timely retraction, or a cold, damp meeting on the banks of the Avon?"

Lord Benjamin hesitated, clearly knowing enough about Dominic's prowess with a pistol to be justly alarmed. A nerve flickered at his temple, and his tongue passed over his lower lip. "Very well, I'll retract."

"A wise decision, to be sure." Dominic gave him a bland smile.

Lord Benjamin flushed. "This won't be the last of it, Fortune! I'll make you rue the past few minutes!"

"Your threats don't frighten me, but you would do well to remember mine."

Lord Benjamin stepped away, then cast a dark glance at Polly. "If you think this will deter me, you're wrong. You're mine, sweet lady, and I won't rest until one way or another my ring is on your finger."

Dominic's hold upon his temper loosened. "Just leave, Beddem, before I kick your plump posterior into the middle of next week!"

Lord Benjamin lost no more time about hurrying away, swiftly disappearing into the press of people beyond the ferns.

Dominic turned quickly back to Polly. "Are you sure you're all right, Polly?"

"Yes, I . . . I . . ." Tears filled her eyes.

He quickly pulled her into his arms, safe in the knowledge that such an act was hidden from view. "You're safe now, Polly. He'll have to deny everything he claimed before, and he won't dare to blacken your name, because he knows I'll come after him."

"Would you do that? Go after him on my account?"

"Of course." He smiled and touched the amethysts encircling her forehead.

"I thought . . ."

"Yes?"

"That you thought little of me after my foolishness in the labyrinth."

"Is that what it was? Foolishness?" His blue eyes were quizzical.

"It's how I imagined you saw it. What else could I think when you cut me so very cruelly here a short while ago."

"I cut you because I saw how cozy you seemed to be with Beddem during that cursed *ländler*, immediately after which I heard him telling friends you'd accepted him."

"It's not true! I didn't want to dance with him, and I certainly didn't accept his proposal!"

"I know, because I overheard your conversation a few minutes ago. But until then, I believed it."

"After all I'd said to you concerning my feelings toward him?"

"I fear so." He held her gaze. "You certainly danced willingly enough with Hightower."

"As you did with Lady Georgiana," she replied.

"Is that why you did it? To spite me?"

She looked away.

He smiled. "You are indeed jealous, are you not," he said softly.

"Annoyed, not jealous," she replied, managing to meet his gaze again. She mustn't let his rescue cloud her judgment. He still seemed too close to Georgiana for comfort.

"I don't believe you, Miss Peach," he murmured.

"I'm telling the truth."

"As you were when you claimed there was a cat called Bodkin?" he asked lightly.

She flushed and glanced away again. "No doubt you find me most amusing, sir." *But Georgiana you find fascinating . . .*

He put a hand to her chin and tilted her face so that she had to look directly at him. "What are you thinking?"

"I was wondering about your feelings for Lady Georgiana," she replied honestly.

He gave a faint smile. "What feelings?" he breathed, and suddenly bent to brush his lips briefly over hers.

She put her hands to his chest to hold him away, not because she wished to, but because she was afraid he was toying with her. "If your kisses are false, please don't . . ."

"Why should my kisses be false? I promised you an answer tonight, and now you have it." Before she could say more, he kissed her again, this time drawing her into his embrace and dwelling upon the moment with a warmth that threatened to melt her soul.

She knew it was wrong to indulge in such caresses, knew he might still be amusing himself with her, but she could not help responding to him in a way no proper young lady should. He had the power to release all her inhibitions, to make her blood course wildly, and to command caution to fly with the winds. Georgiana became a distant memory. Nothing mattered except him, nothing at all.

Chapter 28

Meanwhile, the brownies of Bath were thoroughly enjoying themselves at the ball, but Ragwort was enjoying himself more than most. The unwise sipping of a convivial glass or six from the punch bowl in the tea room had resulted in his face becoming rather red and shiny, his laughter and bonhomie a little too loud, and his steps a little wobbly as he introduced Bodkin to his vast circle of acquaintances. He recounted Nutmeg's sad tale, slurring some of the words, and as each brownie promised to do what he or she could to trace Bodkin's missing sweetheart, Ragwort delivered such a hearty slap to their shoulders that he almost knocked several of them over.

At first Bodkin thought his companion was simply reveling in his night out, but gradually the rambunctiousness became so embarrassing that he understood what Ragwort had meant about alcohol not agreeing with him. "I say, Ragwort, don't you think you should go easy?" he ventured, concerned.

"Nonsense! I'm having a high old time," Ragwort replied, clouting him heartily on the back. "Don't be so stuffy, relax a little. Here, have a glass yourself." Grabbing the ladle from the punch bowl, he poured a very liberal measure for Bodkin, who declined in dismay.

"Er, no thank you, old chap, I fancy you're drinking enough for both of us," he said with a sigh.

Ragwort suddenly saw something and seized Bodkin's arm excitedly. "Look, do you see who I see?"

"I've no idea," Bodkin replied, searching every face, human and brownie, in the vicinity.

"It's my Caraway!" breathed Ragwort, his face rapt with delight. "She's back—Caraway's back!"

"Where is she? I don't know what she looks like."

"Over there, helping herself to those meringues."

Bodkin saw the brownie in question. She was matronly, and still very pretty, with her fur curled exactly the way Nutmeg curled hers.

"I'm going to speak to her," Ragwort declared purposefully.

Bodkin held him back, for in his present state, Ragwort wasn't likely to endear himself. "Will she like it if you do? I mean, you've never said why you and she fell out, but—"

"Oh, stuff and nonsense, I'm going to her." Shaking himself free, Ragwort wove his way unevenly toward his former ladylove. Bodkin followed.

Caraway blinked and almost choked on her meringue. "Why, Ragwort!" she gasped, watching him sway from side to side as he beamed at her.

"When did you return? Are you coming back to Royal Crescent? Have you given that scoundrel Bindweed his marching orders?" The last was added on a note of remembered resentment.

Caraway flushed. "Bindweed wasn't a scoundrel."

"Oh, yes, he was. He knew you were mine, but still he crept all around you, showering you with presents, and even naming his new honey after you."

"And why shouldn't he name the honey after me?" she replied indignantly. "It was a very charming gesture, and as for creeping around me, he was merely there for me when I was upset about you and your drinking. Look at you now—you're three sheets to the wind, and the evening isn't halfway through yet! Don't you ever learn?"

Oh, dear, thought Bodkin, deciding to pour what oil he could on waters that threatened to become very troubled indeed if Ragwort continued on this particular tack. "Er, hello, Caraway, I'm Bodkin," he said, bowing.

She looked hesitantly at him, then bobbed a little curtsy. "Hello, Bodkin. Are you Ragwort's friend?"

Ragwort nodded. "Yes, he is, and very fine friend, too!" Then he belatedly realized she'd spoken of the hated Bindweed in the past tense. "So Bindweed's gone? For good?"

She gave him an arch look. "That's for me to know, and you to find out," she replied.

"Oh, be fair, Caraway, just tell me he's gone," Ragwort begged.

"Seeing you in your cups again doesn't please me, Ragwort. I came back in the hope that you'd learned your lesson, but it's clear you haven't. Right now you don't compare very well with Bindweed!"

Ragwort's face fell. "But I've been very good since you left, Caraway," he protested. "Tell her, Bodkin. Tell her I wouldn't have any mead with you."

"It's true, Caraway," Bodkin said. "I invited him to share my mead, but he said such things did not agree with him."

She hesitated. "You wouldn't fib to me?"

"Certainly not," Bodkin replied earnestly.

"And this is the first time he's gotten in this state since I left?"

"I haven't seen him like this before," Bodkin answered honestly, omitting to mention that he'd known Ragwort only for a day.

She drew a long breath, and then her eyes softened as she looked at Ragwort. "Well, maybe I'll overlook this lapse," she conceded.

Ragwort's face brightened again. "You will? Does that mean you're my sweetheart again?"

"Don't rush, Ragwort, it merely means I'm prepared to speak to you again."

"Dance with me," he begged.

"Oh, I don't know about that."

"Please," he implored.

"All right, I'll partner you for the next *contredanse*, but only provided you behave yourself between now and then," she said, and with that he had to be content, for she turned and pushed away through the press of humans and brownies. In a moment she'd vanished from view.

Ragwort gazed after her in rapture. For a long moment he could not move for joy, but then an unstoppable tidal wave of exultation swept over him—to say nothing of the continuing surge of rashness from the punch he'd consumed—and suddenly he felt he had to *do* something! The urge to laugh, skip, jump, and leap was too much to resist, and with a whoop of delight he bounded from the room.

Caught unawares, Bodkin stared after him in dismay. "Oh, no! Ragwort, she said you had to *behave*!" he cried, then gave chase.

Ragwort was oblivious of plunging into the very misbehavior Caraway abhorred. He threaded across the octagon as fast as he could, then hastened into the ballroom, where he rushed around and around the edge of the floor until he should have been out of breath. Except that he wasn't. He was still so overjoyed about Caraway that his energy and emotion was irrepressible. Suddenly his glance fell upon a fine arrangement of flags, one of which had a particularly long pole. His eyes lit up, and he grabbed it in order to vault in all directions, using the pole as a lever. Higher and higher he went, forgetting that the flag's strange antics were bound to cause a stir. As the flag jerked here and there, apparently of its own volition, many ladies screamed in alarm, while others fainted clean away. Gradually the orchestra stopped playing, and there was an uneasy buzz of conversation as everyone pressed back from the seemingly possessed flag. The master of ceremonies was too startled to do anything except scurry around, flapping his scented handkerchief, and the Duchess of York, highly strung at the best of times, was so rigid with shock she had to be tended by her ladies, who were all of a bother themselves. The duke seemed as bemused as he had been at the review.

Dominic and Polly were just returning to the ballroom, numerous stolen kisses further on than they had been before, but a sliver of overdue wisdom had crept into Polly's wonderful glow of rash happiness. He'd avoided answering her anxious question about Georgiana. *"I was wondering about your feelings for Lady Geor-*

giana," she'd asked. *"What feelings?"* he'd replied. *What feelings indeed.* She should be wary. Georgiana wasn't a distant memory, but was very much in the present. Polly knew she should keep him at arm's length until she was sure Lord Benjamin's sister no longer meant anything to him, and that in the meantime, she had to behave with considerably more decorum than she'd displayed so far. But decorum was not going to come easily, for she was prey to the most beguilingly treacherous emotion of all, desire. These were her thoughts as she and Dominic reached the entrance to the ballroom, but then they both immediately halted in amazement as they saw the weird scene within.

As invisible as ever, Ragwort was now in ecstasy, and with a huge effort he vaulted up to the first chandelier. Dropping the flag to the now deserted floor, he began to swing wildly to and fro, so beside himself with delight that he whooped at the top of his lungs. More ladies screamed, and the beginnings of panic rippled through the elegant onlookers.

Dominic stared. "What in God's own name—?"

"It's Ragwort," Polly said without thinking, for she recognized the brownie's voice.

Dominic eyed her. "Who?"

Polly blushed. "Oh, nothing . . ."

"Would this Ragwort have anything to do with the mysterious Bodkin?" he inquired shrewdly.

Her cheeks went even more pink, and she didn't reply. The second chandelier began to swing, then the third and fourth as the invisible brownie hurled himself from one to the next, and so on.

"Well, if there is a cat on those chandeliers, I'll eat my best top hat," Dominic murmured dryly, then he glanced at her. "How eloquent your silence is, Polly."

Ragwort was now well into the rhythm of it, traveling from chandelier to chandelier like a chimpanzee, then all the way back again. Droplets of crystal fell to the floor and shattered, and the candle flames smoked and flared, many of them extinguishing in the draft he caused. Dominic quickly drew Polly into the space behind the tiers of sofas as he guessed what would happen next. He was right. As more and more candles went out, the ballroom became noticeably more dark and eerie, which proved too much for the hitherto rather stunned audience. Led by the musicians, who discarded their costly instruments with a confused clatter, everyone stampeded either toward the octagon, or the passage that went around the outside of the building. There was much indecorous elbowing and shoving, even from the duke, although the duchess had such a fit of the vapors that she had to be carried out.

It wasn't long before the ballroom was empty, except for a considerable number of dismayed brownies, but Ragwort remained blissfully unaware of the disturbance he'd caused. He continued to swing deliriously on the chandeliers, heedless of Bodkin, who now stood below him, imploring him to come down. More brownies crowded the door from the octagon, among them Caraway, who did not look at all amused; indeed her face was very stormy as she watched Ragwort make a spectacle of himself.

Suddenly one of the chandeliers gave way and came crashing to the floor, bringing Ragwort with it. The ballroom became even more dark as shattered crystal flew in all directions, for there were now only a few candles still burning, and most of the light came from the doorway to the octagon. Ragwort landed with a bump he didn't seem to feel at all, for he sat up with a stupid grin on his face and waved a hand at Bodkin "G'night, Bodkin, my friend," he said, and promptly lay down to go to sleep.

Dominic and Polly emerged from behind the sofas, staring in dismay at the broken chandelier, which glinted like diamonds in the darkened ballroom. Dominic looked at Polly. "I think it's time you explained a thing or two," he murmured.

Chapter 29

All the brownies rushed forward to Ragwort, who was already snoring very loudly indeed. Only Caraway remained behind. With a toss of her head and a disparaging sniff, she turned and stalked back to the tea room.

Dominic heard the patter of numerous bare feet, and ran his fingers through his hair. "All right, Polly. I know they're there, whatever they are, so would you please explain? Who or what are Bodkin or Ragwort? And don't say they're cats!"

She knew she had to tell him. "They're brownies," she said simply.

"They're what?" He stared at her, his gray eyes quizzical in the dim light.

"Surely you know what brownies are?"

"The same as elves, pixies, fairies, and bugaboos, and as mythical," he replied.

"If they're mythical, how do you explain all this?" She waved a hand at the flag and fallen chandelier.

He couldn't answer.

She smiled then. "Well, at least one thing is proved, you cannot have had anything to do with Nutmeg's disappearance."

"I don't understand."

Briefly she related the astonishing tale of Bodkin's furious departure from Horditall House, and did not spare her uncle or Lord Benjamin.

Dominic listened in amazement. "Is this really true?" he asked.

"Every word of it. What happened at the review was Bodkin's work. He was angry with me because he thought I'd betrayed his friendship, and when you found me on your terrace, I was chasing him to try to explain." She looked earnestly at him. "Dominic, when I was with you in your drawing room, something helped me adjust my shawl. It had to be a brownie. A belt buckle was found in your room, and Ragwort insists there hasn't been one in your house since Caraway left, so we're certain it must have been Nutmeg."

"And you suspected me of involvement?"

"You could have been."

"But now I'm exonerated?"

"Yes."

He smiled in the semidarkness. "Forgive me, Polly, but what if I'm a superb actor? What if my apparent ignorance of brownies is all camouflage?"

"I don't think it is. Indeed I stood up for you when it was first suggested that you might be in league with my uncle and Lord Benjamin."

He put a sudden hand to her cheek. "Did you?"

"Yes."

He put his lips lingeringly to hers. "What a fair champion I have," he whispered.

She drew away, aware of her decision to be more careful where he was concerned.

He looked inquiringly at her, but did not pursue the point. "So Beddem has a mysterious page from Nostradamus, does he?"

"He's purchasing it, but I don't think he has it yet. If he did, I think he would have used it by now in order to make money out of Nutmeg and rid himself of all duns."

"Your uncle doesn't have financial problems, so why is he involved? Just to make more money?"

"That's all I can think, unless . . ."

"Yes?"

"Well, I'd like to think he doesn't know about Lord Benjamin's plans. Maybe he's been gulled in some way."

"Is he gullible?" Dominic asked doubtfully.

"Well, yes, very much so where titles and royalty are concerned," Polly said, listening to the scuffling and low urgent whispering coming from the middle of the ballroom floor, as Ragwort, still snoring, was extricated from the heap of splintered crystal that had once been an exceedingly valuable chandelier. From the nearby card room came the sound of human voices as the more daring of the male guests plucked up courage to see if the ballroom was safe to enter yet.

Dominic caught Polly's hand. "Come on, we'll go to my house and talk more. Maybe we'll find Nutmeg," he said.

"I . . . I don't think I should go to your house . . ." she began.

"Why? Because it would be improper?"

"Yes. Look, Dominic, I know how shockingly I've already behaved, and I don't want to make it worse by going to your house again."

"Which is more important? Your reputation, or Nutmeg's rescue?"

"That's not fair."

"Oh, yes it is."

She hesitated, then gave in. "Nutmeg's rescue, of course," she conceded.

He smiled and kissed the tip of her nose. "I'm glad you said that, for it confirms my opinion of you. Besides, I've already said that if the worst come to the worst, I'll make an honest woman of you."

She caught his glance. "If you say that again, sir, I will consider it a definite proposal," she warned.

"If I say it again, it *will* be a definite proposal," he replied, leading her toward the door to the octagon.

She glanced back to where she knew Bodkin would be with the other brownies. "Bodkin, I've told Sir Dominic everything, and we're going to his house to search for Nutmeg!" she called in a low voice.

"I'll come as soon as Ragwort has been put to bed," Bodkin's voice answered.

Dominic's face was quizzical. "Oh, Polly Peach, when I think of how you were all innocence when you swore it was a cat!" he murmured, beginning to usher her across the octagon, but suddenly she halted on hearing her uncle's voice in the card room. He was complaining loudly about the interruption, which he neither understood nor cared about, because he'd been in the middle of a very promising hand.

Polly glanced at Dominic. "I had best give a convincing and acceptable reason for my departure," she said, and slipped into the crowded room, where it seemed most of the gentlemen at the ball had now congregated. Hordwell was just inside the door with Lord Benjamin and several other gentlemen, and she noticed how careful Lord Benjamin was to avoid her eyes.

Hordwell saw her, and his frown deepened. "Ah, miss, and what do you have to say for yourself?" he demanded.

"If you are referring to the so-called betrothal to Lord Benjamin, I expected him to explain that he'd completely misunderstood me. I will never marry him." Her tone was clear enough to interrupt the general discussion about returning to the now silent ballroom. Heads turned, and Lord Benjamin's neck went very red, but other than that he gave no sign of even being aware of her presence.

Hordwell's displeasure intensified. "This is very ill done, Polly."

"My sentiments exactly," she replied, giving Lord Benjamin an accusing look.

Hordwell shuffled slightly, not wanting the rather delicate discussion to continue in public. "That's as may be, that's as may be," he muttered, raising one of his walking sticks to prod his cards, which lay facedown on the green baize. "This ghost nonsense has ruined my game," he complained.

"Ghost?"

"That's what is believed to have brought the ball to a standstill."

"Oh."

"Did you see what happened?"

"Er, no, I was in the tea room," she said, crossing her fingers behind her back.

"Well, I want you stay safely by my side now, in case we have any more spectral goings-on. Sit down here, my dear." He indicated a chair.

"Actually, Uncle, I came to ask you if it would be all right if I went home. I have one of my headaches and feel quite unwell."

His lips parted in dismay. "Go home? But I want to finish this hand!"

"By all means do so, Uncle. I'll be safe enough in the carriage, and will be sure to send it back here again afterward."

"I don't know . . ."

"Please, Uncle, for I would hate to ruin the rest of your evening." She smiled winningly.

"Oh, very well."

"Thank you, Uncle." She gave him a very quick kiss on the cheek, then hurried away before he could change his mind.

As she and Dominic made their way quickly through the deserted vestibule to the cloak room, she explained what she'd told her uncle. "I'll get what I need of my things and leave a note for him. I know what he's like when he plays cards—he doesn't come home until sunrise. I'll be at the hotel by the time he reads it."

"Hotel?"

"I've taken a room at the Sydney Hotel," she said, and explained that even before tonight, Lord Benjamin's disgraceful behavior had made it quite impossible for her to remain in his house. "It was very silly of me to allow my uncle to persuade me in the first place, and even sillier for me to have remained once Lord Benjamin returned. In a way it is all my own fault," she finished.

"*Your* fault?" Dominic was aghast. "Don't ever think that, Polly, for the blame lies entirely with him. A lady should be able to enter his house without fearing his unwelcome attentions. What is your uncle thinking of? How can he permit such things to take place?"

"Uncle Hordwell is too beguiled by titles to believe Lord Benjamin would do anything, and he puts my protests down to unreasonable female moods. He thinks that once I'm married, I will be the happiest creature in England."

"Happy with Beddem? Dear God above . . ." Dominic drew a long breath. "I won't call him out, but I have to confront him privately. My own honor demands it. Do you understand?"

Polly gazed at him. "Do you think so highly of me, Dominic?"

"You must know I do," he replied softly, drawing her close in order to press his lips to her hair. Then he helped her with her cloak, and she raised the hood to hide her identity. They went out into the night, where a very nervous crowd, predominantly ladies, was waiting. Several acquaintances called out to Dominic for information, but as he and Polly walked quickly away, he replied that he knew nothing. Soon the only sound was their footsteps as they hurried with all speed toward Royal Crescent.

She went quickly into 1 Royal Crescent and packed all her things, folding clothes as tidily as she could, then went downstairs to the library to write an explanatory note to her uncle. Giles came when she rang the bell. She told him she wanted her things taken to the Sydney Hotel, and that she would be escorted safely there. She hurried out before the footman could ask any awkward questions, such as who was going to escort her. Once outside, she took a deep breath of the cold night air, determined that she would never set foot over that particular threshold again.

Chapter 30

As soon as they arrived at Dominic's house, they conducted another very thorough search, but came upon nothing to suggest that Nutmeg was there; indeed the brownie might as well be a figment of the imagination. Not even when Bodkin arrived shortly afterward, having tucked Ragwort safely in his attic bed, did she intimate her presence. But if Dominic still nursed any doubts that brownies were fact, those doubts were soon dispelled when Polly persuaded Bodkin to make himself visible.

Dominic stared at the small, shaggy being in the middle of the drawing room carpet. "Good God," he muttered, hardly able to believe his eyes.

Bodkin was a little offended. "Is there something wrong with me?" he inquired, smoothing his fur self-consciously.

"Forgive me, it's just that I'd never seen anything quite like you before."

"I'm just an ordinary brownie, you know. We all look like this."

Dominic smiled at him. "And very agreeable you are, too."

Mollified, Bodkin hauled himself into the nearest chair, but as he made himself comfortable, his tail resting neatly on his lap, he gave a huge sigh. "What am I going to do about Nutmeg?" he asked.

Dominic ushered Polly to another chair, then went to a decanter of cognac to pour a small measure for Bodkin. He pressed it into the brownie's hands. "I suppose it's all right for you to drink this? I mean, your friend would appear to have something of a problem."

"I'm quite all right," Bodkin replied, promptly draining the glass, then holding it out to be refilled.

Dominic obliged, then poured himself some as well. He looked inquiringly at Polly. "Would you care for anything?"

"No, thank you."

Bodkin gave another long sigh. "Ragwort told me that Nutmeg wouldn't be able to communicate if someone had her belt, but what I can't understand is why she can do something like adjust your shawl, Miss Polly, yet cannot touch someone's arm to let them know she's there!"

Dominic spoke. "Or how she can bring towels," he said.

Polly and Bodkin looked inquiringly at him. "Towels?" they repeated.

"Yes. Someone female brought towels when I was taking a bath, and the maids are forbidden to enter under such circumstances."

Bodkin looked close to tears. "Oh, why can she do that, but not communicate when we need her to?"

"Maybe in spite of everything, she still has to go about her tasks," Polly suggested.

Dominic nodded. "That sounds about right," he said.

Bodkin nodded. "Yes, I suppose so. Oh, what if she's in here with us now?" A thought occurred to him, and suddenly he dropped his empty glass onto the carpet, luckily without breaking it. They all three watched, hoping the invisible Nutmeg would pick it up, but nothing happened. Clearly she wasn't present. Bodkin was immediately sunk in the deepest gloom. "If only we knew where her belt is," he said, his voice catching.

Dominic couldn't help putting a comforting hand on the

brownie's shoulder. "Well, I think we can be sure that Beddem has it somewhere. Have you searched his room?"

"Every inch of it. The belt isn't there, I'm certain."

"Perhaps he carries it on him at all times," Dominic mused, reasoning that the key to a probable fortune would be very well guarded.

Polly sat up with a start, remembering something that had passed her by at the time. "I think you're right. He and I had a confrontation on the staircase, and when I demanded to know about Nutmeg, his hand started to go quickly toward his pocket. It was a defensive action, as if to protect something. What if it was Nutmeg's belt?"

Bodkin's eyes brightened. "Of course!" He sat up, his eyes glinting. "I'll get it when he's asleep!"

Dominic spoke up quickly to advise caution. "Don't make rash plans, for Beddem isn't likely to leave it conveniently in his pocket when he isn't wearing the coat. If he believes a great deal of money hangs upon Nutmeg, he's going to hide her belt carefully at all times. He may put it under his pillow, or even tie it to his big toe! You can't go clambering all over him trying to find it."

Bodkin was despairing. "Then what *can* we do?"

"Bide our time. If he is keeping it in his coat pocket as Polly suspects, then the answer is to do something when he's wearing said coat. Perhaps he could be persuaded to remove it . . . ?" Dominic's voice died away thoughtfully.

Bodkin's lips parted. "I've thought of a way to make him take off his coat."

"How?" Dominic inquired.

"Miss Polly could go for a walk with him in somewhere like Sydney Gardens, then ask him to sit on the grass. He'd have to take off his coat for you to sit on." The brownie warmed to his idea. "Yes, and then she could ask him for a cool drink from the hotel! He'd have to get it!"

Dominic shifted a little. "No, Bodkin, for Polly must be kept well away from Beddem," he said. "Besides, he wouldn't *have* to take off his coat to sit on grass—indeed I'd be surprised if he did. One only sits upon dry grass, and if it's dry, there's no need to put anything on it, if you see what I mean."

But Bodkin had warmed to the general idea of somehow getting Lord Benjamin to remove his coat. "All right, maybe it shouldn't involve Miss Polly, but we've got to inspect his pockets somehow.

What about the Halloween celebrations tomorrow night? There'll be dancing around the bonfire, and no matter how cold a night it is, you know how fierce the heat of such a fire can be. I don't recall seeing anyone dancing at such an occasion with his coat on, so if Beddem were to be persuaded to take part in the dance, he'd have to remove his coat, or melt."

Dominic sat back thoughtfully. "It's as good an idea as any, but who's going to persuade him to dance? I'd offer, but I don't think his fancy runs in that direction," he said dryly.

Bodkin eyed him a little crossly. "This is supposed to be serious, you know," he chided.

"I know. I'm sorry."

The brownie continued to eye him for a moment, then returned to the matter of Lord Benjamin's coat. "I still think we should persuade him to join the bonfire dancing. Couldn't we hire a lady? An actress, maybe? Or one of those ladies who wait at the top of Milsom Street after dark?"

Dominic cleared his throat. "They aren't ladies," he said.

Polly spoke suddenly. "No, but *I* am. I could do it, Dominic. As a guest at the hotel, I have automatic entry to the gardens, so I don't even need to worry about not having a ticket."

"Polly, I won't hear of it."

"Why not?"

Bodkin wanted to know as well. "Yes, why not?" he demanded.

"Well, there are some insurmountable problems. Far from dancing with him, Polly, it's out of the question that you should even *speak* to him. Then there is your intention to stay at the Sydney Hotel, which will be very pointed, and cause an even greater rift than already exists between you and Beddem."

"Dominic, at the Assembly Rooms you asked me which was more important, my reputation, or Nutmeg. The answer could only be Nutmeg. She's still more important than anything else."

"But, Polly, I don't want you to go anywhere near Beddem."

"We have to do something, and if dancing around the bonfire is the best we can think of, we have to try it. Listen, I have some thoughts on how we could bring it about. I could send Lord Benjamin a conciliatory note from the hotel, saying I've had time to reconsider, and feel I may have been a little hasty. I could suggest a civilized meeting at the Halloween junketing. He will see it as second thoughts about snubbing a title, and since he is very eager indeed to lay hands upon my fortune, I hardly think he is going to refuse me."

Dominic didn't like it at all. "I'd prefer to find a way of searching for the belt that doesn't involve you coming into contact with him."

Polly couldn't help digging in her heels. "My mind is made up, Dominic." she declared, the glint of battle brightening her lavender eyes.

He groaned. "Oh, I am beginning to know that look," he murmured.

"It just might work, Dominic. A written peace offering, a few words in a very public place, then an invitation to dance around the bonfire. Besides, I'm sure you will be gallantly close at hand, ready to defend me if he should step out of line again."

"That goes without saying," Dominic replied, resigning himself to the situation.

"There's only one obstacle."

"And that is?"

"I don't have a costume. Everyone will be in fancy dress."

"Yes, I've acquired a sultan's outfit, or perhaps it's an eastern wizard's outfit. One or the other. If you're really set on proceeding with this business, I can get a costume for you. My former army batman has now retired and presides over the foremost fancy dress emporium in Bath. He owes me several favors, so although most of his stock will no doubt have been taken for tomorrow night, he'll nevertheless be duty bound to find something entirely suitable."

Bodkin was a little bothered. "I'd forgotten that there will be costumes. What if Lord Benjamin has chosen something without a coat?"

Dominic groaned. "Oh, don't look for any more obstacles, for we have enough already. We'll have to hope he turns out in something suitable to our purposes. If he doesn't, we'll abandon the whole thing and put our thinking caps on again. Is it agreed?"

"Yes," the other two replied.

Dominic looked at Polly again. "Are you still absolutely certain you wish to press on with this?"

"Of course," she replied, but deep inside she was conscious of a shiver of apprehension.

Chapter 31

The next morning Polly awoke in her room at the rear of the Sydney Hotel. Dappled sunlight streamed through a crack in the curtains, and autumn leaves rustled in the tall trees that grew just outside. The sound of music, hammering, and shouting came from the gardens, as the final preparations for Halloween got under way. Everything would be ready for six o'clock that evening, when the Duke and Duchess of York would arrive and the festivities begin.

She got up to draw the curtains back and was immediately dazzled by the sun as the leaves fluttered in the breeze. The music came from the hotel orchestra, which was rehearsing on the grand balcony just a little farther along from her window, but the hammering came from halfway up the gardens, beside the enormous completed Halloween bonfire, where a gang of men was erecting the wooden framework for the fireworks display that was to open the evening. Suddenly her apprehension returned, and she took a deep breath to try to quell it. She was the one who'd insisted on the plan, refusing to heed Dominic's misgivings, and now it was up to her to go through with it. Oh, surely nothing could go wrong. There would be crowds all around, Dominic, Bodkin, and Ragwort keeping an especial watch upon her, so what could possibly happen? She lowered her glance for a moment, recalling that there had been crowds all around at the Assembly Rooms, yet Lord Benjamin had still managed to isolate her.

But the evening was still hours away as she looked up again, this time beyond the gardens to the open hills that shimmered in a haze of unexpected warmth. Lazy twists of smoke rose from the chimneys of isolated farms and cottages, the sky was very clear and blue, and the colors of autumn blazed as never before. Her unease slid away, for it was a wonderful morning. Or did it just seem so because on bringing her to the hotel last night, Dominic had taken his leave with a kiss that was so yearning and tender she feared she might die of desire? More than that, he had arranged to meet her in the gardens at noon. Caution had once again flown with the winds, and this morning she was ridiculously happy, but then her

conscience prodded, for the love lives of poor Bodkin and Ragwort were so wretched. Oh, how she prayed tonight's plan succeeded, so that Nutmeg's belt could be retrieved, and Bodkin
reunited with her. She hoped, too, that Ragwort could redeem himself in Caraway's eyes. Then they would all be happy.

A wagon rumbled into the gardens from the equestrian gateway
and made its slow way up the broad walk. It was heavily laden
with turnip jack-o'-lanterns, which by nightfall would all be
placed around the gardens, each one with a lighted candle inside it
so that it shone frighteningly out of the shadows. She watched the
bouncing load of horrible grinning faces and at last saw the significance of Bodkin's enormous pumpkin. He was going to make a
jack-o'-lantern that was so large it would frighten the daylights out
of everyone!

A tap came at the door. "Begging your pardon, madam," said a
hotel maid's voice, "but your uncle has called. He instructs me to
tell you he's just received your note and will await you in the coffee room."

Polly's heart sank. He couldn't long have returned from the Assembly Rooms, where she hoped the cards had been kind, for that
would mean he'd be in a less angry mood than would otherwise be
the case. "Please tell him I'll come down directly," she called back.

"Yes, madam."

Polly washed hastily, spent ten minutes struggling with her hair,
then opened the wardrobe, where her clothes from Royal Crescent
now hung neatly, Giles having sent her luggage as requested. She
selected the yellow-and-white gingham, composed herself as best
she could, then went nervously downstairs. The meeting with her
uncle was bound to be awkward, no matter what his mood, for she
was defying his wishes in no uncertain manner. But he was going
to have to accept that she wasn't going back to 1 Royal Crescent,
nor was she going to marry Lord Benjamin Beddem. She would
fling herself on the mercy of the courts before she'd do that! Or
seek sanctuary in Bath Abbey. Anything but spend the rest of her
life as Lady Beddem.

The coffee room had been decorated overnight for Halloween.
Sprays of rowan and ash had been arranged along the pelmets, traditional protection from the wicked spirits roaming free on this one
night. Paper witches and ghosts adorned the walls, and fishing nets
were suspended from the ceiling like immense webs, with large
black spiders dangling menacingly above the tables. The room was

crowded, and she immediately realized that the sole topic of conversation appeared to be the previous night's events at the Assembly Rooms. The ball was said to have been subjected to a truly horrid haunting, and one particularly loud lady swore that with her own eyes she'd seen every single chandelier fling itself to the floor. The same woman insisted that the ballroom was so badly damaged it would be months before another function could be held there! The goings-on were linked to the debacle of the review, and the general consensus was that premature Halloween spirits were the cause. So much for Bodkin the Boggart and Ragwort the Inebriated.

Her uncle was seated at a table by a window that looked down Great Pulteney Street toward the heart of Bath. He wore a maroon coat and gray breeches, and his walking sticks rested on the windowsill. Polly stood before the table, waiting to gauge his attitude before she sat down. "Good morning, Uncle Hordwell," she said quietly.

He looked reproachfully at her. "Good? I see nothing *good* about it, missy! You have disobeyed my wishes and obliged me, an invalid, to come here in order to reason with you." He made his displeasure even more plain by declining to stand up for her.

"I know I'm a grave disappointment to you, Uncle, and I apologize, but you have to accept that in this one thing I refuse absolutely to bow to your wishes," she replied steadily.

His face was red with anger. "You refuse? We'll see about that. Oh, do sit down, wench, for my neck aches if I look up."

She took a seat, and almost immediately a waiter appeared at the table. "May I take your order, madam? Sir?"

"I don't require anything," Hordwell growled, still subjecting Polly to his reproving gaze.

She smiled up at the waiter. "Coffee, warm bread rolls, and honey, if you please," she said.

As he hurried away, Hordwell made a disparaging noise. "You should be too ashamed to eat."

"Uncle Hordwell, the only reason you don't want anything is because you'll have to pay for it. If you wait until you're back at Royal Crescent, you'll be able to eat at Lord Benjamin's expense."

"Impudent minx!" he cried, a little more loudly than he'd intended. A fleeting hush fell as all eyes turned toward their table, and he quickly lowered his tone to continue. "It ill becomes you to criticize me, missy! You are a trial to me, a great trial, and by running here like this . . . Oh, words fail me." He sat back with a labored sigh.

"Uncle, I had no choice but to come here. You know that last night's supposed acceptance of Lord Benjamin's proposal was all invention on his part."

"Invention? Oh, no, Polly, according to him you have a very cruel heart. You accepted one moment, then retracted the next. You made a fool of him last night, missy, and I expect you to apologize most sincerely."

Chapter 32

Polly's eyes flashed with indignation. "*Apologize?* Uncle, I would rather make overtures to Old Nick than say I'm sorry to Lord Benjamin Beddem!"

"Polly—" Hordwell began angrily.

She broke in. "What he's told you simply is not true, for I did *not* agree to marry him. The only reason he's admitted that the so-called betrothal is at an end is because Sir Dominic threatened to call him out unless he did!"

Hordwell's eyes widened. "Call him out? What's this? What has Fortune to do with it?"

"He rescued me from Lord Benjamin's despicable clutches. Far from being gallant when he insisted on taking me home, my noble would-be husband behaved atrociously. He trapped me in a corner and threatened to destroy my reputation unless I became his bride. Sir Dominic overheard and dealt with him. That's why Lord Benjamin returned to the card room and told you the betrothal was over. It had nothing to do with my caprices."

"I don't believe it!" Hordwell replied. "Lord Benjamin wouldn't conduct himself thus. He's an aristocrat through and through."

"And aristocrats aren't devious and unpleasant? Oh, Uncle, you know full well that blue blood makes no difference to a man's character. My father had a very low opinion of the aristocracy, and not without reason."

"Your father was a mere bank clerk!"

"He *owned* the bank! And don't speak disparagingly of him—after all it's *his* fortune that Lord Benjamin is pursuing so single-mindedly."

Hordwell flushed. "You're a very outspoken miss, and no mistake."

"It's how I was brought up to be."

"Dragged up, more like," he muttered.

"Are you saying that your only sister was less than a good mother to me?"

"No, of course not." He scowled as the waiter brought her order.

She glanced up at the man. "Would you please bring some coffee for my uncle? And one of those enormous toasted currant buns?"

"Very well, madam." He hurried away again.

Hordwell's scowled increased. "I don't want anything—you already know that."

"You adore toasted buns, and anyway, I shall pay for it," she said, giving him a quick smile.

He softened a little. "Polly Peach, you are a regrettably uppity chit," he declared.

"Uppity maybe, but I'm honest, too. Uncle, I've told you the truth about Lord Benjamin, and you have to accept that I will *never* consent to be his wife."

For a long moment he studied her face, then slowly nodded. "Yes, I believe you about everything, my dear."

She breathed out with relief. "And you won't badger me anymore to marry him?"

"No, you have my word upon it. Oh, this is a pretty pickle. I'll have to quit the crescent as well, and I do so enjoy it there."

"Come here."

"And pay?" he exclaimed, appalled.

"Then go back to Horditall."

"Not without you, missy."

"I can't leave Bath just yet."

"Why not, pray?" he inquired, as the waiter brought a toasted bun that oozed with melting butter. A spoonful of fine greengage preserve was heaped beside it.

Polly waited until they were alone again, then answered. "I just have reasons for wanting to stay, Uncle," she said, not thinking there was any point in mentioning Nutmeg again, for he was bound to continue denying all knowledge of the matter.

Hordwell spread the preserve on the bun and took a large bite. "Oh, this is splendid, splendid," he muttered, closing his eyes with pleasure. After a moment he looked at Polly again. "Sir Dominic Fortune appears to figure somewhat in all this, my dear. Am I to presume this is a fact of some significance?"

"Of course not," she said quickly, wondering what he'd say if he knew the true extent of Dominic's entry into her life. What would he say if he knew she hadn't come straight to the hotel from the ball last night? What would his reaction be if he learned she'd indulged in far too many improper kisses, that she longed to surrender completely to a man she'd known for only a day or so?

Hordwell studied her. "Hmm. I'm not the fool you take me for, missy, so maybe it's better that I don't know what you've been up to." He glanced across at a nearby table, where a gentleman was deep in a newspaper, the headlines of which were rather wild. HALLOWEEN MYSTERY. POLTERGEIST AT BALL. DUCHESS OF YORK COLLAPSES IN SHOCK. ASSEMBLY ROOMS WRECKED. "Polly, what exactly do you think went on at the ball last night? Those of us in the card room knew nothing about it until it was all over. We went into the ballroom and saw the broken chandelier on the floor, but the rumors were all too ridiculous for words. I simply do not believe in ghosts."

"It had nothing to do with ghosts, Uncle—indeed I'm surprised you haven't worked it out for yourself."

He was puzzled, but then his eyes cleared. "*Brownies?* Is that what you're saying?"

"Yes." She explained about Ragwort and all the other brownies at the Assembly Rooms, then added, "They're all searching for Nutmeg, you know, and sooner or later they'll find her. Sir Dominic is helping as well."

He shifted on his seat. "I know nothing about Nutmeg," he muttered.

"I may as well be honest with you. I know you've been telling me fibs about Nutmeg. You and Lord Benjamin *did* do something with her, didn't you? Come on, Uncle, admit it. Her belt buckle was found in Sir Dominic's bedroom, which was Lord Benjamin's room, and there have been one or two occurrences that prove she's there."

He gave a long sigh, then nodded. "You're right, my dear, I did allow Lord Benjamin to take her."

Even though she already knew he was guilty, Polly found the admission upsetting. "Oh, Uncle, how *could* you!"

He looked shamefaced. "With your marriage to him in mind, I wanted to please Lord Benjamin. He and I were examining the house she looked after in Horditall, with a view to extending it considerably and turning it into a gentleman's country residence. I wasn't even thinking about brownies—indeed I'd forgotten all about them, but then she brushed past Lord Benjamin on the stairs, and he reached out instinctively and caught her by the belt. He couldn't see her, of course, but he knew what he'd caught and became very excited. He said he'd been wanting a brownie because the one at his house had left, and he knew he could keep Nutmeg just by taking her belt. There was nothing I could do, for he was right, and when he swore upon his honor to look after her, I said nothing more. Being most methodical, I entered the matter in my ledger, and he immediately took her to Bath. I didn't like to admit it—indeed I was a little ashamed of my ineffectuality, which is why I've insisted all along that Nutmeg simply walked out. But there really wasn't anything I could have done, Polly. Once he had the belt in his keeping, Nutmeg was his."

"Poor Bodkin's heart has been breaking over her," Polly said reproachfully.

"I know, but I thought he'd get over it. I'd forgotten all about it until you arrived at the crescent."

"Do you know *why* he wanted her?" Polly asked after a moment.

"Eh? Well, to be a house brownie, I suppose."

She told him what the page of Nostradamus would achieve for Lord Benjamin, and he was appalled. "This is the first I've heard of it! Mean and grasping I may be, but you have my absolute word that I would never knowingly be party to such cruelty."

She smiled. "I'm so glad you say that, Uncle, for I confess I did fear . . ."

"My sins are many, but there are lines which even I draw." He paused, then exhaled a little guiltily. "My dear, I fibbed to you about something. You asked if he'd cozened me for money, and I denied it. But he did. It was about two weeks ago, and I happened to be with him when he used the loan to make funds available for drawing upon an account in a French bank. He said it was to support an elderly sick aunt who was too unwell to travel home to England, but I believed it was to fend off the most pressing dun. Clearly it was really the final payment for this unholy page. I can therefore only presume that said page will arrive at any time."

"Oh, no. This makes it more urgent than ever that we rescue Nutmeg." Polly decided to trust him fully. "Uncle Hordwell, if I tell you something in the strictest confidence, will you *promise* not to divulge it to Lord Benjamin?"

"My dear, I am so disillusioned with Beddem that I would rather cut out my tongue than be his crony any longer. Of course you may speak in confidence."

She revealed the plan for that night, and he became more dismayed with each word. "Oh, no, my dear, I don't like the sound of that at all! What is Fortune thinking of? You cannot possibly be permitted to write to, speak to, *or* dance with a base insect like Beddem. It will be dark, and there are bound to be countless hidden places, all Vauxhalls are full of them. Heaven alone knows what he might attempt if he gets you in his clutches again!"

Something struck her. "Maybe it can be finished *before* tonight. You see, now that you're an ally, it occurs to me that you may be able to help."

"How?"

"Well, you said earlier that you would have to leave the crescent, but if you stay and pretend you still approve of Lord Benjamin in every way, you'll be able to search for Nutmeg's belt. You can tell him you think I'm coming around after all, that I haven't entirely dismissed the thought of marriage. Promise him that you'll continue to press his suit upon me, say anything you like, but just stay there. He only has to be persuaded to take off his coat, and then have his attention diverted. There may be such an opportunity, and if you can get the belt, there will be no need to press on with our plans for the gardens tonight."

Hordwell looked intently at her. "Which will be all to the good. Very well, my dear, I'll stay there, and do all I can to find the belt."

"There's just one thing more. You must let Bodkin know you are now his friend, otherwise . . ."

"Yes?"

"Otherwise he has unpleasant things in store for you."

"I see. Well, how do you propose I tell him anything?"

She hesitated. "One of Lord Benjamin's footmen, the one called Giles, is a friend of Ragwort's. If you tell him you are now on Bodkin's side, he'll tell Ragwort, and—"

Hordwell interrupted. "Ragwort? Ah, yes, the brownie who caused the trouble at the ball. So if I tell this footman, I'll be let off the proverbial hook?"

"I hope so."

"I'll speak to Giles directly I return," Hordwell replied, beginning to get up painfully from his chair.

"What of your toasted bun and coffee? Aren't you going to finish them?" Polly asked.

He smiled as he eased himself around the table on his walking sticks. "My dear, I feel I must atone for my sins without further delay. There will be other toasted buns, I'm sure."

She rose as well and hugged him tightly. "I love you, Uncle Hordwell," she whispered, so glad of this new rapprochement that she was almost in tears.

"I can't imagine why," he replied frankly, kissing her cheek.

"I love you in spite of your horrid attempts to make me marry Lord Benjamin, because I've always known that behind your social ambition, grumbling and penny-pinching, there is actually someone rather nice struggling to step forward."

"Nice? Upon my soul, I've never seen myself in that light before," he muttered, and began to shuffle from the room.

She saw him safely into his waiting sedan chair, but held the door a moment before closing it. "You will be careful, won't you, Uncle? Lord Benjamin isn't at all the noble fellow you've always thought."

"I realize that now, my dear, and of course I'll be careful," he promised, "but you must be careful, too. I still do not like this notion of yours to send a note to him. No matter how carefully you word such a communication, he is bound to misconstrue it. I only trust I can find Nutmeg's belt before tonight, for I wish at all costs to prevent you from ever having to speak to him again."

"All will be well, I'm certain," she replied, then closed the door and nodded to the chairmen. She watched as he was conveyed down Great Pulteney Street, and when the chair disappeared in the throng of traffic near Laura Place, she went back into the hotel to compose her letter to Lord Benjamin. When that was done, she would prepare for her midday tryst with Dominic.

Chapter 33

Bodkin had taken his time about getting up that morning. He still slept in the hayloft, even though Dominic—and Ragwort before him—had offered a proper bed, and while Polly was with her uncle, the brownie was lying idly in the hay. His hands were behind his head, and his legs were drawn up and crossed, so he could swing a foot pensively up and down. His jack-o'-lantern lay in a shaft of sunbeams beside him and was now a picture of grim perfection after a final session of carving and whittling that had gone on almost until dawn. Bodkin was quietly pleased with his creation, which was bound to outshine anything else at Sydney Gardens that night. Old Hordwell and beastly Lord Benjamin were going to suffer greatly before he was done.

Bodkin smiled with grim contemplation. Polly's uncle was easy enough, for being an invalid, he couldn't exactly flee from any horror, so the mere appearance of the jack-o'-lantern in front of him should be sufficient to frighten him. But Lord Benjamin was a different matter. What would be the best way of terrifying the clammy pink aristocrat? Just appearing before *him* wasn't enough. Perhaps he should be harangued by a terrible ghostly voice? Or should he be pursued around the bonfire? Driven into the labyrinth, then stalked? Chased into the canal? Maybe all four! Yes, all four would do nicely.

The brownie sat up, dipped a finger in the honey, and turned his thoughts to Polly and Dominic. Ragwort had been so right about them, for if they weren't lovers yet, they were bound to be soon. He licked his sticky finger, thinking that Polly would make a very nice Lady Fortune, but then his smile faded as he remembered Georgiana. He'd seen Dominic importuning that disagreeable lady at the review, and saw how Georgiana fluttered her lashes at him at the ball. It was quite clear that Lord Benjamin's nasty sister presented a threat to Polly's happiness, and for that she had to pay a penalty. Boggart shone briefly in Bodkin's eyes as he decided to treat Georgiana to a few Halloween shocks. He beamed at his jack-o'-lantern. "Now then, my horrible friend, you mustn't let me down tonight," he declared, patting it on the head, then licking his honey-drenched finger again.

Suddenly the brownie remembered his bees. He'd have to consult them without further ado, for they had things to do tonight as well. First they had to be persuaded to remove themselves from Royal Crescent to Sydney Gardens, then he wanted them to await his signal to fly into action against those he regarded as the enemy. A swarm of angry bees would cause some very satisfactory havoc, to say nothing of stinging a few well-chosen hides! Putting his honey pot away, the brownie groomed his fur with clove balm, then scrambled down from the loft.

As Bodkin went to his bees, Hordwell returned to 1 Royal Crescent, intent not only upon finding Nutmeg's belt, but also upon letting Bodkin know he was no longer in the enemy camp. Unfortunately, it was Giles's day off, and the footman wouldn't return to the house until that evening, when—unknown to any of his fellow servants, of course—he'd promised to take the Royal Crescent brownies to the Halloween celebrations in a pony cart borrowed from a shopkeeper friend. His absence meant there was no immediate way for Hordwell to let Ragwort know of his defection. All Polly's uncle could do was leave a sealed note below stairs to be handed to Giles the moment he returned. In the meantime, Hordwell sincerely hoped Bodkin's promised campaign against him would not commence before darkness fell.

Dominic was just awakening. He lay naked and drowsy in his vast four-poster bed. He'd been enjoying a very erotic dream, the spell of which still enveloped him. His body was aroused, and the blood flowed warmly through his veins. He closed his eyes, trying to recall the dream woman to whom he had just been making such passionate love. A confusion of feelings ran through him. Did she have raven hair and dark eyes? Or tumbling blond curls and eyes as misty blue as lavender? A glance at the clock on the mantelpiece told him it was ten; in two hours he would meet Polly at the gardens. Blond curls and lavender eyes . . .

After a moment, he flung the bedclothes back and got up to open the curtains. Dazzling sunlight flooded in, but before he could look out properly, he heard a sound behind him and turned sharply. Nothing seemed there, yet he felt certain he wasn't alone in the room. A thought struck him. "Bodkin?" he called, but almost immediately cast the notion aside, for the brownie would reveal himself. Maybe it was Nutmeg! "Nutmeg?" he said urgently. "Is that you?" There was still nothing, but for a moment he was sure he saw a footprint on one of the rugs. Before he could pursue the matter further, a footman knocked tentatively at the door. "Sir Dominic?"

Dominic reached for his gray paisley dressing gown and quickly pulled it on. "Yes?"

The door opened, and the footman entered with the little silver tray of strong black coffee with which Dominic started every day. "Good morning, sir," he said, placing the tray beside the bed.

"Good morning."

The man hesitated. "Sir Dominic, Lady Georgiana Mersenrie has called."

Georgiana? Dominic glanced quickly out of the window again and saw the familiar carriage drawn up at the curb.

"She is demanding to see you immediately, sir," the footman said.

"Is she indeed?"

"I informed her ladyship that you had yet to awaken, but she insists, sir."

Georgiana had clearly been making herself very difficult, Dominic thought. At that moment there was a disturbance downstairs, and he heard Georgiana's outraged tones as she lost patience and hurried up the staircase, pursued by another anxious footman.

The footman in the bedroom looked uneasily at Dominic. "Er, do you wish to see the lady, sir? Or shall I have her ejected?"

Eject Georgiana? Her noise would be heard clear to Bristol, Dominic thought. "No, I will see her," he said.

"But you are in your undress, sir," the footman reminded him.

"It won't be the first time she has seen me thus," Dominic replied wryly.

Georgiana appeared in the doorway. Her face was flushed and angry, and the plumes and ribbons of her stylish leghorn bonnet were all aquiver. She wore a cerise pelisse over a rich butter-cream muslin gown, and a heavy white ringlet of false hair fell over her shoulder. Her dark eyes were bright and accusing, and everything about her heralded a confrontation.

Dominic nodded at the footman. "That will be all," he said quietly.

The man began to withdraw relievedly, although not quickly enough for Georgiana, who almost pushed him out and closed the door behind him. Then she turned to face Dominic. "Where did you go last night?" she demanded.

"Go?"

"You left the ball immediately after that odd 'ghost' business." Her glance moved over him, lingering slightly below his waist, because his dressing gown did not cover him quite as completely as he thought. A little extra color flushed into her cheeks, and she straightened from the door. "Well? Where did you go?"

"I came here," he replied truthfully, hastily pulling his clothes more effectively around him.

"Why didn't you say good night to me? After all, you'd promised me another dance, and the least you could have done was—"

"Forgive me. In all the excitement, I'm afraid you slipped my mind."

It wasn't the right thing to say. Her eyes flashed. "So I ceased to be of consequence, did I?" She moved to the window, where she rested a graceful hand against the shutter and stared down toward the river far below.

"Georgiana, a great deal was happening."

"You were with *her*, weren't you?"

Dominic went to pour himself a cup of coffee. "I don't follow you," he murmured.

"Oh, yes, you do. That Peach creature!"

"Miss Peach is an acquaintance."

Georgiana turned furiously, her plumes and ribbons quivering again. "She's more than that! I saw you with her last night, Dominic. You were kissing her behind that standard. No doubt you thought yourselves well concealed, but I found you."

"Then I know there is no point in denying that I was indeed kissing the lady in question," he said, putting the coffeepot down on the tray.

"Did you bring her here?"

"Georgiana, I really have no intention of explaining anything to you."

She came toward him, halting so close that he could smell the sweetness of her perfume. "Don't I have a right to know if you're being unfaithful to me?" she asked.

"Frankly, no, although I have had the decency to inform you in writing that I now accept your choice of Hightower, and will not embarrass you further."

"I've already told you I received no letter." She met his gaze without so much as a flicker.

"No?" He didn't believe her.

She slowly untied her bonnet ribbons. "I'm deeply hurt to think you'd inform me of such an important matter in writing," she said, tossing the bonnet aside.

"It's no more than you did to me," he reminded her.

"That was different. I was overwrought, and not thinking clearly."

"You seemed composed enough to me."

"I wasn't, believe me." Suddenly she gave him a seductive smile and came close enough to put a hand against his chest where his dressing gown was parted. Her eyes were dark with desire. "Oh, Dominic, I need you to make love to me now," she breathed, bending forward to put her lips to the dark hairs on his chest.

He closed his eyes for a moment as she reawakened the sensuous tendrils of his waking dream, but then reality swept back. Blond curls and lavender eyes were what he wanted, what he needed.

Just as he was about to extricate himself from Georgiana's advances, a resounding crash rang out, and she leapt back with a squeal as the silver coffee tray somehow fell from the table. Dark coffee splashed all over the pale perfection of her butter-cream muslin gown, leaving a dark brown stain that would be very difficult indeed to remove. Georgiana was inconsolable. She burst into tears and rushed to the washstand to see what she could do to lessen the damage.

As Dominic stared down at the tray, the word "brownie" flashed into his head. He cast around for any sign of Nutmeg, or of Bodkin, but saw nothing. Yet how else could the tray have fallen?

Georgiana turned angrily from the washstand. "How could you be so clumsy, Dominic!" she cried.

"I didn't do anything," he protested.

"You must have!" Her expression was furious.

"Georgiana, I've already told you that I didn't do anything," he replied patiently. Oh, how many times had he seen her in a temper like this? Too many to mention. He began to wonder what he had ever seen in her.

She correctly interpreted the expression in his eyes. "If you didn't want to make love to me, you only had to say so. There was no need to do that with the tray."

He didn't reply, for there was no point.

"It's that Peach creature, isn't it? Is *she* the wife you've decided on? She and her inheritance, that is."

Dominic met her eyes. "I have no need to seek a fortune, Georgiana, for I have more than enough of my own. As to whether Miss Peach is the bride I am about to seek, it really has nothing to do with you anymore."

"But you do want her?" Georgiana pressed.

"If I do, she is the one I will inform, not you, and I will do so when I meet her at Sydney Gardens at noon. Now, I will send a footman to the White Hart so that your maid can bring you another gown, and as soon as you've changed, I wish you to leave."

But as he went to the door to call for a footman, he heard her whisper, "It isn't over yet, Dominic, not by a long shot."

Chapter 34

It was half past eleven, and Polly was in the hotel writing room, finishing her short letter to Lord Benjamin. The room was at the rear of the hotel, with French windows that opened onto the orchestra's balcony. She had been writing to the strains of Mozart and Handel, but as she put her quill down to read the letter, the musicians were enjoying a well-earned rest.

Sydney Hotel, October 31st, midmorning.
   Lord Benjamin.
   Now that some hours have passed since events at the ball, I feel I may have been a little hasty in my judgment. I was very upset, as you know, and said things I wish now had been left unsaid. It would make me feel a great deal better if you could overlook my conduct, as indeed I shall overlook yours, so that perhaps we can attempt to be agreeable toward each other. I have already conveyed my feelings regarding this to my uncle, who will no doubt confirm that contrary to what I have said thus

far, I have not entirely discounted your proposal. Tonight I will attend the Halloween festivities in Sydney Gardens, at which I trust to speak civilly with you again. I sincerely hope to see on your countenance a kindness that will obliterate all past unpleasantness.

> I am, sir, yours in all sincerity,
> Polly Peach

She drew a long breath. Under the circumstances of their last parting, had she been too conciliatory?

A maid came up to her. "Begging your pardon, Miss Peach, but Lady Georgiana Mersenrie has called and wishes to speak with you."

"Lady Georgiana?" Polly repeated, thinking she'd misheard.

"Yes, madam."

"One moment." Polly quickly addressed and folded the letter, then held sealing wax to the lighted candle on the desk. After applying her seal, she handed the letter to the maid with some coins. "Please see that a running footman takes this without delay, then show Lady Georgiana in to me."

"Very well, madam."

The maid hurried away, and Polly got up from the desk to go out onto the balcony, feeling somehow that she wanted to face the *chienne* in sunlight. The musicians were lounging casually on their seats, drinking tea and talking among themselves, and in the gardens the workmen by the bonfire and fireworks stands were laughing together. There was rhythmic chanting as other workmen hauled on ropes to erect the purple-and-gold royal pavilion Polly had seen on Claverton Down. Soon a red carpet would be laid to it from the broad walk, so the Duke and Duchess of York would not have to step upon the possibly damp grass of an autumn night.

The rear entrance to the hotel was directly below the balcony, and maids carried out covered trays to tables beneath the trees. Pairs of waiters brought large silver bowls of punch, some alcoholic, some not, while footmen took benches and folding chairs to strategic points in the gardens, for those of a less energetic disposition. Halfway between the hotel and the bonfire site, a shallow pit had been dug so that a whole pig could be roasted on a spit, and the jack-o'-lanterns had now been unloaded from the wagon for two boys to gradually disperse them to their places in the trees and bushes. Jingling bells announced the arrival of the hobbyhorse and morris dancers that were traditional on Halloween, although these particular ones hardly resembled those to be found in country villages. The *beau monde* did not appreciate truly rustic things, so the morris dancers were clad in cloth-of-gold and boasted more ribbons and feathers than Miss Pennyfeather's entire stock. The hobbyhorse was so sumptuous it might have entertained the Sun King at Versailles. A poor farm laborer would not have recognized them!

Apart from all this, the usual business of the Vauxhall was also in progress. People strolled on the walks, laughter issued from the labyrinth, and horsemen and women exercised their mounts on the rides. A breeze stirred, and some autumn leaves fell, shining like polished brass and cooper in the bright sunlight. Polly caught one as it drifted past.

"Is that how easy you think it is to capture what you want, Miss Peach?" inquired Georgiana's voice from just inside the writing room.

Polly turned. "You wish to see me, Lady Georgiana?" she inquired coolly.

"Yes, Miss Peach, I certainly do." Georgiana's dark eyes glittered as she stepped into the sunlight. She still wore her cerise pelisse and leghorn bonnet, but the spoiled butter-cream muslin gown had now been replaced by one of the softest ice-green silk. "It grieves me to have to speak with you on such a delicate subject, but I fear there is no alternative."

"What delicate subject might that be?" Polly inquired, but knew it could only be Dominic. She braced herself for whatever was about to come.

"Why, Dominic, of course. Strange to say, I wish to spare you the humiliation that undoubtedly awaits if you keep your assignation with him."

Polly drew back uneasily. How did Georgiana know about that? The answer followed swiftly, for it could only be because Dominic himself had told her. Polly's self-confidence faltered, then retreated as caution swept back too late from the winds. Compared with Georgiana's glorious raven beauty, what chance had Polly Peach's pale prettiness ever had? *Oh, fool, fool!*

Georgiana smiled. "You can hardly be surprised that I know, Miss Peach, for he was bound to tell me."

"Bound to?"

"Of course, for he has proposed, and I have accepted. He came to me before dawn today and spent several very passionate hours in my arms. At your, er, assignation, he intends to tell you quite bluntly that he has been leading you on. My advice is to stay inside and save your dignity."

Polly's heart plunged. "I don't believe you."

"Why would I lie? Why would I come here to warn you?"

"For spite?" Polly suggested.

Georgiana gave a light laugh. "Well, I suppose you would think that, wouldn't you? However, I have proof that he is mine, although I trust you will forgive me if I don't reveal the full contents of what is a very tender and loving letter." She took a folded sheet of paper from her reticule and held it up so that Polly could read the top portion. *October 30th, 1800. Royal Crescent. My dearest Georgiana . . .*

His dearest Georgiana? A lump constricted Polly's throat, for the letter had been written only yesterday. A snatch of words from the ball rang through her consciousness again. Her own voice speaking to Dominic, *"I was wondering about your feelings for Lady Georgiana."* His reply, *"What feelings?"* He had avoided a direct answer, and she, poor idiot, had let her emotions run free.

Georgiana came to stand beside her, resting cool gloved hands on the balcony rail. "Spite is not my motive, Miss Peach. I am genuinely concerned, and have no wish to grind you with my heel."

"Lady Georgiana, given your attitude hitherto, I find your apparent magnanimity now impossible to believe." Polly's emotions were spinning. After all last night's kisses, Dominic had so far dismissed Polly Peach from his mind as to invite the greatest cat in England to be his bride? More, he intended to humiliate her when she kept their assignation?

Georgiana smiled again. "If you will not believe what I say, or the loving evidence of his letter, at least you must accept that I could only know about your noon assignation if he told me."

Polly didn't respond. Her heart was thudding so wretchedly that she was sure the other would hear, and she had to place her hands very firmly on the rail in order to hide their trembling.

Georgiana went on. "He found you amusing, my dear, that's all. You were nothing more or less than a passing conquest. That's the way of it, I fear, green young creatures like you so often fall prey to a talented seducer."

"He didn't seduce me!" Polly cried, then turned away in embarrassment as the musicians nearby all turned to stare.

"No? He says he did. He says it happened last night, after you left the ball together."

"It's not true," Polly whispered.

"Possibly, but the fact is that he *says* that's what happened. Men will boast of their conquests—imagined or otherwise—will they not? And I fear that we women pay with our reputations. So you see, if you keep that appointment with him, you will feel very foolish indeed."

"Dominic wouldn't say such things of me," Polly said in a choked voice.

Georgiana straightened. "You think not? Well, go out there at noon and find out. Take this visit of mine as the friendly gesture it is, Miss Peach, and be advised to stay inside. He's mine, and the truth is now sealed with a betrothal." She removed her glove to reveal a dazzling diamond ring on the fourth finger of her left hand. "It was his mother's," she murmured, turning her hand so the jewels caught the sunlight.

"What of the Marquess of Hightower? Were you toying with him as Sir Dominic would seem to have with me?" Polly asked, struggling not to show how devastated she was.

"No, I wasn't toying with him. Indeed I had every intention of marrying him, but true and passionate love outranks everything, my dear, even one of the grandest titles in the land." Georgiana slipped her hand back into her glove. "Ah, well, my good deed is done, and whether or not you pay heed to my advice is up to you. Good-bye, Miss Peach, for I doubt we will meet again." With that she swept from the balcony.

Cruel heartbreak grasped Polly, and she closed her eyes as tears began to well down her cheeks.

Meanwhile, as his niece's happiness crumbled into misery, Hordwell sat in the library at Royal Crescent. He was trying to read the daily paper as he waited for Lord Benjamin to arise, that gentleman having been brought home from the ball in such a drunken stupor that four footmen were needed to carry him to his bed. Hordwell was anxious to start searching for Nutmeg's belt, and so was far too agitated to concentrate on the newspaper. He didn't know Bodkin and Ragwort were in the room with him. They were seated on the pelmet, and would have indulged in much mischief at his expense, had not Ragwort been still so much the worse for wear that all he could do was sit with his aching head in his hands. Never again would he touch alcohol! Never! And as if a headache and churning stomach were not bad enough, he knew he'd cooked his goose with Caraway. Oh, why had he drunk so much?

The wretched brownie closed his eyes as he thought of all the things he'd done. Not that he remembered anything; his mind was a blank from the moment he'd spoken to Caraway. Bodkin told him he'd swung from the ballroom chandeliers, breaking one of them, and that Caraway had been so disgusted with him that she'd walked off in a huff. He felt unutterably awful!

At last Lord Benjamin came downstairs. He, too, was suffering the aftereffects of the night before, having had far too much cherry brandy. Wearing a gray-and-gold embroidered dressing gown and a tasseled cap, he came gingerly into the library, intent upon some hair of the dog. "I'm surprised you're still here, Hordwell," he grunted, pouring himself a hefty measure of cognac.

"Still here?" Hordwell replied brightly. "Why, of course, my friend. Why should I not be?"

"Because of my trials at the uncaring hands of your niece." Lord Benjamin flung himself on the sofa. "God, I feel ill."

"Then drink up and you will soon be a little better," Hordwell advised, smiling in a way he hoped was disguising the blistering rage he felt toward his host. Lord Benjamin sipped the cognac, then looked across at him. "I'm told she's gone to the Sydney Hotel. Is this so?"

"Yes. I've already been to see her."

"Then you'll know my supposed crimes. None of what she says is true, you know."

"I'm sure it isn't."

Bodkin glowered at his former master. How like the miserly old curmudgeon to dismiss Polly's word and believe Lord B instead.

Lord Benjamin sat up suspiciously. "What's going on, Hordwell? Why are you being so amiable?"

"Because Polly has explained everything. Oh, I did indeed think the worst of you at first—it was natural that I should—but after I visited her this morning, and we spoke a while, I am sure it can all be resolved."

"Resolved?"

"The match, dear sir, the match." Hordwell eyed the pockets of Lord Benjamin's dressing gown, wondering if either of them contained Nutmeg's belt.

Bodkin watched him curiously. What was the old skinflint up to?

Lord Benjamin gave a mirthless chuckle. "The match? Hordwell, she won't even hear of such a thing. You know it, and I now know it, too, so pray do not insult my intelligence by pretending otherwise."

"Polly's mind isn't finally made up on the matter. She feels she may have acted a little precipitately last night, and now wishes to be reconciled with you."

Lord Benjamin stared at him. "Eh?"

"Perhaps it would be more accurate to say she wishes to start again. You see, I believe she has reconsidered the advantages of becoming Lady Beddem."

"Maybe I don't want her anymore," Lord Benjamin replied churlishly and emptied his glass.

"I concede that Polly herself may not be to your liking, but what of her fortune?" Hordwell ventured.

Lord Benjamin got up to replenish his drink, then looked at the other again. "I say, Hordwell, if she *is* coming around . . ." he murmured, stroking his chin, which had yet to be shaved.

"Oh, she is, I'm sure of it. In fact, she intends to send you a note of some sort, by way of an olive branch. She trusts to see us at Sydney Gardens tonight, and I think you may be sure of a gracious and encouraging reception." Hordwell got up painfully from his chair and grasped his walking sticks. "Dear heaven, I think the cure has made me worse, not better," he muttered, then smiled at the other. "My dear sir, you know what women are, their minds are in all directions at once, but then, they are the weaker sex." Determined to glance inside Lord Benjamin's dressing gown pockets as he passed, he made his way uncomfortably toward the door.

"The weaker sex? That's true," Lord Benjamin replied, not noticing the surreptitious inspection.

Hordwell paused at the door. The pockets appeared to be empty, apart from a handkerchief. Did that mean the belt was up in the bedroom? If Lord Benjamin was about to have breakfast, maybe there would be a chance to look.

From high on the pelmet, Bodkin continued to watch him. The brownie's curiosity was now truly stirred, because he had observed the old man's interest in his host's attire. Why on earth would Hordwell be interested in Lord Benjamin's pockets?

Hordwell cleared his throat. "I say, are you about to have breakfast?"

"Eh? Why do you ask?" Lord Benjamin looked inquiringly at him.

"Oh, just idle curiosity."

Lord Benjamin grinned. "Hordwell, old friend, your news about Polly has made me feel so much better that breakfast is the last thing on my mind. I think I will dress and go for a stroll. But first I'll have another glass."

Plague take the fellow, Hordwell thought, for the belt was bound to go out on the walk as well. But he said, "Oh, how excellent. Well, I think I'll go and sit in the garden." Then he hobbled out.

Bodkin had already clambered down the curtains and slipped from the room with him. The brownie was astonished to hear Hordwell muttering under his breath. "Curse the villain for deciding on a walk!" He then made his slow way along the passage toward the door to the gardens, and Bodkin followed, determined to find out what was going on.

In the library, Lord Benjamin waited until he heard the garden door close, then he rang for a footman. The sound of a bell aroused Ragwort briefly from his sufferings. The brownie looked blearily around, wincing as his poor head thumped relentlessly.

A footman came quickly. "My lord?"

"I want you to go to the White Hart and secure one of their fastest post chaises for an hour after nightfall. It is to wait by the canal at Bathampton. Is that clear?"

"By the canal at Bathampton, an hour after nightfall. Yes, my lord."

"And tell them I wish refreshments to be provided in the vehicle, for I intend to make a long journey."

The footman bowed and withdrew. Lord Benjamin then raised his glass. "Why wait upon a woman's caprices, eh?" he murmured, and drained the glass in one gulp.

Ragwort's wits weren't sufficiently about him for the significance of what he'd just heard to make sense. He longed for sleep to make his headache go away, so he shuffled into a more comfortable position on the pelmet, lay on his side, and put his hands beneath his head.

Chapter 35

It was an hour before sunset, and Polly was still in her room with the curtains drawn. She had been there ever since Georgiana's departure, and at first had wept heartbroken tears into her pillow. Just after noon, a maid had come to the door to tell her Sir Dominic Fortune had called, but Polly had declined to see him. He'd sent the maid back twice, but in the end had gone away. After a while Polly's tears subsided, and now she lay gazing at the leafy shadows moving against the curtains, but the dappled light reminded her of the diamonds in Georgiana's betrothal ring. She felt so terrible that she no longer knew if she could even attend the Halloween celebrations, let alone carry out the plan regarding Lord Benjamin. She didn't want to face anyone right now, not even her uncle. She certainly didn't want to encounter Dominic or Georgiana—that would be too much.

She got up and went to the washstand to dab cold water on her face. Through a crack in the curtains she saw that the sunlight was now rich and golden, tinged with the first hint of crimson, signifying the gradual closing of the short October afternoon. There was about an hour of daylight left. Perhaps a little fresh air would restore some of her courage, she thought, and went to the wardrobe to take out her cream silk gown, gray velvet spencer, and the pink straw hat that providentially had a little net veil to hide her tearstained face. When she was ready, she picked up the pink pagoda parasol, intending to raise it the moment she was in the gardens. If held at a calculated angle, it would provide another shield from curious glances.

She emerged from the hotel and set off up the broad walk toward the classical temple at the top of the gardens. The orchestra was rehearsing a final time, repeating a portion of Handel's "Royal Fireworks Music" until the lead violinist was satisfied. Shadows were very long now, and autumn leaves rustled beneath her shoes. A group of gentlemen laughed together as they played bowls on one of the greens, and she could hear the thud of hooves on the rides. The royal pavilion was fully erected and ready, its golden tassels shining in the slanting sunlight. The bonfire was complete, too, but there was still occasional hammering from the complicated fireworks scaffolding. The display was clearly going to be splendid, Polly thought, watching as a man held a lighted taper to a rocket in order to check that it went off at the correct moment and angle.

But as the rocket soared skyward, then exploded with brilliant lights against the copper and crimson of the sinking sun, it wasn't a firework that Polly heard and saw. Instead, the noise became the cannon reports at the review, and the lights were Dominic's smile as he accepted her offer of a lift in her carriage. Fresh tears pricked her eyes, and to quell them, she hastened on, trying to push all images of Dominic from her mind.

As Polly dressed for her walk, Bodkin had been hurrying along Great Pulteney Street. He was accompanied by his bees, which flew above the chimneys so as not to attract any attention. He'd given up trying to ascertain what Hordwell was up to, and since there was still no sense to be gotten out of Ragwort, the brownie was going about his private plans. Reaching the hotel, he hurried through to the gardens just ahead of Polly, who could not see him. He led his insect friends to the tallest tree, a beech that stood almost in the center, and as they swarmed busily against one of the topmost branches, the brownie grinned to himself. "That's my proud beauties," he murmured approvingly, then turned to retrace his steps to the hotel, intending to visit Polly for a while. Almost immediately he saw her familiar pink parasol bobbing up the broad walk toward him. He was about to greet her when he saw how upset she was. Wondering what was wrong, the brownie allowed her to walk past him without making himself heard or seen. Last night she had been so happy, and when Dominic had kissed her good night at the hotel, her joy had been palpable. Now she was crying. Why? he wondered.

Unaware of Bodkin's presence, Polly tried to focus her attention upon anything and everything except Dominic. She saw preparations for some of the traditional Halloween games that were played by only children and young men, ladies seldom deigning to stoop to the undignified exuberance required for such pastimes. The games included ducking apples and candle circles, and divining hazelnuts that sometimes exploded very dangerously. There was also the equally hazardous sport of revolving rods, which had an apple at one end and a lighted candle at the other. The object was for a circle of players to jump up and catch the apple in their teeth without becoming splashed or burned by the candle. Many a nasty injury was acquired this way, but that did not seem to lessen the popularity of the game.

At another game, that of plunging one's head into a half barrel of water, in order to pick up with one's teeth the prizes at the bottom, two street urchins hung around looking decidedly furtive. Suddenly they both dove their arms into the barrel, snatched prizes, then ran for all they were worth. The splash of the water in the barrels again brought back a memory for Polly, that of a rain-swept night, and Dominic's strong arms as he lifted her from the water butt. Her lips quivered, and more tears sprang to her eyes, so again she hurried on, Bodkin watching with increasing dismay.

The music from the hotel balcony had faded now, and music of a different sort drifted across the gardens. The morris dancers were rehearsing in a grove opposite the temple, and Bodkin watched as Polly observed them for a while. He could see how deliberately she had lowered her veil, and how quickly she adjusted her parasol if anyone came near. He hated to see her this unhappy, but couldn't think how best to approach her. Sympathy often made tears worse, as he himself knew only too well when she had comforted him about Nutmeg, so he bided his time, hoping an obvious moment would present itself.

Together yet apart, Polly and the brownie continued to watch the dancers, whose bells jingled and ribbons and feathers fluttered as they twisted and turned to their age-old dance. The gold of their costumes was quite dazzling, as was the magnificent hobbyhorse, which made splendid equine noises as it cavorted around. Tears fell on Polly's cheeks, for instead of morris music, she heard the ball at the Assembly Rooms, and felt Dominic's lips upon hers behind the ferns and standard.

She turned quickly away and walked around the temple to look at the labyrinth. Because a maze was bound to be popular on such a night, it, too, had received attention. She knew from a hotel maid that the entrance had become a ghostly place where hidden men would wail and rattle chains, and that further in it was swathed with fine white muslin to look like the webs of huge spiders. The spiders themselves were fixed in such a way that they would swing down into people's faces should the muslin be touched. More men in flowing robes were to be stationed at various points, ready to jump out with horrible moaning sounds when anyone drew near. Jack-o'-lanterns with green candles inside them were placed everywhere, and in the very center—if anyone proved stout enough to get that far—there was a coffin from which a terrible fiend would rise like an ancient Egyptian mummy come to life. But as Polly stood outside, looking at the tall clipped hedges, all she could think of was how Dominic had kissed her in their depths.

She was crying now, and dabbed her cheeks with her handkerchief as she hurried on up the slope toward the bridges and canal cut, where there were fewer people. Surely there couldn't be anything here that would make her think of him! She reached the first bridge and stood at the top of the arch to watch the water below. Many of the little pleasure boats were in use, and they, too, had been made ready for the night ahead. Jack-o'-lanterns sat on poles at their sterns, black wooden witches on broomsticks at their prows, and muslin had been draped over their canopies to completely enclose those inside. More lanterns had been suspended from the bridge, and in a very short while now their reflections would shimmer in the dark shining water.

Bodkin drew near and sat on the top of the retaining wall, still watching her. How could someone who had been so happy and buoyant the night before, be in such disarray now? Something made him glance around, and he saw none other than Dominic walking purposefully toward the bridge. "Now we'll see what's what," the brownie muttered, plucking a blade of grass and twirling it attentively. Polly was too deep in thought to be aware of anything. She had managed to contain her tears a little, and now turned her parasol unhappily.

"Well, you've run me a merry dance today, and no mistake," Dominic said softly to her.

Chapter 36

Polly whirled about to see Dominic standing on the bridge behind her. He was dressed in a charcoal coat and cream breeches, with a green silk waistcoat, and an emerald pin glittered in the folds of his neckcloth. A silver-topped cane swung in his gloved hands, and as he had removed his top hat, the breeze riffled his dark hair. His eyes were quizzical as he awaited her response.

"A . . . a merry dance?" she repeated, unable to think of anything else to say.

He was too close for either the veil or the parasol to conceal the marks of her tears, and he looked at her with swift concern. "Polly? What's wrong? What's happened? Is it Beddem?"

She drew back. "No, I haven't seen him. I . . . I've sent the agreed note, though." Oh, why hadn't she stayed inside? she thought.

He came nearer. "Why have you been crying? If someone has hurt or upset you—"

"It's nothing," she interrupted, turning quickly away to look at the canal again.

"I don't believe you, Polly. We had an arrangement to meet at noon, but you didn't come, and when I called at the hotel, you refused to see me, not once, but three times. So I came back to try again and was informed that you'd been seen coming out here for a walk. I think I deserve an explanation, don't you?"

This was too much! She turned sharply to face him again. "No, sir, I don't. After what you've done, how *dare* you demand an explanation!"

"After what *I've* done? I don't understand, Polly."

"I think it best if we are a little more formal from now on, sir. First names seem singularly inappropriate, if not downright improper."

"Well, I don't agree. Damn it, Polly, this is stupid! If I'm supposed to have done something, the least you can do is tell me what it is, then maybe I can put things right!"

"You can never put this right."

He came to stand next to her and placed his top hat and cane by his feet. Then he took her gently by the arm and made her turn to face him. "I'm going to get to the bottom of this, Polly. Tell me what it's about, or so help me I'll pursue you everywhere until you do!"

"You already *know* what it is!"

"Look at me, Polly. Do I seem as if I know?"

She searched his face, still so beloved in spite of his cruelty. The sunset shone in his eyes, like the fires of passion, except that it was

Georgiana who would know his kisses from now on. "Why do you seek to humiliate me even more?" she whispered.

"*Humiliate* you? Polly, I would rather die than do that," he said softly.

"Is that why you've bragged about seducing me? And why you've asked Lady Georgiana to be your wife?" she asked.

He stared at her. "Why I've *what*? Polly, I've never bragged about seducing you, I wouldn't stoop to such a base thing! As to proposing to Georgiana, I assure you that nothing could be further from my thoughts."

"But, she called upon me and said—"

"To Hades with what she said. She's furious because she was given her *congé* this morning."

"But she's wearing your ring!"

"Three diamonds?"

"Yes."

"Her mother's."

"She . . . she said it was *your* mother's."

He shook his head. "To my knowledge, it has been in the Beddem family for two centuries. Believe me, her visit to you was an act of pure spite because I would not take her back."

"Take her back? But I thought she sent you away in favor of Lord Algernon."

"She did, but she now professes to have undergone another change of heart."

Polly was silent for a moment as she tried to keep hold of a myriad of thoughts at once. "And how fares *your* heart, Dominic?" she asked then, unable to fend off memories of his response at the ball. He'd avoided answering a direct question then, and might be doing the same again now. Had he really given Georgiana her *congé* this morning? Had Georgiana's visit really been an act of spite? What if *he* was the one being untruthful?

He raised her veil suddenly and looked deep into her eyes. "Why do you always doubt me, Polly?"

"Because you toyed with me before, in the labyrinth, and then at the Assembly Rooms. You promised to reveal the truth of your kisses at the ball. Instead, you gazed adoringly at Georgiana and bestowed upon me a glance so cold that my rejection seemed clear enough."

"A painful sense of insecurity and hesitance is not *your* sole prerogative, Polly," he interrupted gently. "I saw how warm you and

Beddem appeared to be, and I too drew the wrong conclusion. I confess to such jealousy that I admit to behaving badly. But shortly afterward, so did you with Hightower."

She colored, recalling how she'd turned her face toward Lord Algernon during the cotillion.

"How tellingly you blush."

"I . . . I concede that I was unwise with the marquess, but I only did it because I was so hurt by you. That doesn't excuse it, I know, but it is why I behaved as I did."

"So we both reacted foolishly. Polly, I thought I explained myself later on, and that you understood why I'd been so haughty . . ."

"Oh, yes, you explained, but so much that you say is ambiguous. You hide behind such a sophisticated screen that I cannot tell if you mean anything. I want to believe, oh, I admit that I do, but I think I am a fool for even entertaining warm thoughts of you. For instance, you say you gave Georgiana her *congé* this morning, yet only a day or so ago you told me how much you loved her. And yesterday you wrote her a very warm letter."

"Letter?" For a moment he was puzzled, but then his eyes cleared. "Polly, if she pretended it was a love letter, she lied, for it merely informed her that I accepted that my liaison with her was over once and for all. It was couched in friendly terms, for I saw no reason to be disagreeable, but what I really wanted to write was that I was so disenchanted with her atrocious behavior, that I could barely feel civil toward her. So there you have the very *unambiguous* explanation. The contents certainly were not what she led you to understand, and she is in the past now. I mean every word and hide behind no screen, sophisticated or otherwise."

Polly looked away, suddenly feeling so vulnerable and unsure of herself that she couldn't even meet his gaze. "But I know that a man who has had Lady Georgiana Mersenrie as his mistress is bound to regard someone like me as insignificant."

He smiled. "Insignificant? Oh, Polly, nothing could be further from the truth. Do you really think I would be so shallow as to overlook you in favor of someone like Georgiana? Your criticisms of her were all so true, and even when I was most in love with her, I was never blind to her faults. I knew all along that she was hard, selfish, cruel, and ambitious, but I was dazzled. However, the moment I met you, her failings became too apparent to ignore. Whenever I looked at her, I found myself thinking of you, and whenever I saw you, I could not stay away from you. My eyes stray constantly to you, I listen for your voice, long for your laughter and smiles. Insignificant? That is something you will never be. Do you honestly imagine I would have pressed my kisses upon you if I did not want you?"

"Do you really mean that?" she breathed, still afraid to reach out, afraid of being gulled.

"Yes, of course I do, Polly. I don't want you to misunderstand anything I'm about to say. There must be no hint of concealment, uncertainty, or deviousness. I have no hidden thoughts, no sly agenda, nor any desire to amuse myself at your expense. Look at me." He took her parasol and propped it against the balustrade of the bridge, then took her hand. "Polly, I just told you I wanted you, but it's far more than that. I love and need you, and I think you love and need me. Tell me I'm wrong, and I will walk away, never to bother you again."

She could only stare at him.

His finger slid sensuously over her lips. "I adore you, Polly Peach, and if you would consent to be my wife, I will be the happiest man alive."

"D . . . do you really mean this?" she whispered incredulously.

"I swear upon all I hold most dear. I came here to Bath to find a wife and expected to make a marriage of convenience. Instead, I've fallen in love. Say you'll be my bride, Polly."

Her heart had its way once and for all, and a foolish, rather wobbly smile lit her face. "Nothing would make me happier than to be your wife, Dominic," she breathed.

"Oh, my darling . . ." He caught her close, his lips finding hers with a hunger that played no games, extended no shadows, and hid no secrets.

As her arms slid around him, she knew he was truly hers. It was really happening; it was fact not fantasy, and she felt wonderful. Her doubts and fears soared away, rapture filled her entire being, and she became the very essence of joy.

It was a long, long moment before Dominic drew back from the kiss. His gray eyes were dark with love and desire, and he cupped her face in his hands. "I want to shout our love to everyone in the gardens," he said softly.

She smiled mistily, her vision blurred with happy tears, but then plain facts impressed themselves upon her delight. "I'd like to shout it, too, but such news would soon be all over Bath, and we have yet to undo Lord Benjamin. If our plan is to work, he has to think I'm still unattached. Unless, of course . . ."

"Unless, what?"

"Well, my uncle might find Nutmeg's belt before then, although it's a little late now, so I guess he hasn't been successful." She explained about Hordwell's defection from Lord Benjamin's camp.

"So the old miser has a heart after all?"

"I always knew he did really—it was just well hidden."

"Will a mere baronet do for his niece instead of a duke's son?"

"I'm sure so." She smiled again.

Bodkin had heard everything, and his face was creased by a silly grin. He was more pleased about Polly and Dominic than they would ever know, for he considered them to be an absolutely perfect match, two halves of the same whole. As for the news about Hordwell, well, he was pleased about that, too. For Polly's sake he was relieved that the old miser had a good side after all.

The brownie got up from his rather uncomfortable seat on the retaining wall and strolled back down through the gardens, where long dark shadows now stretched more thickly than before. But then his smile faded as he recalled what he'd learned about Georgiana. The more he heard about that lady, the more vile she became. In fact, she was almost as wicked as her brother, and tonight she would receive the same Halloween punishment he would!

Chapter 37

It was five o'clock. Darkness had fallen, and Halloween had begun. Groups of children and young people, known as guisers, thronged the streets of Bath. They were dressed in strange costumes, from ghosts and devils, to witches and animals, and knocked at doors, demanding gifts of sweets or fruit, and threatening mischief if none were forthcoming. Some fireworks glittered against the starlit sky, but the festivities in Sydney Garden were still an hour away.

Jack-o'-lanterns sat by most of the doors at Royal Crescent, and in many windows, too, their flickering faces quite eerie now daylight had gone. Guisers scurried from house to house, and Georgiana watched them from the drawing room window of Lord Benjamin's house. She was dressed as Diana the huntress, in a flowing white muslin gown, with a leopard skin fixed around her waist. She carried a quiver of arrows and a little golden bow, and her green velvet mantle was keeping warm over a chair near the fire. She had fallen back on her plan to marry Lord Algernon, and expected him to arrive for her at any moment in his carriage. She'd decided to leave for the gardens from Royal Crescent because from this window she could watch Dominic's front door. His little Peach would have none of him now. She smiled vindictively, and the jewels sprinkled in her dark hair flashed in the candlelight as she glanced down at the ring she had now returned to her right hand. It had been almost too easy to trick dear Polly. And, oh, how pleasant it had been.

Lord Benjamin spoke behind her. "You'll never get Fortune back, Sis."

She turned irritably. "And what makes you think I want him?"

"I know you, Georgiana, and I know Fortune. If he's sent you on your way, that's the end of it," he said frankly, going to pour himself a glass of cognac. He, too, was dressed for Halloween as a large red devil, complete with horns, tail, and pitchfork. The costume was stretched to the breaking point by his rather too plump figure, and whenever he bent over or sat down, the stitches looked as if they would burst.

Georgiana scowled at him. He was very good at giving out advice, but hopeless at taking it himself. If he imagined the Peach's Bank heiress was going to fall into his arms after all, he was very much mistaken. "Brother mine, if home truths are the order of the evening, I think it is time to acquaint you with a few," she said, going to him and taking his filled glass for herself.

He scowled, and then turned to pour himself another. "And what, pray, do you imagine I need to be told?"

"That your heiress prize is the object of Dominic's affection, and he of hers."

"Maybe, but she is still prepared to consider marriage to me."

"You think so?"

"I have Horditall's word for it."

"And you have *my* word that she's only interested in Dominic.

I've seen it in her eyes." Georgiana swirled her glass and savored the bouquet. "You're right about me, though, I do still want him. It's rather quaint, is it not? You want the Peach's Bank fortune, and I want Dominic."

"I will have the fortune, my dear," he replied, returning to his chair and easing himself carefully into it. "Actually, I intend to enjoy two fortunes, although the second one will take a little longer. Dear Polly's coffers will drive the duns away and make me very comfortable in the meantime."

Georgiana's attention was on his costume. "Are you sure that outfit is up to the strain? If a seam should go—"

"It fits perfectly well."

She shrugged. "Well, for heaven's sake stay away from the bonfire, or you'll melt in the heat."

"I intend to stay away. Curse the world, I'm hot enough now." He ran a finger around the high, tight throat of the costume.

Georgiana's gaze rested intently on his face, and abruptly she changed the subject. "What is this second fortune you mentioned a while ago?" she asked.

"Nothing that I intend to speak of just yet."

Her curiosity was kindled. "Oh, tell me, Benjie," she pleaded.

"No. All I intend to say is that it involves something a little, er, supernatural."

"Something nonexistent, more like," she replied flatly.

"Oh, it's very real, I promise you," he replied. "You'll see soon enough. In fact, the whole world will soon see."

"What are you talking about?"

"All in good time."

Losing interest, she looked outside again. The guisers had almost reached the far end of the crescent now and would soon move on. Someone had clearly refused to heed their demands, for a small group had removed a portion of railing and were carrying it across the common. They took it halfway down the slope, hid it among some bushes, then ran laughing back to the road to make their way to Marlborough Buildings.

Lord Benjamin looked at her. "I said I will have the Peach's Bank fortune, and I will. It's all in hand."

She turned. "What are you up to?"

"That old fool Horditall has assured me she'll be all agreeability at the gardens tonight, and—"

"I cannot see that she'll do any such thing. Benjie. She's head over heels in love with Dominic."

"Horditall said—"

"But is he being truthful?"

"Why wouldn't he be?"

"I don't know, but I certainly wouldn't trust him. Miserly and grasping he may be, but deep down he loves his niece. Don't place too much faith in him, that's my advice. Anyway, what were you saying about her agreeability?"

Benjamin was distracted by her warnings about Hordwell and had to collect himself. "Eh? Oh, yes. Well, I mean to make full use of the darkness to bundle her—tied and gagged—into one of those pleasure boats on the canal. I'll row her to Bathampton, where a carriage will be waiting. Then I'll carry her off to Gretna Green and force her into marriage."

Georgiana's lips parted in astonishment. "You're not serious!"

"Oh, I am. Perfectly." He smiled. "It cannot fail, especially if you help me."

"Me? How?"

"By keeping Fortune occupied. If he is interested in her, he's bound to stay close tonight, and that won't suit me. I don't care if he's ended it with you. I want you to be at your most adorable, fetching, and bewitching. Just keep him busy, whether or not he wants it."

"I don't think Dominic will take any notice of me." It galled Georgiana to admit it, but she saw no point in pretending otherwise to her brother.

"Listen, Sis, you want her out of Fortune's way, don't you?"

"Yes."

"Then help me."

After a moment, Georgiana nodded. "All right, but only provided you tell me about this second fortune."

He pursed his lips reluctantly. "You probably won't believe me even if I tell you."

"Tell me, and we'll see."

He undid a few buttons on the breast of his costume and reached inside. When he drew his hand out, it seemed empty, and Georgiana raised an eyebrow. "Is this a game of imagination?"

"Come here and put your hand on mine," he invited, and she obeyed. Her fingers touched something that wasn't there, and with a gasp she snatched her hand away.

He chuckled. "Oh, it's there, all right, Sis."

"What . . . what is it?"

"A brownie's belt."

"A *what*?" She knew nothing about browniedom.

"A brownie's belt." He told her about Nutmeg and the page of Nostradamus.

Georgiana stared at him. "You mean, you really think you can make this brownie visible?"

"I'm sure of it. Nostradamus was infallible. I expect the page any day now, because I borrowed the last payment from Hordwell. It was forwarded about two weeks ago."

"If you make money out of this, I want a share," she said suddenly.

He shook his head. "Oh, no, Sis, it's going to be mine, and mine alone."

"I won't help you tonight," she threatened.

He laughed. "Oh, I think you will. You want Polly Peach to be out of sight and out of mind."

She colored angrily and turned away.

Lord Benjamin watched her as he pushed the belt back inside his costume. "Tell me something, Georgiana. Why in God's name do you suddenly want Fortune so much? I thought you were admirably sensible when you tossed him aside in order to pursue Hightower. Now you want to undo all your careful work? Why? Hightower is in the palm of your hand, and he'll make a duchess of you."

"Algie is a fool, and I will never love him as I do Dominic."

"Then have them both. Marry Hightower and take Fortune to your bed."

"I know now that I want Dominic as my husband as well as my lover," she said softly.

Lord Benjamin shrugged. "As you like." He glanced at the clock on the mantelpiece. "What's keeping Hordwell? He should have been down here about ten minutes ago."

"He's probably gone to the library. That's where he's usually to be found, isn't it?"

"Yes, he's part of the damned furniture."

At that moment a carriage drew up outside. It was the marquess, and a few moments later he was shown up to them. Georgiana thought the footman's face looked a little odd, as if he was finding it hard not to laugh, and when Lord Algernon entered, she saw the reason why. The future Duke of Grandcastle was also garbed as a red devil—a very tall, skinny one, indeed the very opposite to bulging Lord Benjamin.

The devils stared at each other in dismay, then the marquess gave a scornful snort. "Dear me, Beddem, you look a very tight squeeze."

Lord Benjamin was annoyed. "I suppose you think *you* look excellent?"

"As a matter of fact, I do."

"I'm sorry to disappoint you, but you put me in mind of a scarlet beanpole."

Lord Algernon stiffened angrily, and Georgiana stepped hastily up to him. "Ignore him, Algie, and help me with my mantle," she said.

He hastened to comply, and shortly afterward escorted her down to the waiting carriage. As they drove off, the other carriage arrived to convey Hordwell and Lord Benjamin to the gardens. On finding the library empty, Lord Benjamin became curious. Georgiana's warnings about the old man rang loudly in his ears, and he decided to go upstairs to see what was going on. He found Hordwell's room empty, and was just becoming truly suspicious when he heard soft sounds coming from his own room. His eyes became cold as he moved softly toward the door to press his ear to it. Sure enough, the sounds were coming from within. He flung the door open and caught Hordwell in the act of hastily closing a drawer.

"What's the meaning of this?" Lord Benjamin demanded, stepping inside and closing the door.

Hordwell stared at him in dismay. "I . . . I . . ." There was nothing he could say, for it was clear that he'd been going through his host's things. His dismay was on another account, too, for the devil costume ruined the plan.

Lord Benjamin's foot tapped. "Well? I'm awaiting your explanation."

"I have none," Hordwell confessed, sitting resignedly on the edge of the bed.

"What are you looking for?" Lord Benjamin studied him carefully, and the truth suddenly dawned. "It's the belt, isn't it?" he breathed, remembering how Polly had accused him.

Hordwell said nothing, but Lord Benjamin knew he was right. Quickly, he went to a wardrobe and divested his dressing gown of its belt, then wrenched open the drawer where he kept his hand-

kerchiefs. Before Hordwell realized what was happening, a monogrammed cambric square had been forced into his mouth, and his
hands were being tied behind his back. He struggled futilely, but
Lord Benjamin got another cord to tie his ankles together. Then
Hordwell was bundled fully onto the bed, where he lay looking
fearfully up at his former friend.

Lord Benjamin drew out Nutmeg's invisible belt and shook it.
"You were wasting your time, for I always keep it with me. It
wouldn't do to lose it now I'm so close. Soon I'll be making a veritable mint out of that brownie, just as I will out of your niece." He
gave an unpleasant laugh.

Hordwell wriggled and tried to call out, but could only make
muffled noises.

Lord Benjamin smiled and went around the bed, drawing all the
curtains. Before he pulled the last one, he looked down at his prisoner. "Don't waste your strength trying to attract attention, for I
will tell the servants that on no account are they to enter my room
until the morning. By then it will be too late, for I will be well on
my way with Polly." Hordwell's eyes widened, and he strove to
say something, but Lord Benjamin smiled all the more. "Good
night, Hordwell, you may as well try to sleep. *Au revoir.*"

Drawing the last curtain across, Lord Benjamin left the room
and closed the door firmly behind him. As he went downstairs, he
issued the necessary orders about his room to the footman who
opened the front door for him. A moment later his carriage drew
away from the curb, en route for Sydney Gardens.

Chapter 38

Darkness had fallen, and the Royal Crescent brownies had gathered in the mews, waiting for Giles to bring the borrowed
pony cart that would convey them to Sydney Gardens. They stood
excitedly in the faint pool of light cast by a turnip jack-o'-lantern
someone had placed on the wall of Dominic's garden. The Hal-

loween night exuded an air of mystery and the supernatural, and some of the brownies giggled nervously, while others glanced uneasily skyward, knowing there really were witches and other horrid entities that would harm even brownies.

Ragwort had just joined Bodkin in the hayloft in the nearby mews. He had fully recovered from the previous night's overindulgence, and was in fine spirits again, even managing to be philosophical about Caraway. Then Bodkin revealed the pumpkin jack-o'-lantern. "There, Ragwort, what do you think of *that*, eh?"

Ragwort gave a startled squeak and backed fearfully toward the ladder that led down to the stable below. "What is it? Does it bite?" he cried, his eyes as round as saucers.

Bodkin caught him before he fell off the edge of the loft. "Don't be silly, of course it doesn't bite, it just looks as if it can. You won't come to any harm. It's just a jack-o'-lantern," he said reassuringly, pulling his friend near again. "Well? What do you think?" he asked again.

Ragwort swallowed. "*Just* a jack-o'-lantern?"

Bodkin preened a little. "Well, perhaps that doesn't do it justice. It's *the* jack-o'-lantern, the finest that ever was! And it's mine!"

Ragwort recovered a little. "It . . . it's certainly the biggest one I've ever seen. What have you made it from?" he asked, touching it with cautious fingertips.

"A pumpkin, all the way from America," Bodkin declared proudly, taking a handkerchief to lovingly polish his handiwork.

"A pumpkin, eh? I've heard of them, but this is the first I've seen. I say, it really is *splendid*, isn't it? You're going to cause a real stir, Bodkin."

Bodkin beamed as he got the stout cord ready to tie the jack-o'-lantern on the pole so he could carry it over his shoulder. "I'm going to chase Lord Benjamin with it, and his horrible sister, of course," he muttered.

"Lord Benjamin's sister? Why?"

Bodkin explained what he'd learned by the canal bridge, then concluded, "Hordwell is on our side now, but Lady Georgiana made Miss Polly very unhappy for a while, and must be punished."

Ragwort nodded his agreement. "And quite right, too. Still, at least Miss Polly's happy again now, eh? Soon she'll be Lady Fortune!"

Bodkin nodded and sighed. "If only I was that happy. And you," he added.

"We'll find Nutmeg, I'm sure of it," Ragwort said soothingly, then sighed. "As for me, well, maybe Caraway and I aren't meant for each other."

"I think you are."

"If we are, I have no one to blame but myself for the present situation. I was stupid last night and cannot blame her for not speaking. If it weren't for the punch bowl, maybe I'd have her on my arm tonight."

Bodkin's eye suddenly brightened with determination. "We're both going to win our sweethearts back!" he said vehemently. "Come on, help me get the pumpkin down the ladder. We'd better join the others, or we might get left behind, and I don't really want to carry my jack-o'-lantern all the way to Sydney Gardens. You throw it down, and I'll catch it, but please be careful, because it's not as strong now I've hollowed it out." He dropped the pole over the edge, then climbed down the ladder.

Ragwort grunted as he picked up the heavy pumpkin. He grunted again as he heaved it down to his friend waiting below.

Bodkin's knees buckled as he caught it, and he was glad to put it down on the straw-littered cobbles, then fixed it firmly to the pole. "Oh, I'm really looking forward to chasing foul Lord Benjamin with this. After Miss Polly has tricked him into taking off his coat, of course."

"His coat?"

"I haven't really spoken to you since last night, have I? Well, we think he always keeps Nutmeg's belt on his person, so tonight Miss Polly is going to ask him to join the dance around the bonfire. He'll have to take his coat off in the heat, then his pockets can be searched." Bodkin heaved the pumpkin and pole over his shoulder.

Ragwort exhaled slowly. "There's just one small problem."

"Problem?"

"Lord Benjamin isn't wearing a coat—he has a devil costume. It's all in one piece, very tight, and doesn't have any pockets. He can't possibly take it off to dance, and the only way he can conceal something like Nutmeg's belt is by tucking it right inside. Bodkin, my friend, you'll have to think of something else."

Dismayed, Bodkin put his load down again. "We were afraid of this. Now we'll have to abandon the plan."

"This particular plan, maybe, but there must be other ways."

"What do you suggest?"

Ragwort shrugged. "I don't know. Maybe we could frighten the wits out of him with the pumpkin, then jump on him and hold him down while he's searched! No one will see us because we're invisible!" He paused in surprise. "I say, that's not a bad idea, is it? It will be dark, and there'll be so much happening in the gardens that he'll just look as if he's fallen over."

Bodkin began to grin. "And if he doesn't have the belt on him, but has hidden it somewhere else, the threat of my bees will soon persuade him to divulge its whereabouts! I say, Ragwort, I like your idea much more than ours."

"It's settled then," Ragwort declared, pleased. "We'll tell the other brownies on the way, and as soon as we get to the gardens, we'll let Miss Polly and Sir Dominic know there's had to be a change of plan."

Bodkin nodded. "All right, but come on, we've talked too long. The pony cart will be in the lane in a minute, so let's get the pumpkin out of here." Swinging the heavy pole over his shoulder again, he led the way out of the stable.

The other brownies turned with startled gasps on seeing the enormous jack-o'-lantern for the first time. Eyes widened, and there were murmurs of mixed admiration and nervousness as they milled around to examine it. Caraway sidled up to Ragwort. "Is it yours?" she asked, forgetting she wasn't speaking to him.

"No, it's Bodkin's," he replied reluctantly. Oh, if only it *were* his, how marvelous he would appear now! Caraway's eyes moved admiringly to Bodkin, and Ragwort's jealousy stirred. "He already has a sweetheart, so don't think you can—"

Incensed, she interrupted. "I wasn't thinking I could anything, Ragwort!" With a toss of her head, she stalked away.

His lower lip jutted, and he would have sunk into his former gloom again, but for another pair of shining brown eyes. The young lady brownie from number twenty-six smiled shyly at him, and he smiled back. Maybe things weren't so bad after all, he thought.

Caraway saw the exchange, and suddenly it was her turn to be jealous. She immediately singled out her rival. "Ragwort's mine, you keep your sticky fingers *off*!" she hissed, and with an alarmed gasp, the other brownie backed away.

Giles arrived with the borrowed pony cart, and Ragwort made himself visible to his human friend. "This is very good of you, Giles," he said gratefully.

"It's nothing," the footman replied.

Bodkin and Ragwort waited while the other brownies clambered on. Then they lifted the pumpkin carefully on, hid it under a blanket and climbed aboard themselves. As they made themselves comfortable, Giles handed Ragwort Hordwell's explanatory note.

"This was waiting for me at the house. It seems Mr. Horditall is now your friend."

"Yes, we already know," said Ragwort, smiling at Bodkin.

But Bodkin didn't smile back. "I know he's one of us now, but . . ."

"But what?"

"I can't forgive him because no matter what, he still let Nutmeg be taken in the first place." Bodkin glanced back at the unlit windows of Dominic's house. "I'll come for you tonight, Nutmeg, my love," he whispered, vowing that nothing, *nothing* would be permitted to stand in his way on this most important Halloween of his long life.

Giles took up the reins. "Come on, lads, time is marching on."

They wriggled down in the cart with the others, and as the cart rattled out of the mews, anyone who merely glanced at it would have thought it empty, but if closer attention were paid, they would have heard the excited whispers and smothered laughter of brownies setting out on the most important night of their year. From down in the town there came the distant sound of cheering as the Duke and Duchess of York set out for the gardens with their entourage.

In Sydney Gardens, the spit roast had been cooking for some time, and the smell of sizzling pork hung on the cold, still air. The orchestra was playing a Mozart minuet, and the crowds had been arriving for some time. Laughter and chatter resounded, the gardens twinkled with jack-o'-lanterns, and the bonfire was ready to be lit. Polly was almost ready to leave her hotel room. Dominic had sent her a costume as promised, and she liked it very much. It consisted of a crimson velvet cloak that was embroidered all over with golden stars and crescent moons, and fastened over the left shoulder with a large brooch in the shape of a black cat. The cloak did not envelop her, but parted easily to reveal most of the cream gown she wore beneath. On her head she wore a crimson velvet witch's hat that was stitched all over with golden spangles, and she was to carry a hazel twig broomstick that was propped up in readiness against one of the chairs.

The room was candlelit, and the embroidery on her costume glinted in the gentle light. She looked at herself in the mirror. She was very nervous now the time had come. Could she carry out her part of the plan? It was going to be very difficult to be pleasant to such a toad as Lord Benjamin, but somehow she'd have to manage it. She glanced at the clock on the mantelpiece. It was a quarter to six. Dominic should arrive at any moment.

He knocked at the door. "Polly?"

"Yes?"

He came in with a flourish, so that his lime green cloth-of-gold robe swung richly. He was dressed as a sultan, with a white silk turban adorned with a jeweled aigrette, and Polly thought he looked very romantic and dashing indeed. After bestowing a very eastern bow upon her, he smiled. "And how do you like being a witch?"

"I like it very much," she replied.

"It suits you, for you have indeed bewitched me," he murmured, stepping over to pull her into his arms.

Their kiss was as fierce as if they'd been parted for days, instead of just an hour or so, and intense emotion flared through Polly like wildfire. She was a woman who was now hopelessly, helplessly in love. It was a long moment before he slowly released her, and his eyes were very dark in the candlelight as he whispered, "I adore you, Miss Peach."

"And I adore you, sir," she whispered.

They turned as the sound of cheers carried from Great Pulteney Street. The royal carriages were drawing near. As a fanfare blared, Polly and Dominic went to the window to watch. There was an expectant stir in the gardens as everyone moved toward the equestrian entrance, through which the duke and duchess's cavalcade would appear. Nearly everyone was a witch, ghost, wizard, goblin, mummy, devil, or druid, while the remainder had opted for a variety of other outfits, some of them so peculiar as to be unidentifiable.

A jingle of harness rang out as the royal carriages swept in. Loud cheering began, but there were one or two boos because the duke and duchess hadn't truly entered into the spirit of things by wearing fancy dress. The duchess looked rather tense, Polly thought, recalling some whispers she'd heard in the coffee room. It was being said that events at the Assembly Rooms had proved rather too much, and the duchess had been obliged to languish in a darkened room. Tonight was her first appearance in public since the ball.

The cheers died away as the cavalcade came to a standstill beside the royal pavilion. Polly and Dominic could only just see through the trees as the duke handed the duchess down, and then they both approached the bonfire for the ceremonial lighting. A flame flickered, then grew larger and more vigorous, until suddenly the bonfire seemed to burst into life. Renewed cheers rang out, the first rockets shot upward like glowing arrows, and the orchestra began to play the much rehearsed and labored over "Royal Fireworks Music." As the display got fully under way, the duke and duchess retreated to the comfort of their pavilion.

Dominic drew Polly away from the window and raised her hand to his lips. "Now remember, I will escort you to the bonfire, where there is plenty of light, then I will leave you. I will behave formally, so Beddem's suspicions aren't aroused. Then I will remain within sight and sound, so I can be with you again in a second if necessary." He put his hand to her cheek. "Are you sure you want to go ahead with this? If not, you only have to say . . ."

"It's only a dance." She paused. "But I wish we had something better in mind than just the hope that Lord Benjamin will take off his coat in the heat of the bonfire. It seemed an excellent notion last night, but now it seems rather feeble."

"I know, but when it comes to a new and amazingly effective plan, I'm afraid my mind is blank."

"So is mine." She gave a brave smile that masked her dreadfully churning stomach. "There's only one other thing."

"What's that?"

"I wish I knew if Uncle Hordwell has been able to tell Giles he's now on our side. If he hasn't, Bodkin may go ahead with whatever he's planning."

"I'm sure Hordwell will have managed somehow."

"Yes, I suppose so." She smiled sheepishly. "You think I'm worrying unnecessarily, don't you?"

"Just a little. After all, Hordwell's had plenty of time. Now then, let's go down." He went to extinguish the candles, then led her from the room.

Chapter 39

The fireworks were quite spectacular as they popped and sparkled to the music from the hotel balcony. Cries of delight echoed from the onlookers, whose faces glowed in the leaping light of the bonfire. Heat-blackened potatoes were already being raked from the pit beneath the sizzling roasting pig, and a small queue waited, appetites sharpened by the cold night air. Smoke drifted across the gardens, where several hundred ghostly jack-o'-lanterns flickered, and the bursts of light from the fireworks found mirrors in the fountains and cascades. The Halloween games were all well under way, to an accompaniment of uproarious laughter and shouting, and from the depths of the labyrinth came the expected shrieks and squeals. Many of those shrieks came from brownies, because the human presence was easily matched by its invisible counterpart.

The pony cart from Royal Crescent disgorged its load at the riders' entrance, and Bodkin kept well to the bushes as he carried his pumpkin to a suitably secret spot in order to light it. Accompanied by Ragwort, he crouched in the shadows of a clump of bushes, looking all around for a sign of Polly or Dominic. There was a rustling next to them, and both brownies shrank away with squeaks of alarm, but it was only Caraway. "Hello," she said.

"Caraway! You gave us quite a fright!" Ragwort said with relief.

"Can I help you?"

"There's nothing to do, except find Miss Polly and Sir Dominic as quickly as possible," Bodkin replied, returning his attention to the crowds.

"I could do that," she offered.

They glanced at each other, and then Bodkin nodded. "All right, but be quick. It's important."

She slipped away again, and Bodkin looked at Ragwort. "She's still interested in you, my friend."

"I doubt it," Ragwort replied heavily.

"Didn't you see her sending that lady brownie away—the one who had the audacity to smile at you back at the mews?"

"Did she really?"

"Most definitely." Bodkin glanced up at the sky as crimson and gold rockets exploded against the velvet darkness. "Ragwort, you look for Miss Polly and Sir Dominic as well. I have to light the jack-o'-lantern. I'll get a lighted twig from the bonfire."

Before Ragwort could reply, Bodkin scrambled away and ran across the open grass toward the bonfire. Alone with the pumpkin, Ragwort was immediately uneasy. He half expected it to give an unearthly groan or roll itself against him. "Just behave yourself, right?" he muttered, getting up to look for Polly and Dominic. As he, too, ran away from the grass, the jack-o'-lantern gazed after him, as if biding its time.

Bodkin had reached the bonfire. Where were Polly and Dominic? he wondered. And Hordwell and Lord Benjamin, come to that. The brownie scanned all the firelit faces, but didn't see any of the ones he sought. Except . . . Georgiana and Lord Algernon were among the many couples dancing a *ländler*. The marquess's face was as red as his costume, and perspiration stood out on his forehead. Even his devil's horns seemed to droop, as if wilting in the heat. Everyone was conscious of the tremendous heat, and those gentlemen whose costumes permitted it had already dispensed with their coats or jackets. Suddenly it all became too much for Lord Algernon, and he stopped dancing. Georgiana had no sympathy; indeed she was very cross and walked away, the tail of her leopard skin swinging irritably to and fro. He gazed unhappily after her, sighed, then made his way toward the refreshments to quench his thirst with several large glasses of iced lime cup.

Bodkin continued to observe Georgiana, and as he watched, she halted. Something had caught her attention on the far side of the bonfire. It was Polly, who had commenced the original plan by standing on her own, watching the bonfire. She was trying to look natural and unconcerned, but the brownie could see how nervous she was as she waited to see if Lord Benjamin would approach her in response to her note. As the *ländler* came to an end, so did the fireworks. A final rocket soared into the night sky, sprinkling golden lights against the stars, then the moments seemed to hang before the jingle of morris bells and wheezy notes of a hurdy-gurdy announced the morris dancers. Everyone clapped in time as the gaudy hobbyhorse leaped all around, and the morris men showed off their slow, skipping steps.

Georgiana walked toward Polly, and Bodkin followed, momentarily forgetting his jack-o'-lantern. Polly didn't sense her enemy's approach. The heat from the bonfire was tremendous, and the morris music so hypnotic that she gave a start as Georgiana appeared at her side. "Why, good evening, Miss Peach."

"Lady Georgiana." Polly tried to sound composed, which under the circumstances wasn't very easy.

"I'm surprised you're still here in Bath. I thought that by now you would have taken yourself back to your rustic nest."

Bodkin looked vengefully up at her. What a waspish tongue the creature had. The boggart in him was aroused, and his tail began to lash slowly but threateningly to and fro. He felt like jumping up and sinking his teeth into her fingers, which were temptingly close.

"Leave Bath? Why on earth should I do that?" Polly answered.

"We both know why, my dear," Georgiana murmured.

Polly was all wide-eyed innocence. "Oh, I suppose you're referring to Sir Dominic. Please do not concern yourself about me, for I wish you every joy and happiness."

Georgiana was taken aback. "I beg your pardon?"

"Don't be so surprised, Lady Georgiana, for I mean it. I only feel sorry for the poor marquess, who clearly worships the ground upon which you tread. His hopes must have been cruelly dashed. Actually, I'm truly glad we've had a chance to speak like this, because I wish to be your friend. After all, I now have every expectation of soon becoming your sister. Your dear brother has been most patient and understanding with me, and tonight I intend to make amends for my past stupidity."

A mask settled over Georgiana's face. "I'm sure Benjamin will be more than willing to meet you halfway, Miss Peach," she murmured, glancing across the bonfire and perceiving Dominic's gaze upon them. He'd been there for several minutes now, watching very closely. Something was going on, but what? As she looked, Dominic's hem flicked a little oddly, as if a child had tugged it. He glanced down, seemed to listen for a moment, then hurried away. Georgiana watched him disappear in the general direction of the equestrian entrance, then she gave Polly a brief smile. "If you will forgive me, I've seen someone I wish to speak to," she said, and slipped away to follow him.

Bodkin paused only to pick up a small glowing stick from the fire, then hurried after Georgiana. His tail was twirling almost to a blur, and he decided it was time for his bees to go to work on Diana the Devious, so he pursed his lips to give the warbling whistle that would summon his friends from the beech tree. He was so attuned to them that he immediately heard the first stirrings of their battle buzz. He whistled again, and the buzz intensified to something that was almost a roar, then they swooped down to him in a long column. He pointed at Georgiana. "There is your target. Teach her a lesson!" he cried, and the column set off after her. Bodkin watched with delight, his tail revolving at such a rate that once again his rear end was almost lifted from the ground. "Chase her, boys! Chase her!" he yelled.

The bees were now loud enough for everyone to hear, and people began to glance around in puzzlement. Bees? At night? Then they saw the flying phalanx, and there were screams of alarm. Georgiana heard the angry buzzing and turned to look back. Her eyes widened with horror as she saw what was coming toward her. Realizing she was their target, she gave a screech like a scalded cat and ran for the royal pavilion, which offered the only likely shelter within easy reach. Etiquette and protocol were completely forgotten as she stumbled breathlessly into the royal presence and tried to hide behind Harry Dashington. He had that very day been promoted to aide-de-camp to the duke, and was togged in his finest regimentals, but Georgiana seized his arm, spilling his glass of champagne all down his front. As he smothered a rather ungentlemanly curse, the bees swept into the tent. He staggered backward in alarm, knocking into several nearby gentlemen, who tumbled into others like dominoes. There was pandemonium as the bees zoomed around the tent, trying to catch Georgiana as she dashed from useless hiding place to useless hiding place. The duchess gave a squeal and collapsed in the duke's arms, and courtiers scurried in every direction as the swarm twisted and turned on their quarry's trail.

Georgiana was now quite hysterical. How could she escape? *Water!* That would save her. Seeing a large fountain about fifty yards away across a bowling green, she gathered her skirts and fled out of the tent, elbowing the duke aside so violently that he and the duchess tumbled ignominiously onto a sofa. Georgiana ran like a hare, with the bees only inches behind her, then flung herself into the pool where the fountain splashed from a stone pedestal. She scrambled and splashed to get behind the silver curtain of falling water, then pressed herself against the pedestal. Thwarted, the bees buzzed angrily overhead, watching and waiting for the moment she dared to emerge. But Georgiana had no intention of emerging. If necessary she would stay there all night!

By now, the bees had caused consternation throughout the gardens. Several ladies swooned with shock, not the least of these being the unfortunate Duchess of York, who on coming around gave way to a fit of the vapors second to none. The duke was scarcely less shaken, for he wasn't accustomed to being shoved roughly aside. It wasn't good for his dignity! He sent a courtier to summon his carriage, and within minutes the royal cavalcade had quit the gardens at a canter that threatened to overturn each vehicle as it swept hectically into Great Pulteney Street.

Meanwhile, Bodkin had run back to his precious jack-o'-lantern. He found Dominic, Ragwort, and Caraway waiting for him, and made himself visible for Dominic's sake. Dominic was about to hurry back to keep a watchful eye on Polly, but Bodkin prevented him. "Let Caraway go—she'll be faster than you. Go on, Caraway. Miss Polly's by the bonfire." As Caraway dutifully hurried away again, Bodkin looked at Dominic. "Have you been told about the change of plan?"

"Yes. I wish I'd been told by the bonfire, so I could have removed Polly from all risk of Beddem," Dominic replied a little crossly, for he'd given Polly his solemn word that she would be safe at all times. There had been no need for him to come here, but Caraway had said it was very urgent indeed.

Bodkin pressed his lips together and nodded. "We didn't think," he confessed. "Anyway, Caraway will bring her now. What do you think of the new plan?"

"It's good—I approve."

"All the Royal Crescent brownies are ready to help, so with us all we'll overcome Lord Benjamin and strip him if necessary. But before we get to that, I intend to pursue him with my jack-o'-lantern." Bodkin held the lighted stick to the candles in the pumpkin, then stamped on the stick until it no longer smoked. As the candle flames grew stronger, and the terrible face shone in the darkness, the brownie rubbed his hands with anticipation. "Oh, I'm going to enjoy all this," he declared.

But then Caraway ran breathlessly back. "Lord Benjamin has Miss Polly!" she cried.

Guilt and alarm lanced searingly through Dominic. He tore off his robe and turban. "Which way have they gone?" he cried.

"Up the hill toward the canal!"

As Dominic ran to the rescue, Bodkin turned to Ragwort and Caraway. "Alert the other brownies, then go after Sir Dominic.

Miss Polly must be saved!" They nodded and hastened away. Bodkin then turned to his jack-o'-lantern. "Your moment has come, my laddo," he said, making himself invisible once more. Then he heaved the pole onto his shoulder, and stepped from the bushes.

A gentleman had just quieted his hysterical lady on a bench beneath a leafy arbor about twenty yards away, but then the giant jack-o'-lantern emerged into view, apparently moving magically on its own. The lady promptly delivered such a broadside of uncontrollable screams that her unfortunate companion didn't know what to do. The lady's hysteria attracted attention, others turned, saw the jack-o'-lantern, and scattered in the utmost panic as Halloween no longer seemed quite the time of fun it was meant to be. Bodkin paid them no heed as he set off after Dominic. Ragwort and Caraway had begun to collect the other brownies, who came from all directions to hurry behind Bodkin and the jack-o'-lantern. The only signs of their presence were the little indentations of their feet in the grass and their low, determined voices.

The candles in the pumpkin flared and guttered, and the huge jack-o'-lantern could be seen quite clearly as it bobbed up through the gardens. The result was more mayhem than ever; indeed the elite of Bath were reduced to utter chaos. One half thought it was a trick that was too clever by far, the other half that it was a supernatural visitation. There were more screams, more faintings, as the remnants of Halloween frivolity collapsed. Fashionable witches, wizards, goblins, and devils dove for cover beneath handy bushes, or scuttled for sanctuary in the temple and sham castle; morris men scattered, bells jingling; and the hobbyhorse picked up its skirts to gallop after them.

Bodkin remembered his bees and whistled to them. As they abandoned the fountain to obey his commands, Georgiana put her head tentatively through the curtain of water. The first thing she saw was the giant jack-o'-lantern, and with a most unbecoming wail, she drew hastily back out of sight again.

Chapter 40

The cause of all this pandemonium—Polly's abduction by Lord Benjamin—had taken place the moment Georgiana and Bodkin left her. She was just scanning the crowds around the bonfire for Dominic when Lord Benjamin suddenly blocked her view. He'd been waiting for his sister to carry out her promise regarding Dominic, then made his move as soon as Georgiana hurried away. "Good evening, Miss Peach," he murmured in as civil and agreeable a tone as could be imagined.

Her heart tightened in dismay. "Lord Benjamin!"

"I trust your letter still holds good, and you wish to warm the atmosphere between us?"

She stared at him, her courage suddenly almost deserting her now that the final moment had arrived. Her eyes flew for reassurance to where Dominic had been a moment before, but he'd gone! She glanced back to Lord Benjamin, and incongruously she thought how ridiculous he looked, squeezed so tightly into his costume that his face would have been red and sweating even without the bonfire's assistance. *The costume! He had no coat!*

"Miss Peach?" he prompted, giving her a sleek smile.

"Forgive me, Lord Benjamin, I . . . I've been anticipating this moment so much that now it's here, I'm all at sixes and sevens." Did she sound convincing? Oh, how she prayed so! What was she going to do now? Because of his costume, their plan had fallen at the first fence!

"I fear we have been unnecessarily at odds in the past, but all should be well from now on. It would please me immeasurably if you and I were to be true friends, Miss Peach, er, Polly . . ."

"It would please me too, Lord Benjamin. I . . . I mean Benjamin."

At that moment Bodkin's whistle rang out as he set the bees on Georgiana, and Polly turned, distracted, but Lord Benjamin took her hand. "It's disagreeably warm here. Shall we walk where it's cooler?"

And darker, she thought with alarm, and quickly endeavored to divert him. "Oh, look, something's happening," she said as the first onlookers spotted Bodkin's bees.

He wasn't to be put off. "I'm sure it's nothing," he murmured, drawing her hand firmly over his sleeve.

Polly was in too much of a quandary to think of any reasonable way to resist. Nutmeg's fate remained uppermost in her thoughts, but everything felt as if it were going horribly wrong. Where was Dominic? she wondered. He must be somewhere nearby, because he'd promised, and so had Bodkin and Ragwort. Yes, they were all keeping watch. She overcame her alarm and accompanied Lord Benjamin away from the bonfire, toward the canal, which lay hidden in its cut at the top of the garden. Suddenly she remembered Hordwell. "Where is my uncle?" she asked "I haven't seen him tonight, and—"

"I fear he felt indisposed, and so elected to remain at the house," Lord Benjamin interrupted smoothly.

An icy finger of renewed disquiet passed down Polly's spine. Something was wrong! Her uncle would have sent a message if he was unable to come tonight, of all nights. Her steps faltered, but Lord Benjamin walked calmly on, and his hand rested so strongly over hers that she had to go with him. Should she scream? But even as she thought it, a chorus of screams came from behind. It was caused by the appearance of Bodkin's jack-o'-lantern, but she didn't know that. To add her screams would be futile. *What was happening? Where was Dominic?*

Lord Benjamin didn't care what was happening behind them; he was concerned only with getting Polly to the canal, and thence to the carriage waiting at Bathampton. Georgiana must be succeeding in diverting Fortune, he thought, quickening his steps just a little. He spoke cordially to Polly, as if the atmosphere between them was lighthearted and carefree, although he knew it wasn't. "I think you and I could do very well together, Polly. Granted we've known only friction until now, but deep inside I think we are very well suited. Don't you agree?" His gaze was fixed ahead, where the canal bridges, decorated with small green jack-o'-lanterns, had now appeared through the darkness.

"I . . . I cannot really say," she replied, frantically glancing behind again.

"Cannot say?" He affected to be a little injured.

She stumbled over a suitable reply. "Well, one cannot know such a thing until one is married."

He kept walking. "I find your frankness most refreshing," he murmured, steering her to the westernmost of the bridges. The pleasure boat he had secured was waiting beneath it at the foot of stone steps that were set against the retaining wall. In a few short minutes now, dear Miss Peach—and her fortune—would be on their way to Gretna Green.

As they reached the top of the steps, Polly's increasing fear at last spilled over, and suddenly she pulled away from him. "I . . . I want to go back," she said.

The time for false smiles was over. He seized her arm and propelled her down the steps to the narrow towpath. She screamed and struggled, and with a curse he clamped a hand over her mouth. Her spangled witch's hat fell as she tried to beat him off with her fists, but he was far too strong. In a blur she saw how the jack-o'-lanterns on the bridges cast a baleful green light over the waiting pleasure boat, with its single lantern at the stern. The muslin draped over its canopy resembled a shroud, and the black wooden witch silhouetted at the prow seemed about to take to the air as the boat rocked gently at its mooring.

Lord Benjamin hauled his prize across the towpath, then into the boat, which swayed alarmingly as Polly fought every inch like a wild cat. He forced her beneath the canopy, where a handkerchief and a coil of rope lay on the seat. After forcing the former into her mouth to silence her, Lord Benjamin made short work of binding her hand and foot so she could only lie helplessly in the bottom of the boat. Then he stepped out from the canopy again, carefully pulled the muslin over so she couldn't be seen, and undid the mooring rope. Seizing one of the oars, he shoved it against the bank.

At that moment Dominic appeared at the top of the steps. "Stop, Beddem, or so help me I'll kill you!" he cried, producing a pistol from inside his coat.

Lord Benjamin's lips parted in dismay as he feared the game was up, but then he reasoned that Dominic wouldn't dare fire for fear of hitting Polly, so he didn't even acknowledge the challenge as he began to row strongly in the direction of Bathampton. The canal passed out of the gardens in only a few yards, and he would get away! Dominic scrambled down the bank and began to take off his boots as quickly as he could, the better to swim, but help was already at hand in the form of Bodkin and his magic jack-o'-lantern.

The brownie ran breathlessly onto the bridge, untied the pumpkin, and threw it at the departing pleasure boat. As always, his aim was perfect, and the jack-o'-lantern hit Lord Benjamin on the head, before rolling overboard into the water, where by good fortune it landed upright. Still intact, with its candles miraculously alight, it bobbed up and down, its leering face seeming eminently well pleased as Lord Benjamin slumped senseless over the oars. Wavelets rippled across the canal, obligingly carrying the drifting pleasure boat toward Dominic, who was soon able to pull it to the bank. He immediately stepped aboard to gather Polly in his arms and take her to safety. Laying her gently on the towpath, where Bodkin's brownie friends crowded around, he removed the handkerchief from her mouth, then untied her.

"Forgive me, my darling," he whispered as she sat up. "Let you down. This wouldn't have happened if I'd—"

She caught his hands and kissed them both, then smiled up at him. "I know you wouldn't have willingly left me, and you've saved me now, so nothing else matters. I love you, Dominic," she whispered.

"As I love you," he breathed, sinking his fingers into the warmth of her hair and pulling her lips up to meet his.

The watching brownies, sentimental souls, gave unanimous sighs, for if there was one thing brownies adored, it was romance.

Lord Benjamin began to groan as he came around, and Dominic quickly took the rope and jumped lightly back onto the boat to bind Polly's abductor. Bodkin ran from the bridge to jump in the boat with his pole, which he stretched out to guide the pumpkin toward him. Then he lifted it out of the water and carried it triumphantly ashore to the cheers of his friends. Above their cheers there was the buzzing of the bees as they waited to see what Bodkin required of them.

Ragwort mustered the brownies. "Bring Lord Benjamin ashore," he ordered, and as one they scrambled into the boat. On the count of three, they managed to haul Lord Benjamin onto the towpath, where they pinned him down by sitting and standing on his outstretched arms and legs. He was terrified, for although he couldn't see his assailants, he knew they were brownies, and that they would show no mercy to someone who'd planned such a terrible fate for one of their number.

Then Bodkin stood over him, a foot on his chest, and made himself visible. "Where's Nutmeg's belt?" he demanded.

Lord Benjamin stared up at him, for this was the first time he'd actually seen a brownie. Lord Benjamin's tongue passed dryly over his lower lip, and he swallowed, too frightened to speak.

Bodkin jumped up and down on him. "Where's her belt?" he cried furiously, his tail beginning to lash. "If you don't tell me, I'll set my bees on you!" The mood of the other brownies turned to anger as well, and some of them urged him to let the bees do their worst regardless. The swarm buzzed threateningly and descended a little closer, so Lord Benjamin could see them against the starlit sky.

Dominic had drawn Polly gently to her feet, then turned as Caraway tugged his coat, then held up Polly's witch's hat, which she'd rescued intact from the foot of the steps. He thanked the brownie and smiled at Polly as he placed the glittering hat tenderly on her head. Then he glanced down at Lord Benjamin. "You'd be wise to divulge the belt's whereabouts, Beddem."

As Lord Benjamin's full lips pressed defiantly together, Bodkin pointed up at the eager bees. "Tell me, or it will be the worst for you," he warned, then gave a brief whistle. A solitary bee flew down and perched on the end of his lordship's nose. Lord Benjamin's eyes almost crossed as he tried to focus on it. Perspiration ran down his forehead, and he began to tremble from head to toe. Like the jelly at the review, Polly thought.

Bodkin gave him one last chance. "Tell me what I want to know, Beddem."

The bee buzzed on Lord Benjamin's nose and wriggled its abdomen to show how ready it was to sting. Lord Benjamin capitulated. "The belt is inside my costume!" he cried. "Now get this bee off me!"

Bodkin grinned, whistled again, and the bee flew back to join the rest of the swarm. Bodkin then gave a longer whistle, and with a loud parting buzz, they flew away into the night. By dawn they would be home in their Horditall hives.

The brownies set about divesting Lord Benjamin of his costume. They ripped the seams, showing no consideration at all as they pulled and tugged. In moments it lay in red tatters on the towpath, and the second son of the Duke of Lawless was left in only his unmentionables. With a triumphant whoop, Bodkin held up the precious belt. Nutmeg would soon be safe in his arms again! He danced a jig on the towpath, so happy that he couldn't speak.

His joy was temporarily halted by Polly's anxiety as she looked down at Lord Benjamin. "Where is my uncle?" she demanded.

"I caught him searching my room, so I tied him up and left him on my bed."

"He's an old man . . . if you've hurt him—"

"You only have to untie him."

Polly breathed out with relief, and Dominic took her hand, squeezing it gently.

Ragwort nodded at the other brownies, and they bundled Lord Benjamin back into the boat and pushed it out onto the water. Bound with his own rope, he could only lie there. He knew it was unlikely that he'd be found before daylight, and he could only hope the rest of the night wouldn't get too cold. His plans were in as many tatters as his costume, and both prospective fortunes had slipped through his pudgy fingers. The duns would get him now, and before long he'd be languishing in jail. He gave a huge, resigned sigh. Plague take all brownies. And Polly Peach!

On the towpath, he was already forgotten. Bodkin recovered his voice. "Come on, let's free Nutmeg!" he yelled, and rushed up the steps, followed by all the others.

Polly and Dominic remained on the towpath, except for the jack-o'-lantern, of course. Its candlelight swayed gently, dealing a soft glow to everything as Dominic pulled Polly close to kiss her forehead. Then he gazed into her eyes. "I know you say it doesn't matter now, but my conscience is still great. I shouldn't have left you, no matter how urgent Caraway told me it was."

"Dominic—"

"I might have lost you tonight!" he broke in, closing his eyes with emotion. "I could not have lived with myself if any harm had befallen you because of my idiocy."

"If you insist on blaming yourself for your part, then I must take even more of the blame for being so foolish as to let him bring me here. All's well now, and that's what really matters." Suddenly she thought of the celebrations. "Let's see what's happening," she said, and gathered her skirts to hasten up the steps.

Dominic followed, and together they hurried toward the temple, from where they could see everything in the gardens. The fireworks were over, and the bonfire had begun to collapse now, but the flames still leaped high. The crowd—what was left of it, for most had fled for home, hotel, inn, or lodging—was now gathered quietly in the light of the bonfire. The carefully prepared supper had barely been touched, but the punch bowls were nearly empty as rattled nerves were steadied, then steadied again. The trees and shrubs still twinkled with little jack-o'-lanterns, and the hotel orchestra had found the spirit to play again. Sweet notes drifted through the night, like a soothing lullaby.

Dominic gave a low laugh. "I think this Halloween will go down in history as the night Bath picked up its genteel petticoats and had the vapors," he murmured.

"And all because of Bodkin," Polly said.

He nodded. "Yes. I sincerely hope he finds Nutmeg now that he has the belt, for I don't think my fragile constitution is up to any more of this."

"Nor mine."

Dominic watched the gardens again, then pointed suddenly. "Look, there's Harry. Who's he putting a blanket around? Why, I believe it's Georgiana!"

"Yes, it is. And how very wet she is," Polly observed with undisguised relish, for Diana the Huntress had become Diana the Drenched. "What on earth happened to her?"

"Well, it's a tale that's bound to please you," Dominic replied, and told her about the bees.

Polly giggled and clapped her hands. "Oh, how wonderful. I wish I'd seen it. What a pity she didn't get a single sting."

"What a very unsympathetic soul you are, Miss Peach," he murmured.

She gave him a look. "If you defend her, I shall never speak to you again."

"One cannot defend the indefensible," he said softly, and pulled her close once more.

The wedding of Miss Polly Peach and Sir Dominic Fortune took place two days later by special license. Harry Dashington was the best man, and Hordwell proudly gave his niece away. The occasion passed without Bath society realizing, because the *monde* had too much else to rattle about, what with the review, the ball, and now the shambles of Sydney Gardens. Newspapers, drawing rooms, hotels, and Pump Room rang with the shocking events, although everyone was very careful not to mention them in the hearing of the Duke and Duchess of York. The duchess was now said to be so prostrate with shock that she would have to take the cure in its most strict and arduous form, and the duke was rumored to be so angry about being elbowed aside by Georgiana that he saw to it she would in future be banned from every royal function. The Marquess of Hightower proved to be no St. George to this particular damsel in distress. He could not forgive her for her lack of sympathy by the bonfire, and was already comforting himself in the company of Lady Margaret Ponsonby-Ponsonby-Muslyn, a rather pretty but empty-headed creature who was probably perfect for him.

Lord Benjamin was the object of much ridicule for having been found virtually in his birthday suit, and ever afterward was to be known as Birthday Ben. Not that he was around to hear his new nickname, for the duns had swiftly seen to his arrest, and by the time Polly and Dominic said their vows, he was already languishing in a Bath bridewell. The name of Hordwell Horditall figured high upon his long list of creditors.

On the day after Halloween, the page of Nostradamus arrived by letter carrier, and Ragwort burned it immediately. The vigilant brownie had been awaiting the post every day, and the moment something arrived that had been posted in France, he knew what it must be. As the sheet of paper for which Lord Benjamin had paid so much went up in flames, Ragwort shuddered to think what might have happened to Nutmeg had it arrived a few days earlier.

Hordwell was delighted with the outcome of everything. His feathers had been considerably ruffled by his ignominious imprisonment on Lord Benjamin's bed, but a decanter or so of good cognac had put him in the happiest of glows, albeit with the promise of a rotten head come the morning. He quickly left 1 Royal Crescent and joined Polly at the Sydney Hotel, where a second room had conveniently become available. A few discreet inquiries soon elicited the information that Lord Benjamin had indeed been lying about his elder brother's supposed disinheritance, which meant that Polly would never have been Duchess of Lawless. Thus Hordwell regarded Dominic as an excellent consolation prize, for his wealth—if not his title—was greater than the duke's. Polly's uncle was satisfied that her husband was a most excellent and worthy fellow; indeed to hear him speak of his new nephew-in-law was to wonder if Dominic was a blend of King Arthur and the Archangel Gabriel! From the Sydney Hotel, he went to Dominic's residence on Royal Crescent, where his happiness was completed by the safe return of his valuables.

Nutmeg had been rescued within minutes of the belt's recovery;

indeed she'd been waiting on the doorstep on Halloween, when all the victorious brownies, with Bodkin in the lead, had streamed along Royal Crescent. She joyfully consented to marry him, and Caraway so forgave Ragwort that *she* proposed to *him*. As a result, on the day that Polly and Dominic married, there was also a double brownie ceremony beneath the mulberry tree in Dominic's garden.

The pumpkin jack-o'-lantern had been rescued from the towpath and had pride of place at the brownie nuptials, serving as the altar upon which the four tiny wedding bands were placed. As a nuptial present for them, Dominic hired Zuder's shop for the night, and every brownie in Bath was invited to the feast. Come the morning there wasn't a single item of confectionery left. Crumbs remained, of course, heaps of them, and spilled honey, smears of cream, blobs of jelly, and numerous other lamentable examples of how brownies should not behave, but it had to be said that a good time was certainly had by one and all.

While the Zuder's party was in full swing, Polly and Dominic slipped between the sheets as man and wife. She lay back, her golden hair spilling over the pillow. "Do you think the brownies are having fun?" she asked.

"I don't know, but we are about to, my lady," he whispered, leaning over her. "I adore you, Lady Fortune," he whispered, bending his head to kiss the soft curve of her breast.

"Lady Fortune. How wonderful that sounds . . ." she breathed, closing her eyes with pleasure.

Outside in the garden, the pumpkin shone beneath the mulberry tree. Bodkin had crept back from the party to light it. He didn't care that Halloween was over. It just seemed fitting that tonight of all nights his magic jack-o'-lantern should be lit.

On Sale October 11, 1999

Lord Dragoner's Wife by Lynn Kerstan

Six years ago, Delia wed Lord Dragoner, the man she'd loved from afar. But after only one night, the handsome Lord mysteriously fled the country...only to return amid scandalous rumors.

Can love bloom again in the shadows of the past—and the danger of the present?

0-451-19861-1/$4.99

Double Deceit by Allison Lane

Antiquarian Alexandra Vale is more interested in artifacts than love affairs, but her diabolical father has different plans for her. Soon Alex is caught up in a cunning deceit with a notorious rogue—but the clever twosome may learn they can't outsmart their very own hearts....

0-451-19854-9/$4.99

The Holly and the Ivy by Elisabeth Fairchild

Mary Rivers's Gran has predicted a wonderful Christmas in London. And when their usually prickly neighbor, Lord Balfour, is increasingly attentive, Gran's prediction may come true—if the merry Mary and the thorny Lord can weather a scandalous misunderstanding and a chaotic Christmas Eve ball!

0-451-19841-7/$4.99

A Regency Christmas Present

Five exciting new stories by Elisabeth Fairchild, Carla Kelly, Allison Lane, Edith Layton, and Barbara Metzger

0-451-19877-8/$6.99

To order call: 1-800-788-6262